PRA

the starlight sisters

the
starlight
sisters

OLIVIA MILES

Rosewood Press

THE STARLIGHT SISTERS

ISBN: 979-8-9904728-0-8

Formatting: Alt 19 Creative

Published by:
Rosewood Press

ALSO BY OLIVIA MILES

chapter one
AMANDA

AMANDA FOLEY HAD a date to plan. Yes, it was with her husband, but it was long overdue—so long, in fact, that Amanda needed to go back to not just last year's planner but the one from the year before that to find the exact date, and even then she had to flip all the way to the very beginning. January. It had been a cold winter night, they'd gotten a corner table at the then-new French place in their small New England town, even though neither of them particularly enjoyed French food. But it wasn't exactly child-friendly, and that was the entire point of a date night, wasn't it? To go somewhere it wouldn't have made sense to bring a restless seven-year-old boy?

Now that boy was already ten.

Amanda's heart sank like it always did when she thought of how quickly Trevor had grown up—what a haze the past two and a half years had been. How long every day had seemed, first bringing her mother to live with them in the underused guest room, then shuffling her to doctor appointments, sitting in waiting rooms, talking to doctors, fighting fatigue every step of the way, only to be sitting here, in the parking lot of the assisted living facility where Amanda had spent most of the last six months, putting off the final visit. It was much easier to scroll through her phone for restaurant options, wondering if any of her nicer clothes would even fit her anymore.

With that thought she set the cookie she'd been eating in the cup holder of her minivan, hoping the chocolate chips wouldn't melt in the summer sun while she was inside, telling herself that it was one more reason to be quick. In and out. Take the box of personal belongings and be on her way. Back to her life. The one that she'd yearned for. Even wished for.

The life that she'd neglected for too long.

Amanda grabbed the bakery box that had been keeping her company on the passenger seat and sighed with dismay when she saw the dent in the pile of cookies. She'd lost count of how many she'd consumed when they were supposed to be a gift for the staff—even though Amanda knew that her mother had treated them all with far more kindness than she'd bestowed on her eldest daughter. Really, if anyone deserved the cookies, it was her, not that her hips would agree.

Amanda stepped out of the car and brushed the crumbs from her tee shirt, feeling the warmth of the sun on her face as she walked the familiar path from her usual parking spot to the front doors, which glided open for her as if expecting her arrival.

"Amanda!"

Amanda felt her shoulders relax at the sight of "Nurse Debbie," as the large and cheerful woman liked to be called. For not the first time, Amanda entertained what life might have been like if she'd had a mother like Debbie. Debbie with her warm smile and compassionate eyes, always quick with a compliment about

Amanda's hair or outfit, deserving or not. Debbie with a laugh that could fill a room and make you want to sit and stay in her company for a bit out of desire, not obligation.

"I set aside Martha's things for you," Debbie said quietly after giving Amanda one of her tight, comforting hugs.

"And I brought these for you," Amanda said, nearly forgetting the bakery box, which had been partially squished in their embrace. "I'm sorry they aren't homemade."

"Darling, you have nothing to apologize for," Debbie assured her, and for a moment, Amanda almost believed it. Or wanted to, at least.

"Someone should have said that to my mother," Amanda joked, only the look Debbie gave her showed that she understood it was no laughing matter.

Amanda was relieved that Debbie didn't try to say the things she heard so often growing up; that her mother loved her in her own way, that Martha just didn't show affection easily, that really, she was so proud of Amanda, even if she didn't show it.

Instead, Debbie walked Amanda over to the reception desk where she swapped the bakery box for another, less inviting one. Amanda glanced inside the open storage box that contained the few things that Amanda's mother had kept in her room: a jewelry box, a faded peach terrycloth robe and matching slippers, and three framed photos: one of Amanda's sister, forever a grinning ten-year-old, a little girl who would never grow up; a faded wedding photo revealing fashions long out of style, even though Amanda's father had walked out on the family when she was fourteen; and a Christmas print of Trevor, circa somewhere around age three. There weren't any photos of Amanda, which Amanda already knew because she'd once pointed it out to her mother, trying for a joking tone to cover her hurt feelings, only to be told that Martha didn't need a photo of Amanda when she "had to" see her every day.

Every day. For more than two years, that's how Amanda had devoted her time. And now, she felt like she was waking up, blinking at her surroundings for the first time. Had this lobby always been so bright, with the sun streaming in through the big bay windows on either side of the front doors? Had there always been a large, colorful floral arrangement on each of the coffee tables in the lobby?

"This won't be the worst of it," she told Debbie, taking the box into her arms.

Just thinking of returning to her childhood home made her stomach tighten with dread. She knew Ryan would come with her to Starlight Beach—but that would require taking time off from his dental practice and canceling appointments. And it wouldn't be fair to Trevor to miss any upcoming soccer games.

No, it would be easier to go back on her own, settle the last of her mother's affairs, and then put Starlight Beach and all the bad parts of her life firmly behind her for good.

"I'm going to miss you," she said to Debbie, knowing that another goodbye was in order.

"You'll come visit me," Debbie said, setting a hand on her shoulder.

Amanda could only manage to nod as a lump formed in her throat. They both knew that she probably wouldn't. This building, like her childhood home, was tainted with difficult memories and moments best forgotten, even if Debbie, like her best friends growing up, had been a much-needed glimmer of light.

Amanda struggled to swallow as she walked out of the building, solacing herself with the promise of the remaining cookie that was waiting for her in the car, trying to run through her list of chores for the afternoon which she'd purposefully planned, knowing that she was always happiest when she was doing things for Ryan and Trevor.

She put the box on the floor of the backseat where it wouldn't tip and slid into the driver's seat. She was just about to reach for the last half of the cookie when her phone rang in her hand and her best friend's name lit up on the screen. Amanda's heart lifted as she connected the call and held the device to her ear.

"You saved me," she said, knowing that it wasn't the first time.

"Don't tell me that you were about to cut your own bangs again," Cassie said, bringing a smile to Amanda's lips.

"Lesson learned twenty years ago," Amanda said solemnly, still remembering the jagged edges that had taken months to grow long enough to tuck behind her ears, each day of which she was met with her mother's pursed lips and disappointed tsks. Feeling her tension rise again, she explained, "I was just about to eat a baker's dozen of cookies. I had to stop by the assisted living facility today."

"Ah." Cassie didn't need to say anything more and neither did Amanda. The silence that stretched was one of a hundred words and complete understanding.

"What are you up to at the moment?" Amanda asked as she transferred the call to the speaker and set the phone in the cupholder beside the cookie.

"Just sketching a few designs for my latest bridezilla," Cassie said airily.

Amanda laughed as she backed out of her parking spot. "Is this the one who wanted the sixty-foot train and veil to match?"

She could picture her friend in her trendy New York loft, surrounded by frothy, ivory fabric waiting to be turned into one of her beautiful creations.

"Oh, she dropped that idea when I pointed out a veil that long would get tangled in the nearest tree branch the moment it caught a breeze. No, this is the one who wants something that, I quote, no one has ever seen before," Cassie said, blowing out a sigh. "Remind me again why I went into this business?"

"That's easy." Amanda smiled as she headed toward the dry cleaners to pick up Ryan's dress shirts. She could still picture Cassie as a young girl, saving up her babysitting money to buy the newest bridal magazine at the old-fashioned pharmacy in their small beach town. Amanda was always more focused on the chocolate milkshakes the store sold at the vintage soda fountain, but Cassie couldn't tear her eyes from the beautiful pages. "You love weddings more than anyone I know."

"Yes, well, right now what I'd love is a vacation."

"You and me both, sister." Amanda grinned, but she couldn't deny the pang in her chest. Cassie wasn't her biological sister, and she knew that no one would ever replace the one she'd lost, but Cassie knew her heart, her thoughts, her deepest worries and fears as well as her greatest hopes and wishes. They were as close as two people could be. Well, other than Whitney, but Amanda didn't like to think of the other member of their trio these days.

"Maybe it would be good for you to take some time away, now that you can…" Cassie said delicately.

Amanda nodded along as she pulled into the dry cleaners' lot. "Well, actually," she said, dread filling her tone as her eyes darted to the cookie sitting in the cupholder. "I have to handle my mother's estate."

Estate was such a fancy term, reserved more for people like the Palmers. Whitney came from an estate; a big, sprawling shingled house tucked behind a high green hedge, its backyard a stretch of private beach, whereas Amanda had grown up on the far side of town, reserved for the types of people who worked hard at their jobs to make sure people like the Palmers had an unforgettable summer.

"You're going back to Starlight Beach?" Cassie's tone was full of disbelief, but Amanda thought she detected another emotion, one even she couldn't quite decipher.

Amanda knew that Cassie had her own mixed feelings about Starlight Beach that had eventually driven her to New York, but it didn't stop her from blurting out her next question anyway. "You're welcome to join me."

What she really meant was, "I need you there." And Cassie knew it.

Amanda reached for the rest of the cookie, but nearly choked on the first bite when Cassie said, "What about this weekend?"

Sputtering the crumbs into her hand, Amanda slapped her chest to get her breath. This weekend was only a few days away. She had her son to think about, and her husband to tell, but who was she kidding? The real reason that she was panicking was because she didn't want to go back at all, and she probably never would unless Cassie came with her.

And Cassie knew it.

"This weekend?"

"Better now than later," Cassie said in her optimistic way. "You need closure. Putting off this visit will just ruin your entire summer if you let it."

Her friend was right, Amanda knew. "You're sure you want to come with me?"

"When have I ever said something I didn't mean?" Cassie replied simply.

Never. And that was what Amanda loved about her. It was what she'd loved about Whitney too—until her words turned hurtful.

"It's been three years since our last reunion," Cassie continued.

Three years. Again, Amanda was reminded of how quickly time had passed, when she was busy just surviving, not living. But now, the memories of that long weekend on the Cape kept rushing back. Whitney, out of sorts, her auburn hair pulled back tight at her neck, instead of blowing in the breeze the way it had when they were younger. The words that had flowed, the silence that had followed.

The reunion used to be an annual thing—even when Trevor was little and Amanda would fret over leaving him for a few days. That was something that Whitney could never understand, amongst other things, it turned out.

"It's hard to believe it's been that long," Amanda replied. More impossible to believe that it had been three years since she'd spoken to Whitney. Once there was a time when the three of them could fill an entire afternoon with their chatter.

"So what do you say?" Cassie asked, and Amanda could hear the smile in her tone. "There's no time like the present."

No, Amanda thought, as her heart sped up. There was no time like the present, especially when she'd lost so much time as it was.

"I'll find us a place to stay. Right on the beach now that we can finally afford it. We're not the same kids we were the last time we were there, Amanda. We're thirty-two years old. We're different now. We'll make it fun." Cassie almost sounded convincing.

Agreeing before she had time to change her mind, Amanda ended the call and looked down at her trembling hands. Only instead of shaking from nerves, or anxiety, like they did so often, this time it was from excitement. She hadn't seen Cassie in three years. Three years! So they'd be in Starlight Beach; they wouldn't stay in her old house. They'd stay somewhere on the other side of town, away from the bad memories, right on the beach, where only good things ever happened. They'd drink wine, talk until they could barely keep their eyes open, and laugh until their ribs hurt.

She didn't even know she was smiling until the nice old man who owned the dry cleaner commented, "You seem chipper today, Mrs. Foley! It's been a long time since I've seen that smile!"

"Well, it's here to stay!" Amanda said triumphantly as she collected her husband's shirts. She smiled all the way to the grocery store, where she filled her cart with bags of fresh produce, waving to neighbors or mothers of Trevor's classmates. Yes, she was still wearing her usual leggings with the oversized cotton tee, and her hair was still in a messy bun, but all that would change once she was back into her old jeans. Maybe she'd start wearing her sundresses again, too. Those would forgive the stress pounds she'd put on recently.

She didn't even see the text from Ryan until she was home, bags unpacked, the box of her mother's belongings still safely hidden in the car: *Getting caught up on paperwork tonight.*

So much for a date night tonight, even though Trevor was sleeping over at a friend's house.

Amanda wandered around the empty rooms of the house. Cooking for one seemed senseless. She'd forgotten to buy cereal. For the first time, she wished that she had pushed harder when Trevor had asked for a dog all those years ago and Ryan refused, citing his mild allergy.

But a pet wasn't what was missing. Or even Trevor or Ryan. There was space in this house, a dream that had been deferred, and now, might come true.

She'd known the loneliness of being an only child, and she'd never wanted that for Trevor. But it was more than that, she knew, that made her chest pull with longing. It was the need to reclaim her life. To take back the years she'd lost. To have the family she'd always wanted.

By the time she took a shower, tidied the house, and made and eaten an unsatisfying salad for dinner in front of the television, she finally heard the sound of the garage door opening.

"Late night," she commented as she walked into the kitchen to greet her husband.

"Long day," was all Ryan said. He looked tired as he pulled a beer from the fridge.

Amanda decided that now was probably not the best time to broach the topic of trying for a baby.

"I decided to go back to Starlight Beach this weekend, to set-tle everything. I'll only be gone a few days," she said. "Cassie's joining me."

Ryan looked momentarily relieved not to have to go to her childhood house, and Amanda was fully aware of the toll these past years had taken on him too. "Cassie's going? That will be great. You don't need to rush back. Trevor and I will be fine on our own."

Amanda opened her mouth to reply but faltered. She knew that Ryan was just being kind, encouraging her to take some time away with her closest friend, but she couldn't help but take his words another way. To see the truth in them. He and Trevor were fine on their own. They didn't need her anymore. Maybe they hadn't in quite some time and that was because her focus had been on another family member.

"I thought we could go for dinner before I head out. Just the two of us," she added, glancing up at him. "Trevor has another sleepover this Friday."

Ryan didn't meet her eyes and his shrug wasn't exactly the reaction she had been expecting—or hoping for. But then she glanced at the clock and figured that it *was* late, that he was tired from a long day at the office.

"It would be nice to have some time for ourselves, wouldn't it?" she pressed, trying to keep her tone cheerful.

"Yeah," Ryan said, looking at her thoughtfully. "It's been a while since we've had a chance to talk."

And a talk they would have, Amanda thought, with a little smile.

"You coming up?" she asked.

"In a bit," Ryan replied, already heading toward the den. Soon the sounds of the television filled the house. It was his way of relaxing, even if he did usually end up falling asleep on the couch for the night.

Upstairs, Amanda paused outside of Trevor's empty bedroom, then sent him a quick text, telling him good night.

Night eventually came the reply.

She told herself that he was probably busy playing video games with his friend or eating pizza in front of a movie, enjoying his summer vacation the way every child should, but all the same her chest felt heavy.

Gone was the rhyme they'd always said, the very one she'd said as a girl, not in the comfort of her bedroom, certainly not with her mother, but outside, on the beach, Cassie and Whitney at her side, their toes sinking into the sand as the waves crashed below the clear night sky.

Starlight, starbright. I wish I may. I wish I might.

She closed her eyes, just like Trevor had once done, like she had too, oh so many years ago, back when she believed in wishes and magic and the possibility of something better—maybe even something wonderful—out there in the universe just waiting for her.

She'd made hundreds of wishes. Some—like being as thin and rich as Whitney or having a mom as cool as Cassie—would never come true. They were right up there with the biggest wish, the biggest regret, the one that had bound the Starlight Sisters together whether they liked it or not. Friends, but not sisters, not like the one that Amanda had lost.

But some wishes had come true. This house. Her husband. Her son.

Opening her eyes, she felt more resolved with her decision. It was time to face her past once and for all. And then...embrace her future at long last.

chapter two
CASSIE

CASSIE STARED AT her open sketchbook and then squeezed her eyes closed, willing the vision to come the way it used to do, so very easily. It wasn't that the bride wasn't specific with her ideas. If anything, she had been too specific, too detailed, and frankly, too demanding. She'd flipped through Cassie's portfolio at a steady pace, pointing out exactly what she liked and didn't like, asking for more of this, less of that, until Cassie's head had spun to the point where she'd actually felt dizzy. Since then, the client had texted and emailed with dozens of more "thoughts" until Cassie had promised her she had enough to work with for now. That she had this under control.

Even though she didn't have anything but a blank page and less than two weeks to hand over something brilliant.

Cassie closed the sketchbook, knowing that she could sit in this chair in the corner of her Soho loft until the natural light turned to the glow of city lights, but nothing was going to change. It would be so easy to blame her client, but the truth was that she'd been struggling long before the bride-to-be had power-walked across her hardwood floors in stilettos. She'd lost her love for what she did. Or maybe it was her passion that had fallen by the wayside. Either way, losing it wasn't the problem.

Not being able to find it again was.

"Cass?"

Cassie craned her neck to see Grant standing in the open doorway of the apartment they shared. It was a large space by New York City standards, one they could only afford with their dual income. A wide-open cube that had once felt so spacious but now felt increasingly limited as their years together brought them firmly into their thirties. They'd have to move if they ever wanted to have children—and she did, she always did, ever since she was a little girl, playing alone on the tree swing her mother had set up, longing for siblings that had never come along.

"You're home early!"

Grant glanced at the watch she'd given him four years ago to mark their first dating anniversary. "It's nearly seven."

"Is it?" Cassie blinked in alarm. And what did she have to show for the day?

"Productive day?" Grant asked since she'd given him no reason to suspect otherwise. Admitting to him that she was creatively blocked would mean admitting it to herself, and she wasn't blocked. No, that was too harsh a word, a label that she couldn't accept. She just…wasn't inspired. Yes, that was it.

She stood now to stretch her back. "Should we get sushi tonight?"

He stared at her. "Boy, you were busy today. Don't you remember? We're having dinner with Mark and Shana at eight."

Was that tonight? Cassie looked down at her bare feet and loose jersey pants, calculating how long it would take her to get ready for a stuffy sit-down affair with Grant's boss and his manicured wife. Their midweek dinners uptown were nothing new, but far from relaxed.

"Shoot. I guess I was…"

"In the zone." Grant smiled. "I know."

Her stomach went a little funny when she considered that he didn't know her as well as he thought he did. To him, she was Cassie Reed, established wedding dress designer, graduate of Parsons, girlfriend of five years who had an undying love of cheap slices of pizza and long, lazy strolls through art museums. Sure, he knew the basics of her past, that she was an only child to a single mother. That her mother was "artsy" and "free-spirited" which were true but forgiving descriptions. That she'd never met her father. That she didn't even know his name. That she may have grown up in a beach town, but that she was a true New Yorker now. Just like him.

She showed him the parts she wanted him to see. The girl she'd always wanted to be.

"I'll be ready in twenty minutes," Cassie promised, hurrying to the closet and then slipping into the bathroom with her most conservative summer wrap dress.

As promised, twenty minutes later, they were walking out the door of their building hand in hand, Grant still in his suit from his day at the office, her in a navy dress that floated around her knees, her long blond curls pulled into a ponytail at the nape of her neck, her sandals gold, her jewelry modest.

"I talked to Amanda today," she said as they turned the corner where it would be easier to flag a cab.

"Oh?" Grant looked distracted as he held up a hand, and Cassie waited until they were tucked into the back of the sedan, destination given, to continue.

"I told her I'd go to Starlight Beach with her this weekend. I found a cute little cottage right on the shore, a last-minute cancellation, so we got it through next week."

"Starlight Beach, huh? Don't you usually take your reunions somewhere else?" Grant craned his neck to study the traffic up ahead.

They did, but Grant didn't know the reasons behind that, or that Amanda, Whitney, and Cassie hadn't been back to the town they'd once loved since they were teenagers. He assumed that when Cassie's mother moved across the country, she had no excuse to visit. But that was only partly true, and the real story, the hard truth, was something that the women didn't even discuss with each other.

"Amanda has to deal with her mother's property," Cassie said, still feeling bad that she hadn't gone to the funeral. Amanda had kept it small, to her little family only. It had been held in Providence, where the family had a plot and where Amanda's sister had been laid to rest.

"Not one of your usual girls trips where you come back still smelling like piña coladas?" Grant grinned.

She couldn't help but smile back, thinking of all those cherished weeks with her friends, until they'd come to a grinding halt. She pushed back the ache in her chest when she thought of their last reunion, how Amanda had left in tears and Whitney had left in silence, and even she couldn't find a way to repair the mess.

"No, it's not one of our usual reunions," she sighed. How could a reunion even be complete without Whitney? She and Whitney still talked, often, though admittedly not as often as Cassie talked with Amanda. Certainly, Whitney would want to come, wouldn't she?

But would Amanda want her there?

Cassie worried her lip as she studied the traffic. She could sense Grant stiffen beside her. They'd be late, but Mark and Shana would understand, and they had a live-in au pair that kept things easy.

"Are you sure you can take the time away from work?" Grant looked at her.

Cassie hesitated but then nodded firmly. She hadn't been back to Starlight Beach since she'd left for college and her mother had decided to try her hand at the Scottsdale art scene. "Amanda needs me, and a change of scenery will be good for my creative flow."

Or so she hoped.

Maybe, it would be good for all of them. Even Whitney and Amanda's friendship.

She leaned her head back and watched the city pass her by, the landscape changing as they pushed through Midtown and finally crossed 59th into the Upper East Side, where Grant's boss lived.

"Let us off at the corner," Grant suddenly said to the driver. "We can walk the rest of the way."

Cassie was relieved to be out in the fresh air again, but Grant's jaw was still tense after he'd paid for the meter. She reached out and squeezed his hand. Grant didn't like to let people down or keep them waiting. It was one of the things she loved most about him. He balanced her out with his logical, orderly ways. He was, as her mother would say without necessarily meaning it as a compliment, "A straight shooter."

Meaning he wouldn't be bouncing from one job to the next, shrugging his shoulders and making do when opportunities fell through, passively waiting for another one to come along. Grant had a plan, with his career, with his life. He was secure. And wasn't that all Cassie had ever craved?

They pushed through the doors of the steakhouse; even though Cassie was a pescatarian (growing up by the water made it impossible to give up fish), she knew better than to suggest another venue. Mark and Shana were already seated at a booth, arms raised to wave them over.

"Cassie." The couple stood and greeted her with familial hugs. Shana paused to look her up and down. "You always look so effortless."

Cassie smiled at the compliment as she took her seat. If only her designs could be that way.

A bottle of wine had already been ordered and now Mark took the liberty of filling their glasses—red, when Cassie much preferred white because the tannins gave her a headache. Well, she'd stick to one glass. It was better that way, really. Mark and Shana might be a fun couple, but there was always the unspoken fact that Mark had brought Grant into the financial firm eight years ago, and he was his direct superior to this day.

"Sorry we were running late," Grant said. "Traffic."

"Next time we'll come downtown," Shana said pleasantly. "I've been meaning to stop by and see some of your gowns, Cassie. A friend of mine has a sister who just got engaged. I'll pass her your name if you'd like."

Cassie reached for her wineglass, eager to cover her tight smile with a sip. "That would be great. Thank you, Shana."

Shana brushed a hand through the air. "It's my pleasure. Although looking at all those wedding gowns might make me start wishing I had a wedding of my own to plan."

Cassie laughed nervously, already feeling anxious at the mere thought of Shana and her Upper East Side friends stopping by her loft. She didn't keep sample dresses on hand, just fabric and materials, and the only gown that was ever on the dress form was her current creation. Always sitting in the corner of the wide-open space they called home, reminding her that she was only halfway to her dream. She'd gotten the career. The stability. But there was still one thing missing. Family.

"And what about you two?" Shana asked, giving a sly smile.

Cassie and Grant were used to these comments. They'd heard them enough times at various weddings they'd attended over the years, or at the firm's holiday parties. You couldn't exactly work in the wedding industry without having people inquire about your marriage plans. The only person who never asked was her mother. Cassie knew that Willow, as her mother preferred to be called ("Mom" was so pedestrian, apparently) could never understand why Cassie would crave the conventional route of an institution like marriage.

Choices, she would say. Options, she would press. It was all about freedom to Willow. Being her own woman, going where her whims took her. Not planning for tomorrow but living for the day.

Sometimes, Cassie almost craved her mother's ability to not worry about little things, until she had to worry for them both. She'd gone from being the little girl who thought it was fun when her mother took their cooking outside over an open fire to agonizing over when the gas would be turned off again, to now worrying if Willow was once again setting up camp instead of sitting down to a warm meal like Cassie was tonight.

She knew better than to offer her mother money. Willow had never cared about such things. And if she saw Cassie sitting here tonight, pretending to be fine with red wine, in a steakhouse, she wouldn't see a woman who had turned her life around from her own sheer will.

She'd see a woman who had let herself down.

Cassie glanced at Grant. She was about to give the same excuse they always did when people asked about their future plans. The one they told each other, even though she was feeling less and less convinced. Yes, getting their careers off the ground had been important to both of them, but now they had made that happen.

"Cassie and I are happy as we are," Grant said, giving her a warm smile.

She tipped her head, waiting for him to say, "For now." And when he didn't, her stomach felt a little funny for the second time that day.

"We wouldn't change a thing, would we?" he asked instead.

Cassie stared at him, feeling her brow wrinkle with confusion, but then, remembering that they weren't alone, she swallowed against the dryness of her mouth and nodded.

"We're very, very happy," she said to the couple across the table, reaching for her wine and taking a large gulp.

Because they were. They were very happy. Except that right now, she felt anything but.

"SO," CASSIE SAID AS THEY walked a few blocks from where the cab had dropped them in Soho. "You changed our story on me."

"Our story?" Grant raised an eyebrow.

"You know." Cassie gave him a playful jab with her elbow. "About our wedding plans."

"We don't have any wedding plans," Grant said simply.

Cassie felt her breath stall in her lungs for a moment. It was true, they didn't, at least not currently, but the way Grant said it made her start to wonder if there would never be any plans, not in the near future, maybe not at all.

"I meant it when I said that we're happy as we are," Grant said, now being the one to give her the playful jab.

Cassie tried to fight her frown, but she couldn't. She'd been with Grant for over five years, the longest relationship she'd ever been in. Certainly longer than any relationship her mother had ever been in. She loved him. She loved their life. She was happy. But she wanted more.

She always had.

"Do you not have any plans to get married?" she asked. They talked about weddings all the time. It was impossible not to given her profession. Sure, they had never talked about their own, but he hadn't proposed yet, and she hadn't wanted to pressure him, but now, the conversation had arrived. Five years later than it should have, perhaps.

"Marriage is nothing but a piece of paper," Grant said.

"I don't see it that way," Cassie said, swallowing back the lump in her throat.

"Well, you have to say that. You're a wedding dress designer," he pointed out.

Cassie shook her head. She wouldn't be using that as an excuse.

"Marriage is a promise. A commitment." Stability. Security. Permanence. Didn't he represent all those things and more? Didn't he want them too? She stopped walking to stare up at him, forcing herself to look into those dark eyes that had once felt so understanding. "And what about kids?"

"What about them?" Grant frowned. "We're both only children, Cassie. I never had any younger cousins. I don't think I'd be very good with kids. And you've never mentioned wanting them before."

No, she hadn't, even though she did. She'd assumed that the topic would come up at some point naturally; it wasn't something you tossed around with someone you were just dating.

Except that she and Grant weren't just dating anymore. They were living together. Sharing a home, rent, and—she'd thought until tonight—a future.

"I guess I figured that everything would happen…organically." She closed her eyes. She sounded just like her mother. Only Willow wouldn't approve of her desire to get married—she didn't believe in being tied to one person or place.

"I always wanted a big family," Cassie told Grant now. "I told you how lonely my childhood was."

Only she hadn't. Just that she'd longed for siblings. She didn't tell him how it felt to shoulder the burden of her mother's choices all on her own, to feel singled out by the looks and snickers the other kids would give her when she walked into school each day or bumped into them in town. How she felt alone, every day, living a life that no one else did or seemed to understand, not even Amanda or Whitney. Especially not Whitney.

"But you had friends," Grant said. "Besides, this is Manhattan. Do you know what it costs to raise a child in this city? One child?"

"I'd never want one child," Cassie said. "I'd want at least two."

Now Grant stared at her, his eyes wide, incredulous. "*Two*? In Manhattan?"

"Well, we could move to the suburbs—"

"What?" Grant practically shouted. A young couple in their twenties stopped their conversation to glance over at them as they passed by. "Can you picture me living in the suburbs, commuting into the city every day? Do you really see yourself being one of those women who drives a minivan and volunteers at school events?"

She knew what he was saying, and no, she couldn't picture herself being that type of mother—even if she didn't plan to parent like her mother had. The soccer games and school board meetings were more Amanda's style, the happy homemaker.

"We could find a way to still be ourselves. That's what people do," she said, but she knew that wasn't completely true. Her mother hadn't been willing to compromise any of her interests or priorities when Cassie came along.

Now, looking at Grant, she had the sinking feeling that maybe, neither could he.

"Look, we don't need to make any big decisions tonight," she said, even though that's exactly what it felt like they were doing, without saying so directly.

If marriage and kids were off the table, then where did that leave them? Continuing as they were? Happy? Or not happy enough?

"We're both stressed out with work," Grant agreed as they continued to walk, now in silence.

Cassie didn't speak again until they were trekking up to their fourth-floor loft. She wondered if, like her, Grant was thinking that it would be impossible to haul a baby stroller up and down these stairs every day.

"We can talk more tomorrow," she said. "Maybe over sushi?"

"I have a late dinner meeting tomorrow," he told her. "Friday will be a long day in the office too."

"I'm leaving Saturday," she reminded him. "For Starlight Beach."

He nodded slowly when they reached their landing, sliding his key into the doorknob and turning it. Cassie flicked on the lights, illuminating the space, from the big white slipcovered sofa where they sat and watched movies, to the stretch of wall that held cabinets and appliances, the long workbench that doubled as a dining space, to the back corner, where her dress form stood bare, reminding her of all that could have been, and might never be.

Reminding her of the design that she wasn't any closer to completing, even as time ticked away the minutes.

"You sure it's a good idea to go?" Grant tossed her a worried look from where he now stood at the open fridge, a beer in his hand. "You have that big client handled?"

Cassie nodded, even though she wasn't so sure about anything in her life anymore, a position she'd promised herself a long time ago she'd never end up in again.

But she nodded firmly all the same because right now, getting away from the city, from her bare dress form, and even from Grant was the best thing she could do.

It might be the only chance she'd have to find some inspiration.

And it might just be the only way to make Grant change his mind about their future—especially if he had the chance to imagine what it might be like without her in it.

chapter three
WHITNEY

WHITNEY PALMER STARED at the resignation letter that she'd been carefully crafting for the last three years. Every time she pulled it up, she found something new to add. Another slight. Another reason for her departure. Fresh wording that would perfectly capture her dissatisfaction, her misery, her longing, and frankly, her resentment.

She'd started it just before she turned thirty and the realization that she'd spent all of her twenties—make that all of her life—doing something she didn't want to do made her dare to contemplate a different path. But now here she was, still in the same office, with the same swivel chair, desk, and view, and deep down, she knew that she'd never finish the letter. Never get the prose just right. Never find the words to justify letting anyone down. Never find it in herself to be that selfish.

Or maybe, that courageous.

Besides, if she marched down the hall to her father's corner office and handed the letter to him, he'd have a good laugh, feed it into the paper shredder, and it would never be spoken of again. She'd go back down the hallway to her office, the very one which she sat in now, and continue about her day and every day thereafter.

That's how it worked in the Palmer family. They were excellent at pretending the bad stuff never happened.

A tap on her door pulled her from her daydream, and with fire in her cheeks, she quickly closed out her document and sat a little straighter, something that was expected of her as the Vice President of the marketing department, even if she'd only received the title because her father owned the company, and his father before that.

Her father stood in the doorway, wearing a finely cut navy suit and his signature bow tie, a tired look in his blue eyes that was probably only noticeable to her. She understood. The man was world-weary. It was one of the few things that they had in common, other than a great backhand on the tennis court.

"Your mother's birthday dinner is Friday," he reminded her.

Whitney knew what he meant by this. "I'll pick up her gift on my lunch break." The gift from her father, that was. She'd already given much thought and care into buying her mother's birthday gift and it was wrapped and waiting on her underused kitchen island at this very moment. She'd done good this year, if she did say so, for herself. A personalized silver jewelry box with a lush velvet interior, not too big, but not too small either. She'd pick up a pair of earrings for her father—from her father—to accompany it, knowing all too well that neither gift would please Whitney's mother, no matter how hard she'd tried to get it right.

"Of course, we all know what she really wants," her father added, sighing heavily.

Whitney again knew what he meant. Their family had a way of communicating through silence. What their mother wanted was for Whitney's brother to rejoin the family fold, even if she hadn't spoken his name in over ten years.

"Your brother will never be the man she wants him to be," her father ground out.

"No," Whitney agreed, adopting her father's frankness. "I think she just wishes that it all could have been…different."

Didn't they all, Whitney especially? It was she who had to make sure she got into the Ivies when Tripp flunked out of Harvard freshman year. She had to maintain a perfect academic record, even though everyone knew that she'd end up working for her father anyway. There was a reputation to uphold, a family name to respect, especially when Tripp was determined to tarnish it. He was the one who was supposed to take over this company one day, to carry down the Palmer bloodline. But Tripp's marriage had been as brief as his known stints in rehab. If there were any children, Whitney certainly didn't know of any, and perhaps, neither did he. And the bigger mess Tripp's life became, the more pressure that was put on Whitney to do her duty. For them both.

"Have you—" Her father hesitated.

"Spoken to Tripp?" Whitney raised an eyebrow. "Not since I heard about the divorce. That was years ago." She squinted, trying to count just how many. She hadn't kept track of her brother's life any more than she kept track of his whereabouts. He wasn't known to stick with a person, place, or job for longer than a few months.

"Well," her father said, backing out of the door. "Thank you for picking up the gift."

Whitney nodded, even though it wasn't a favor or even a choice. She'd been doing it for years. Another family mess to handle, however small. Another attempt to keep her mother happy, and her father as well, by extension.

When he'd left her office, closing the door behind him, Whitney exhaled a pent-up breath and turned her attention back to her computer screen. She pulled up the resignation letter again and tapped quickly at her keyboard: *This is not the life I ever wanted, Dad. This is the life you chose for me. Did you ever even ask what I wanted? Did you ever even care?*

The ringing of her cell phone made her jump, and she closed her eyes briefly before answering it, forcing her most professional voice. "Whitney Palmer."

"Whit?" came the hopeful voice on the other end of the line.

Whitney paused for a moment. "*Cassie?*"

She felt the first genuine smile pull at her mouth in weeks, maybe months. Cassie Reed had always been the sun peeking through the clouds for Whitney, ever since they were little kids splashing in the ocean and running barefoot in the sand. It didn't matter that they were opposites in every possible way, from looks to family circumstances—if anything, that was what had drawn Whitney to her friend. Cassie's life was everything Whitney's wasn't, and Whitney longed to go along for the ride.

"I didn't interrupt you in the middle of an important meeting, did I?" Cassie didn't sound too concerned, only because she probably knew that Whitney would have invited the distraction. It was no different than when they were nine years old, and Whitney was all too happy for an excuse to leave the stuffy dinner table early.

"Hardly," Whitney replied. "I was just fantasizing about being anywhere but here."

"Says the woman who loves her job more than she could love any man," Cassie teased.

Whitney hardly loved her job, but it was a convenient excuse for not being in a serious relationship.

"Even I take a vacation from time to time," Whitney reminded her, hoping that their reunions wouldn't be brought up, especially the last one.

"Alone, mostly," Cassie reminded her.

Whitney couldn't argue that point. She did take vacations alone. She did many things alone. She'd learned over the years that it was easier that way, or at least, safer.

"I'm actually packing a suitcase right now," Cassie went on.

"Work or vacation?" Again, Whitney's mind wandered to exotic locations.

"Neither," Cassie said, her tone turning hesitant. "I'm going to Starlight Beach."

"Starlight Beach?" Whitney's eyes widened and she realized she'd spoken loudly. Too loudly. She glanced at her door, hoping that her father wasn't passing by at this exact moment. Like Tripp, their old summer stomping grounds were never spoken of in the family.

Now, for the first time in years, Whitney allowed herself to visualize the quaint Rhode Island beach town, with its small shops lining cobblestone roads, the ocean visible around every corner, the smell of taffy sweetening the salty air. She hadn't been back to Starlight Beach since her parents had sold their house the summer she was fourteen. She could still remember standing tearfully at the base of the front steps while her father told her in his no-nonsense way to forget this town, and everything in it. But she couldn't stop crying, even when she'd slid into the back of the black sedan beside her mother, who hid her eyes behind her oversized sunglasses, only realizing by the quiver of her mother's lips that this was hard on her, too. She could still remember the crunch of the gravel under the tires as the driver pulled away, and Whitney turned and looked back until the house was so small it seemed like nothing more than a toy. A big, beautiful, white dollhouse, where everything was perfect and nothing ever went wrong.

Or so that's what they would have people believe.

"Did your mother return?" Whitney wondered what could have prompted this visit. The last she knew, the woman was living in Arizona, selling her stained glass in a gallery. She could still picture Willow, her long, sun-bleached hair tied into a loose braid, her kaftan floating in the summer breeze as she walked through town, often barefoot, a dreamy smile on her lips that used to make Cassie cringe in embarrassment.

Whitney had found it charming, but also a little confusing. Willow always moved slowly, as if she didn't have a care in the world, even though Whitney's father wasn't shy in muttering about all the problems that her "little friend Cassie" did have. Money problems. Problems that Whitney couldn't even understand.

Problems that felt so fixable compared to Whitney's own troubles.

"Amanda's mother passed away last week," Cassie said matter-of-factly.

Whitney sat up straighter. "Why didn't you tell me?"

But the question was rhetorical. Cassie hadn't mentioned Amanda in years, not since that awful last reunion when their friend group seemed to break up for good, leaving Cassie floating in the middle. And what would Whitney have done if she'd known? Sent a card? Would Amanda have even opened it?

"It was a small, private ceremony held where Amanda's grandparents were buried," Cassie said, leaving it at that. They both knew who else's headstone was in that cemetery, and their thoughts of Amanda's sister filled a moment of silence. "I didn't go either. No one did. It's what Amanda wanted."

Whitney nodded, even though she knew Cassie couldn't see her. Her words had stopped coming easily when it came to Amanda.

"What happened?" she finally asked, not sure if she still had a right to know.

"She had a degenerative disease," Cassie said sadly. "Amanda took her in over two years ago until she eventually moved into a facility. I think that it was a lot on Amanda," Cassie added.

Given how Amanda's mother treated her after Shelby's death, Whitney could only imagine how difficult the last couple of years had been for her friend, and she pushed back the guilt that rose when she thought of how she didn't even know what her friend was going through.

She'd gotten used to pushing away the guilt. They all had, she supposed, ever since that awful day when Shelby died. But it was always there, just the same, even if it wasn't talked about.

"Why didn't you tell me?" Whitney asked again. She and Cassie didn't talk weekly, or even monthly, but they caught up on the phone at least a few times a year, and there were the occasional texts, too, usually of the "thinking of you" variety when one of their favorite summer songs came on the radio. They were older, busy professionals, bogged down with adult responsibilities.

But Whitney knew that was only part of it.

"Whit…" Cassie seemed to struggle for a reasonable excuse. "You know that things haven't been the same since the last time we were all together."

There was an underlying accusation there, one that said Whitney was to blame for that, and she was. She'd hurt her friend. Hurt herself in the process. And she didn't know how to make it better. That was just the problem.

"I can't imagine how hard this must have been for Amanda," Whitney said. While her mother was distant, Amanda's was difficult in a completely different sense. She seemed to fixate all her misery on her daughter as if picking at her might transfer some of that unhappiness.

"Amanda has to clear out her childhood home. You know how she feels about going back there," Cassie added.

Yes, Whitney did, but only in her own way. Starlight Beach had once been a paradise, a town where only wonderful things happened, a reprieve from her stuffy, city, school-year life. But when Amanda's sister died, everything changed. Not just for her friend. For all of them.

"We're leaving on Saturday. I found a great rental, right on the beach. Last-minute cancellation. I think it was meant to be."

Meant to be. Whitney couldn't help but smile. It was such a Cassie thing to say. Cassie who was eternally hopeful, always convinced that in due time things would work out, no matter how difficult they may seem in the moment.

"I know it's short notice," Cassie continued, and Whitney brought her attention fully back to the conversation. "Amanda hasn't directly said it, but I think it's going to be hard on her, being there again. She could use all the support she can get."

And what Cassie wasn't saying was that what kind of friend would Whitney be if she didn't show up? She'd failed Amanda before, and now she was being given a choice, to fail her again or face her and hope that maybe, somehow, even in a small way, she could make things right.

"I'll go," Whitney blurted before she could talk herself out of it.

Starlight Beach. She never thought she'd see it again. She was strictly forbidden from seeing it again after what happened to Shelby.

She swallowed hard, thinking of the tragedy, the talk, the conversations that seemed to buzz in the air that summer, how a little girl had been struck dead because her sister and her friends weren't keeping an eye on her.

"You will?" Cassie sounded so delighted that Whitney again felt bad for not being able to match her friend's emotions. "What about all your meetings and work?" Cassie asked, underscoring the person that Whitney had become, a woman who buried herself in this office because it was easier than pushing back against her parents, disappointing them, or making things worse for them—and herself.

She realized she was being handed an out. She could claim she had a meeting she couldn't miss, one that she hadn't seen on her calendar. That she couldn't go back to the beach that had brought her more joy than anything or anyone else ever had.

But if Amanda could face it, then who was she to refuse? This was her chance to make things right with Amanda, or at least try.

"I'll bring it with me," Whitney said. It wouldn't be the first time. And it wouldn't be the first time she was vague about her whereabouts, either. In all these years, she'd kept her ongoing friendship from her parents' knowledge, which wasn't difficult, since they weren't interested in her personal choices. Forcing a breezy tone, she said, "What's the point of working for the family business if I can't pull a few strings?"

"I'll be bringing work with me too," Cassie said, even though Whitney knew that it was hardly the same. Cassie was self-made, and she managed to balance her successful career with a relationship. And friends.

And the only thing that Whitney could properly balance were the numbers on a spreadsheet.

"You think that Amanda will be okay with me being there?" Whitney asked, not entirely sure that their friend would agree to this.

Cassie's pause was telling. "Oh. I think...I think it's just what she needs. Besides, it's been years since you last spoke. Years since we've all been together. Isn't it time to put the past behind us once and for all?"

If only such a thing were possible, Whitney thought, knowing how they'd tried to run from it, each in their own way, in different directions. That somehow it had followed them anyway, creeping into their daily lives, changing the course of their direction forever.

But maybe, at least some things could be repaired. Her relationship with Amanda, at least.

And what better place to do so than back where they'd all met and formed their friendships, a bond that could never be broken, even by distance. And silence.

Whitney opened her desk drawer and her eyes slipped to the only personal item she kept in her office. Some people had framed photos of spouses, kids, and even pets on full display. But all she had was this, tucked away where no one could see it. A faded three-by-five of a trio of girls, standing on the beach, their arms slung over each other's shoulders, their cheeks pink from days in the sun. Their smiles were big, their teeth a little crooked.

The Starlight Sisters.

chapter four
AMANDA

AMANDA DIDN'T KNOW why she was so nervous about tonight's dinner—it was just dinner with her husband, a man she had been with since she was a college freshman with wide eyes and yet somehow way too much life experience already. Surely she shouldn't be worried about one more conversation, except that she was, and not just because she was out of practice sitting alone at a table across from Ryan.

She was nervous because tonight was the night that could change everything. If they were going to have another child, then now was the time to do it.

The plan was simple: She'd wear her favorite sundress (well, her third favorite sundress, because the hips were disconcertingly tight when she tried to zip up her actual favorite and the second one had an unfortunate stain on the lap that she must have forgotten to tend to when it happened, probably last summer, or maybe even the one before that), order a salad (light on the dressing), avoid the breadbasket at all cost (well, maybe just half a slice, but definitely no butter), and enjoy a glass of good wine while she still could. Then she'd broach the topic. Maybe, if all went well, which of course it would since Ryan loved being a father, they'd celebrate over a shared slice of chocolate cake, and then come home and burn off the calories the old-fashioned way.

Now, as they drove through the small suburb in Connecticut that they'd lived in since Trevor was in preschool, she glanced over at her husband, thinking of all the things that had changed and yet stayed the same over the years. Ryan's hair was greying on the temples. That was new. But then, he was four years older than her—and his father had gone grey early. Amanda supposed it made him look distinguished, that his clients felt comfortable when they sat down in the dreaded dentist's chair, opening their mouths wide and blinking against the overhead light, knowing that an experienced doctor was about to extract their tooth.

She'd never had the stomach for that sort of thing. Even when she'd worked in Ryan's office for all those hours that Trevor was in school, before she had to give up her position to be available to care for her mother, she'd stayed firmly in the front lobby, greeting patients with a smile, handling easy, tidy tasks like insurance claims and seasonal decorations.

As they passed by the office that she'd helped him set up, from selecting paint colors to hanging artwork, she said, "I was thinking that I might start coming back to the office soon."

He frowned for a minute at the next intersection. "*My* office?"

Amanda laughed. "It's the only one I've ever worked in. Trevor's busy with camp and sports, and then school. And as you said, he doesn't need me as much."

She swallowed against the hurt of that statement but then remembered what they'd be discussing tonight. Yes, now was the perfect time to go back to work for the dental practice. Until the baby came, of course. She and Ryan could resume their twice-weekly lunch breaks at the little café next door, she'd feel more and more like her old self with each passing day, the hardship of these last two and a half years finally fading away behind her.

"I'm not sure that's possible," Ryan surprised her by saying.

She blinked in shock but then realized, of course. He'd hired a replacement for her, three months into her moving her mother into the house, when it became clear that this wasn't going to be a short-term situation.

"I guess that would require firing Katie," Amanda conceded. "That wouldn't be fair."

She shrugged. It was just as well. She'd spend her time preparing for the new arrival, shopping for sweet little clothes and nursery furniture.

She was imagining a pink and white nursery as she climbed out of the car and walked with her husband into the restaurant, wishing that he might have reached for her hand but telling herself that she was being too sensitive, as her mother used to like to tell her, and not kindly. It was a brief walk, and they'd been together for ages, even if they hadn't had much one-on-one time in a while.

She smiled when she thought of their first date—how nervous she'd felt, but excited too, knowing, somehow, that that night was the start of the rest of her life. Like tonight, it had taken her multiple outfits to find one that fit, one that she felt passably confident in, only back then she'd also been on a three-way-call with Cassie and Whitney, Cassie being at her New York design school on scholarship, and Whitney in Cambridge, at Harvard, as planned. How fun it had been discussing her options, promising to give every detail of the evening before she fell asleep that night.

As she scooted into her chair and faced her husband, she couldn't help wishing that for just one night, they were still so young, with their entire futures wide open. That she was still that young girl, giddily chatting on the phone with her friends, dreaming about what life held for her.

She pushed away those thoughts. There was still a lot to look forward to, and a new baby was at the very top of that list.

"Wine?" the waiter asked before they'd had time to study the menu.

"Let's do a bottle," Ryan surprised her by saying. Normally, he was a beer guy, if he drank at all.

She felt her spirits soar. He understood the importance of tonight. He too felt like this was a turning point for them.

They placed their orders to get that out of the way, Ryan surprising her with the choice of broiled fish when he usually opted for steak.

"That's different," she observed.

Ryan shrugged. "Trying to eat healthier."

Amanda couldn't help but feel a jab, and after eyeing the bread-basket, she firmly pushed it to the side when the waiter reappeared with the wine. Was that a passive-aggressive way of implying that he'd noticed her recent weight gain?

But of course not. That was something her mother would have said, not Ryan. Since the day she'd first met him, he'd only ever loved her for who she was, smiling at any of the habits that used to cause her mother to roll her eyes or pinch her lips. He was patient, kind, and caring.

Amanda reached for her wineglass, wondering if Ryan might propose a toast, but he was already drinking from his glass, rather quickly, she noticed.

"You seem to be feeling better," Ryan said. He was sensitive, her husband. And she was a lucky woman.

"I feel like myself again for the first time in years," she admitted. She felt like she did when she first moved into the college dorm, free of that depressing house. She hadn't even known how tense her body had been for so many years until her shoulders could finally relax, and her heart could stop pounding with anticipation every time she opened her eyes in the morning.

"I've been wanting to talk to you," she continued, and this time her heart did speed up, but with excitement, not anxiety. "There's been something on my mind for a while and it wasn't the right time to say anything until now."

Ryan looked warily at her but raised a single eyebrow. "Oh?"

She couldn't hide her smile, and she didn't want to, either. "I think we should have another baby. Trevor's getting older but he's still a kid really and..." And her husband wasn't beaming with joy the way she'd expected him to.

She stopped talking, noticing then the way his cheeks had gone ruddy, the way he pulled at his shirt collar, reached for his wineglass, and then seemed to stop, thinking the better of it.

"Amanda, you don't really mean that. It's the grief talking," he said gently but firmly.

She stared at him, her jaw slacked. Ryan knew every detail of her story, of why she never visited her mother after high school, but why she took her in these past few years, too. He understood that it was complicated. He understood that none of it was easy for her.

But now she wondered if he understood any of it at all.

"I want another baby," she insisted. "I've wanted one for a long time. I've always wanted a big family, you know that. But you were busy getting your practice off the ground and then I wanted to devote some special time to Trevor while he was still little. And then..."

And then. Then she'd put her life on hold. She shouldn't have to explain it.

"Now's the time, Ryan."

He stared at her and then heaved a sigh. "I'm sorry, Amanda, but I don't think now is the time."

Tears filled her eyes and she fought to blink them back. She snatched her wineglass and took a sip, hiding from the other patrons, hoping that no one was noticing her distress.

"But..." She searched his face. "But...why?"

He looked her straight in the eyes, his filled with something close to regret. "The thing is that I've...met someone."

She stared at him as the blood began to rush in her ears. For a moment she could hear nothing else, just the strange tidal wave of her life crashing before her eyes.

"You've...met someone?" she managed to repeat, her voice barely above a whisper. She looked him up and down properly, thinking about the fish, the wine, the way he seemed to have thinned out in the stomach. Even his hair looked a little different.

She set the glass down heavily on the table, spilling a little and staining the white cloth. "Have you been going to the gym? Is this what it's all about?"

"I didn't think you'd be so surprised," Ryan said with a shake of the head. "We've been growing apart for years."

"Growing apart?" Amanda squawked. "I've been busy, taking care of my mother, raising our child—"

"And where did that leave you and me?" Ryan countered, suddenly sounding angry. He glanced around the room and then leaned over the table, lowering his voice. "Where did that leave us?"

Amanda stared at him, speechless. "You mean to tell me that you're punishing me for taking care of my mother?"

"She didn't take care of you," he pointed out, and then closed his eyes, releasing a sigh. "I'm sorry. I shouldn't have said that."

"That's what you're apologizing for?" she cried. She blinked back tears. What Ryan had said about her mother was true. Everything he was saying was true, and oh, it hurt. It hurt so much. She sniffed hard, trying to control her emotions. "You know I felt obligated to take care of her."

"And who was taking care of me?" Ryan replied.

"Some hussy from the gym apparently," Amanda scoffed. She reached for her wineglass and nearly drained it. And then, thinking to hell with it, she grabbed the breadbasket and plucked out a garlic stick.

"Katie is not a hussy," he replied evenly.

"Ah, so she has a name!" A name that made her real. Amanda ripped off a piece of bread with her teeth, wondering if Katie ate carbs. If Katie had blond hair instead of brown like her own. If Katie really did go to the gym and if Ryan did too. Or—

Wait. Amanda's heart started to race as the possibility unfolded.

"Not…Katie from your office," she said slowly. "Not…the one I hired to replace me?"

The look on Ryan's face said everything he didn't.

Amanda closed her eyes, picturing Katie, with her perky smile and deep dimples, her friendly way with clients, how she was always so chipper and eager to help.

Katie, with her size four butt and her ample chest. Her veneered smile, compliments of the very man sitting across from Amanda right now.

Katie who most definitely did not eat garlic breadsticks in three bites and then reach for another.

Katie, who couldn't be a day over twenty-five. Amanda would know; she'd hired her straight out of college!

"You've been having an affair with your assistant," Amanda pointed the second breadstick directly at her husband. "While my mother was dying."

Oh, now the heads turned. Did they ever. The room fell quiet, every eye in the restaurant seemed to narrow, and she could have sworn she saw a few lips curl too. Ryan's cheeks flamed.

Well, good.

"While you were checked out of our marriage," Ryan replied, matching her tone, still leaning, still whispering. "I was the one who saved you from that woman, as you might recall saying. And look, I get that she's your mother, and after what happened with your sister you feel…"

Responsible. Guilty. There were so many emotions but no real words to describe it.

"I was my mother's only living family," she reminded him. "What other choice did I have?"

"Maybe you didn't have a choice," Ryan said sadly. "Maybe this was just the way it was meant to be."

"Meant to be?" Amanda all but shrieked. "You and I were *meant to be*. We have a life together, Ryan. We have a *child*."

Across the room, Amanda heard a cluck of a tongue.

She set down the breadstick and took a deep breath. They had a child. A house. An entire life together. And she wasn't going to let it go without a fight.

"We'll go to counseling. You'll fire Katie and I'll come back to work. We'll…take a family vacation. Reconnect."

But Ryan was shaking his head, nixing every one of her ideas. "You've changed," Ryan said. "You used to be so light and fun, and…and I know that these past two years have been hard on you. I do. But it's changed you."

She stared at him, knowing that what he said was true, even if she didn't want to believe it, or hadn't seen it at the time.

He wasn't talking about the extra pounds around her midsection. He was talking about how she'd finally close the door to the bedroom after a long day, her mother's scowling face still clear in her mind, the harsh words echoing in her ears, even when she'd settle in next to him on the bed to watch the evening news. How she'd shake her head when he told her she looked nice. How she moved away when he reached for her, not wanting to reveal herself to him. Not wanting to see the disgust in her mother's eyes reflected in his.

"I told you," she pressed. "I'm feeling more like myself."

He gave her a smile of encouragement. "And I'm happy for that. For your sake. For Trevor."

Anger and frustration rose in her throat as she tore off another piece of the bread and chewed it forcefully. "You need to end things, Ryan. We need to try. We owe it to Trevor."

Their food arrived then, but neither of them lifted their forks, even when the waiter quickly moved back to the kitchen after setting their plates down with a clank.

"I don't plan to do that," Ryan replied. Then, taking a moment, he said with more insistence, "I can't do that."

"Can't?" Amanda didn't realize she was clutching her knife until she saw Ryan's eyes drift to it and stay there. It was shaking in her hand, its sharp tip pointed in his direction, but she couldn't think about setting it down now. She couldn't think about anything other than the fact that somewhere between leaving the house forty minutes ago and sitting here right now, with a serrated weapon in her hand, she had lost everything that mattered most to her. "I'm your wife! What could possibly be the reason that you can't choose me over her?"

But as the words flew out of her mouth, loud enough to draw the attention of the neighboring diners, who skirted their eyes politely, she knew.

The blow hit her hard, worse than the first one even, and she hadn't thought that such a thing was possible. The knife fell against the plate and then bounced onto the table.

"Katie's pregnant," Ryan replied softly, cementing her fears, inserting the last nail into her coffin filled with hope. "And we're getting married, Amanda. We're going to be a family."

Family.

Her husband was going to have the family she'd dreamed of, only without her in it. Trevor was going to be a brother, but not to her child.

And even though every person in the restaurant seemed to be whispering, scowling, or shaking their head in Ryan's direction right now, she couldn't fully blame him. Not when what he'd said was true.

Not when she'd been a naive fool of a little girl to ever think that wishes would come true and life might get better.

And despite all the vows and promises that she had cherished and Ryan had broken, in that moment, she couldn't help but hear her mother's voice, telling her that she'd gotten exactly what she deserved.

chapter five

WHITNEY

THE ROAD FROM the highway into Starlight Beach was narrow, lined with faded cedar shingle houses tucked behind tall seagrass that grew bigger as the shore grew nearer.

When she was a kid, Whitney would strain her neck for a peek at the old lighthouse, the landmark that confirmed summer was finally here. She'd roll down her window in the backseat the moment that it became visible, when she knew the ocean was close enough to run to, and she'd wanted to do just that. But she also always wanted to slow down and savor the moment of her arrival, knowing all too well how quickly the days would pass, even though she was so eager to spend them.

It all came back to her as she pulled to a stop at the first intersection near Main Street, where the road turned to cobblestone, and the houses were replaced with shops bunched together, close to the sidewalks, their awnings blowing in the ocean breeze. Not quite knowing what had gotten into her, she rolled down the window and took a deep breath, the smell of candy and fish and salty air all mixing to form something strangely wonderful.

Something that felt like summer.

Someone behind her honked their horn, and Whitney quickly pushed through the light, rolling up her window. Focusing. She had to stay focused. Because when she didn't, bad things could happen, like what happened to Shelby all those years ago. And what she'd said to Amanda at their last reunion.

She drove slowly, the familiar sights coming back to her. The town hadn't changed much in all these years, not that this was surprising. Starlight Beach was quaint like that, not built up like neighboring beach towns. There were no big resorts or restaurant chains here. People came to Starlight Beach to relax, to slow down, and even to escape—not that Whitney was expecting anything of the sort. She was here on a mission: to mend her friendship with Amanda.

To get in and get out. And hopefully, this time, to never look back.

She'd planned to go straight to the cottage, hunker down, and get unpacked before anyone else arrived, but one glance at the clock on the dashboard of her Mercedes showed that she still had forty-five minutes before she was scheduled to collect the key at the cottage Cassie had rented for them for the week.

A week of no work. No office talk. No suffering through the glances people still gave each other when she said something in a meeting that they disagreed with. She knew the look, of course. It said: Go along with it. She's the boss's daughter. Someday, she'll be running this place.

But here she wasn't the boss's daughter—and if she had any say in it, no one would even have to know she was a Palmer. She was just a tourist, here for a week. No longer a summer person. No longer someone who could call this place home.

She turned at the next corner, the street opening up to a wide stretch of ocean, the dark blue a sharp contrast with the clear sky, where seagulls swooped and soared. She pulled to a stop just as someone was backing out of a coveted parking spot, deciding that it was as good a place as any to stretch her legs.

From behind the shield of her sunglasses, she saw that the Barefoot Bistro was still in business and thriving from the looks of the people who sat outside on the white wooden deck furniture, sipping drinks and admiring the view.

She hesitated, pulled by the desire to go back to one of her favorite haunts in town, even if her parents had always turned their nose at the place, preferring the Marina Café, or the other white-tablecloth restaurants that lined the shore. Maybe that was why Whitney had loved coming here so much—because she didn't have to worry about manners and posture or keeping one hand in her lap while she ate. Here she could kick off her flip-flops, feel the wind in her hair, and breathe.

She closed her eyes and did just that.

The bistro was shingle-sided like many other buildings in town, its white paint crisp, but her eyes were on the ocean, which was active today, its waves crashing at the shoreline in an almost hypnotic rhythm. She held her breath as she passed tables of diners who were relaxing on the large patio space, wondering if anyone recognized her, but all she saw was a sea of strangers, probably tourists. Knowing better than to expect a table at this hour, especially outside, she walked through the door and into the nautical-themed interior. She briefly scanned the room for a table near the open windows, but when her gaze swept to the bar it stopped there. Screeched to a halt, was more like it.

It couldn't be. Not here. Why here? And why now after all this time?

"Tripp?" The word came out in a whisper, but somehow, even from a good ten feet away, the man seemed to have heard anyway. His broad back was hunched over the bar, his dark auburn hair that curled slightly at the nape of his neck was a dead giveaway, and as he turned, his expression went from curious to angry to resigned all in a matter of seconds. Maybe less.

The surprise, it seemed, was on him.

"Whit?" Tripp frowned at her briefly before his familiar face broke into a grin.

Her breath caught as she stared at him, her heart pounding so hard that for a moment she felt like it would break. It seemed unfair to think that a broken heart could still break, but looking at her brother, feeling that pull of affection that she'd thought she'd laid to rest a long time ago, she knew that it could.

She narrowed her eyes at her brother, studying him closely, looking for the telltale signs of a slight droop at the corner of his mouth, a glassiness in his blue eyes as she tentatively approached. Her gaze landed on the drink in his hand, but unless that was a tumbler of straight vodka, it would appear he was only enjoying a glass of water. Still…

"What the hell are you doing here?" she blurted as she walked toward him, because of all the places, this was the absolute last she expected to find him. And the last place he should be. He knew the deal as well as she did: when they'd left this town, they were to never speak of it again. And they certainly weren't to ever return.

Leave it to Tripp to break another rule.

"I could ask you the same." He seemed amused by her question. "Mom and Dad send you to find me?"

He didn't stand to hug her, and she didn't lean in, even though they hadn't spoken in years, and hadn't seen each other in longer than that. She swallowed hard, not liking to think back on the last time she'd seen Tripp when his then-wife had invited Whitney for a weekend visit to their rundown rental home outside of Burlington, Vermont, only for Whitney to watch her brother bitterly toss back drink after drink. He'd recently lost yet another job (Whitney didn't need to guess why), this time at one of the ski resorts, and though his wife would never say it, they were hurting for money. Whitney had left a large check on the kitchen counter before she'd left a day earlier than planned. It was never cashed.

"Mom and Dad don't know where you are," Whitney told him. "Neither did I. The last Christmas gift I sent you was returned to sender." Not only had he not forwarded his new address, he hadn't shared it either. Now, she understood why. "I'm here to see Cassie and Amanda."

Just saying Amanda's name made her chest tighten up. There was a good chance that this reunion would end as soon as it began.

One problem at a time, she told herself.

"No one in the family has heard from you in years, Tripp," she said.

Not since she'd called him around Thanksgiving that one year, only to hear his slurred words tell her that Vanessa had left him again—this time for good. He hadn't seemed too broken up about it, even though Whitney had liked Vanessa nearly as much as she'd pitied the woman. Tripp wasn't an easy man to put up with—and Vanessa, like Whitney, had given up trying to save him.

"I live here now," Tripp said simply.

Whitney felt the blood slowly drain from her face as her worst fear was confirmed. The din of the restaurant seemed to fall silent around them. She stared at her older brother's face, his features so similar to her own, just larger, and a little more chiseled, and waited for that flash of his grin that used to let him get away with everything at one point in time.

"Please tell me you're joking," she managed to say as her heart began to thump against her ribcage.

But Tripp just smiled mildly and shrugged. "I've been living here for over a year now, if you'd bothered to call."

So they were playing the blame game? Whitney was having none of it. "I seem to recall that the last time we spoke, you told me to leave you alone. In less polite words, of course."

Tripp stiffened for a moment and then reached for his glass. He drank half of it back, making her again question its contents.

He held the glass out to her. His eyes were filled with mirth but there was an edge to his tone. "You want a sniff?"

She wanted to—badly—but Tripp wasn't her responsibility anymore, or so she kept telling herself. But most days, it felt like everyone in her family was her responsibility. That she was the knot carefully, barely, holding them all together. That she'd never be free.

"Why here of all places?" Whitney demanded, knowing that there was no use in rehashing their last conversation or why they hadn't spoken in so long. It had been years ago, and Tripp probably didn't even remember it.

He had a convenient way of not remembering a lot of things, most especially the mess he'd made of his life, or that Whitney had been forced to pick up after it.

"Why not here?" he countered, rather than answer directly.

Whitney felt her anger stir. Yes, Tripp was a rebel, he'd made that clear in small and big ways starting from the time he was seven years old and refused to wear his blazer at the prep school their parents eventually sent them both to, landing him in the headmaster's office at least once a day. By the time Whitney started classes four years later, the teacher saw her last name on the attendance list and cast a worried look her way, only to sigh in relief days later when they realized that Whitney was nothing like her brother. She was a rule-monger. A good girl, as everyone liked to say.

But most days, in fact, lately all days, she hated being cast in that role.

"I don't have time for this," Whitney said now, pushing back from the bar top. "Cassie's waiting for me." It wasn't likely, what with Cassie never being prompt by nature, but maybe she could get into the rental cottage early or sit on the beach while she waited. Maybe she'd close her eyes for a bit and by the time she opened them, all of this would have faded away, like a bad dream.

"Do me a favor," she said, as she stepped back. "Don't ever let Mom and Dad know you're here."

Tripp lifted an eyebrow as if to tell her that was a tall ask. They stared each other down, the restaurant again seeming to go still, as if nothing existed other than their family drama, the unspoken words, and the history that bound them. She saw in the softening of his eyes that he knew it. That he felt it.

Their parents didn't even know that she was here, but Tripp in Starlight Beach? For the past year?

That could only stir up one thing. Trouble. And like always, it would just mean more problems for her.

THE COTTAGE WAS JUST UP the road, and Whitney was caught off guard to see another car already parked out front when she arrived, now just twenty minutes ahead of the agreed-upon time. She scanned the car closely, but the plates were local, meaning Cassie hadn't beat her here—or God forbid Amanda. No, Cassie had promised to arrive ahead of their friend, and Whitney was grateful for that. Cassie had an easygoing way about her that countered Whitney's anxious energy. Cassie would probably mix up a pitcher of margaritas and act like nothing had happened, and maybe eventually, Amanda and Whitney would too. Maybe their little tryst would just fade into the past—but like so many other things, it wouldn't be completely forgotten.

Just never spoken of again.

Whitney texted Cassie to let her know she was here and then stepped out of the car. The cottage was like many others that fronted the wide beach: weathered grey cedar shingles covered the two-story structure, interrupted by plenty of windows with crisp white trim and overflowing flower boxes. Tall hydrangea bushes bloomed on either side of the front porch in shades of blue and purple and wrapped around the sides to where Whitney could make out a peek of the ocean. It was a friendly house, the kind of house that Amanda had always dreamed of living in when they were little—and Whitney had too, not that she had ever admitted as such, not when she lived in a house twenty times the size of it. She had the perfect life; there was no room to complain.

She walked up the steps to the navy-painted front door, noticing upon reaching it that it was slightly ajar.

"Hello?" she called out tentatively, giving the handle a push. "Hello?"

Immediately, a man ducked his head into the hallway from the far end of the house, but even from this distance, Whitney could make out warm dark eyes and a wide grin.

Something in her stomach tightened as he approached, the smile filling his face and crinkling the corners of his eyes. His sandy-colored hair was longer than what she was used to seeing in the office every day and streaked with highlights from days spent in the sun. A slight tan brought a healthy glow to his handsome face that was a sharp comparison to her Vitamin D-lacking complexion.

"Cassie?" The man extended a hand.

"I'm Cassie's friend. Whitney Pa—" She stopped before she could say anything more. Cassie had rented the place, which should be enough, and no good would come from saying her last name around these parts. The Palmer name bore a lot of weight in her native city of Boston, and just as much here once—a reputation that they worked to uphold. Well, all of them except Tripp.

But she'd never seen this man before. Would he know about the big, sprawling house half a mile down the beach that once belonged to her family? The house where they'd live from Memorial Day through Labor Day, each year, up until that fateful summer when they'd boarded up the house for good? Or had the Palmer name faded out into the ocean breeze by now, along with the events of that tragic day?

"Whitney." The man studied her a second longer before his mouth quirked into a grin. "I'm Derek. Derek Chase."

She took his hand, giving it a firm shake like she'd been trained to do from a young age, but she couldn't help focusing on his smooth palm, on the warmth of his skin pressed against hers.

She snatched her hand back. She'd been out of the dating scene for too long, even though she usually preferred it that way. A drink here or there worked for her, sometimes even a casual fling that might last for a few months, revolving around her busy schedule.

She'd gotten used to being alone. Comfortable. Even content. But she'd just had a taste of what she was missing and that…well, that was dangerous.

Her life was best when it was contained. Neat and orderly. When no mistakes could be made. And no one could get hurt.

"I can give you a quick tour if you'd like," he offered, motioning toward the back of the house.

She started to protest. The cottage was small; she could get her bearings in a few minutes, on her own. But for some reason, she didn't want to be alone right now. Maybe it was because she was here, in Starlight Beach. Or maybe it was because she was still recovering from the shock of seeing Tripp, after all this time. And here. Of all places. Or maybe it was just the fear that Amanda could walk through that door at any minute, and she didn't have a clue what she was going to say when she saw her.

"Only if I'm not keeping you," Whitney said.

"Not in the least," Derek assured her. He smiled again and her stomach went all funny. It was silly, she knew, having an attraction like this for a man she'd just met. A man who lived here, at Starlight Beach, of all places. She wasn't the type to have a fling, and that wasn't the point of her visit either.

She followed him into the kitchen at the back of the house, which opened into an expansive living room. As expected, a wall of windows extended from one side of the house to the other, giving a full view of a back porch and the ocean beyond it.

She stood there for a moment, taking it in, watching a little boy fly a kite, a girl who was probably his sister chasing him. She smiled at the innocence of the activity, of the thrills that could be found without money or pretense, and at the memory of days spent doing the very same thing, flying a bright pink kite, building a sandcastle, collecting shells into a bucket.

She'd traveled the world, stayed in the best hotels, and eaten in the finest restaurants, but nothing had ever compared to how she felt here on this beach.

"I never tire of this view," Whitney sighed.

"Oh?" Derek tipped his head. "You've been here before?"

Whitney felt her cheeks grow warm. She turned her gaze abruptly from the window and managed, "Oh, not here. Not this house. But I've been to Starlight Beach before...when I was...younger."

"I'm surprised our paths never crossed," he said. "I used to visit my grandmother here every August."

She stared at him, gauging how old he was, guessing that he was a couple of years older than she was, but then maybe not. Her regularly scheduled Botox appointments that her mother insisted she start as preventative treatment when she turned thirty had kept some of the natural wrinkles she had at bay.

"Maybe they did cross," she said nervously, thinking of how the Palmers were a known family back then, not just for their big house but for the parties that they would throw each summer. Half the town was invited. The other half worked shifts to make it a success.

Her mind shifted to Tripp, how he was back, and their name would have resurfaced by now. Starlight Beach was a close-knit community. Derek probably knew him. But what else did he know?

Derek suddenly grinned. "Nah. I would have remembered a girl like you."

Whitney felt her cheeks positively flame and she looked out to the ocean once more, her heart lifting with the rise of the waves, before turning back to the living room, with its wall of shelves, glass jars filled with shells, and throw pillows in every shade of blue on white slipcovered sofas. It was a cozy space. Informal. A place where she could open the windows, sit, and finally breathe.

"Cassie grew up here. And Amanda, too, the other woman staying with us this week."

"So it's a reunion!" Derek didn't seem to sense how triggering the word was for her.

It was a reunion. Their first in three years. But hopefully, the first of many more to come.

He continued the tour, showing her the three bedrooms upstairs, each with dormer windows overlooking the ocean. One bigger than the other two, and Whitney immediately decided that Amanda should have it. She needed it the most, and she deserved it too. It was the least Whitney could do for her, all considered.

Once back downstairs, Derek handed her a key and then pointed to the kitchen counter, where two others sat on the marble surface.

"I figured you'd each want your own key," he said. "It unlocks the front and back doors."

Whitney knew he probably had to get back to the real estate office, or maybe even another showing, but she didn't want to let him go just yet. She didn't want to be alone in this house, not with the ocean so close she could run out and touch it, not with the memories of all that had happened here encroaching.

Cassie would be here soon. She'd fill the place with life and positive energy.

But for now, Whitney had Derek. And it was more than his handsome face and easy demeanor that made her want to continue this conversation.

"How long has it been since you've been back?" he asked casually, showing no signs of heading to the door just yet.

"Me?" She didn't need to do the math but still, she paused as the reality of it sank in. "About eighteen years."

"That long? That's too bad." He rolled back on his heels, appraising her. "Your family doesn't come every summer anymore?"

"No," she said too firmly, then added, "I live in Boston now."

"Boston's not far from here," he said lightly. "Used to live there myself."

"Oh?" It wasn't surprising, because like he'd said, Boston wasn't very far from here at all. But it felt like a million miles somehow. "You live here full-time now?"

Derek nodded. "Starlight Beach was a magical place for me as a kid. When the opportunity presented itself to move here a few years ago, I took it."

Well, there it was. Any thought she had that she and this man might...have something...vanished. She couldn't have any connection to Starlight Beach. She shouldn't even be here.

"This was my grandmother's house," he continued. "Of course, it needed work when I inherited it. You know how these old properties can become if they're left unattended. The ocean air can wreak havoc."

Whitney still wondered what had become of her house, just down the shoreline. If it had stayed empty for long after they'd absconded from it, or if another family had quickly moved into it. If they'd been happy there. If they'd been lucky enough to stay.

"Well, I live close by, so be sure to reach out if you need anything. I left my number on the key ring," Derek added.

She looked down at her hand, where sure enough his name and phone number were written on the plastic keyring as if inviting her to find an excuse to call. To talk.

To...nothing.

There was nothing for her left in this town, nothing good anyway. And stumbling upon Tripp was proof of that.

chapter six

CASSIE

THERE WAS NO sense in worrying, Cassie told herself for about the hundredth time since she agreed to come on this trip. It was a line her mother had used for as far back as Cassie could remember. "Does worrying change the facts?" she'd ask. It didn't, sadly. And worrying, Cassie eventually came to realize, only made the situation worse than it already was.

But still, Cassie was worried right now—very worried—about too many things to count.

Worry number one: Whitney was already at the cottage.

She had texted when she arrived, and Cassie could only hope that the lack of pings from her phone that sat cradled in the cupholder of her rental car meant that Amanda hadn't shown up yet.

Still, Cassie's foot pushed a little harder on the gas pedal as her eyes darted around for cops. A ticket would just delay her arrival, leaving the possibility of Amanda walking in to find Whitney without any warning.

Again, Cassie cursed herself for not arriving earlier, but (cue worry number two!) her current bridezilla had called late last night, insisting on a morning meeting, which had lasted longer than anticipated. And when was Whitney ever late for anything? Unlike Cassie, Whitney operated on a schedule, one that led to paths of success, one that guaranteed that everything in her life was always calm and peaceful and exactly as she wanted it.

Whereas Cassie's life wasn't going according to any plans, or intentions, no matter her effort.

She glanced down at her phone again, sitting dark and silent beside her, thinking of Grant, otherwise known as worry number three. They'd said a stilted good-bye as she packed up her suitcase this morning, and for the first time since they'd met, Cassie had almost felt relieved to be away from his company.

There was meaning in that, she knew. One that Willow would tell her to explore.

One that Cassie wasn't ready to confront.

One that she could only worry about.

But all thoughts of Grant and the wedding dress and the difficult client vanished when the dunes parted and there, not more than a quarter of a mile in the distance, was Starlight Beach. She slowed her speed for the first time since she'd taken the wheel, wanting to take the sight in, to commit it to memory, even though, as her gaze lingered on the cedar-shingled buildings that lined the cobblestone road in town, she knew that it was all there already. Maybe not in her mind, but in her heart. A part that had been tucked away, closed off, not forgotten but perhaps denied.

She swallowed hard as she passed the candy store, where she'd stolen more than her share of salt water taffy. She'd always suspected that old Mr. Whittaker who owned the place knew what she was up to—but if he did, he'd never said anything. Maybe he didn't think it was worth it. Or maybe he knew just how precious those candies were to her; how impossible it was to come by a treat like that unless Willow was going through one of her dumpster diving phases. Once, she'd thought she saw him standing at the window, watching her from across the street when she'd crammed the soft piece of candy into her mouth, but instead of frowning, she could have sworn she'd seen him smile.

Cassie's heart pulled tight as she took a fleeting glance at the old storefront with its pink- and-white-striped awning rippling in the breeze, which, like many in town, had been passed down through the generations. Mr. Whittaker must have been at least seventy when she left for college. Had his son taken over by now? Or grandson?

The thought that some things had undoubtedly changed in the fourteen years since she'd last been here made a lump form in her throat, even though she knew that she wasn't the same little girl who had been desperate enough to grab a handful of sweets and dash out a door. She'd left all that behind—for a better life. For security.

Thinking of Grant and her current life back in Manhattan, she nearly snorted at that thought.

Dune Road was just ahead. She didn't need directions to find the cottage. There were dozens of them on this stretch of beach—good-sized homes with a priceless view of the Atlantic—and the one she'd rented was grey with a navy front door and a weathered wooden welcome sign that hung over the doorway.

She smiled when she spotted it but nearly kept going when she saw that there was not one but two cars parked in the small driveway.

Panic quickened her pulse as the car slowed to a stop. Surely Amanda hadn't arrived already. She would have called. Or

Whitney would have texted. Or maybe they were both waiting inside right now for her to explain herself.

A new worry started to turn in her stomach.

And what would she say if this were the case? That life was too short to waste time fighting with your best friends? It was true, but it seemed callous, all things considered. Amanda was going through a tough time, and the last thing she needed was more stress.

What she needed most were her best friends. Both of them. Even if she didn't know it yet.

As Cassie pulled to a stop and stepped out of the car, breathing in the salty sea air in giant gulps, she longed to do a runner, just like that little girl who would sprint from the candy shop on Main Street. She could be back in New York before dinnertime. She and Grant could go to that Italian place on the corner they liked so much. They'd order a bottle of wine to share, he'd apologize, and then so would she, and by the next morning, it would be as if their little argument had never happened.

And that was just the problem. She wasn't her mother, who could live life pretending her troubles didn't exist.

But sometimes—like right now—she wished she could.

The door to the cottage flew open and Cassie instinctively squatted down, hiding behind the rental car, not much unlike the little girl who would duck behind trees to indulge in her stolen sweets.

There was some muffled laughter. And a voice—a deep voice.

Carefully, Cassie slowly stood, her shoulders sinking with relief when she saw a man standing on the small front porch, but her heart soared when she saw Whitney standing in the doorframe.

She hadn't even realized how much she had missed her friend until she was sprinting at full speed toward the door, and Whitney, always so reserved and proper, broke out into a grin and jogged down the short set of stairs to meet her. They body-slammed into a long, hard hug, and for one perfect moment, everything in the world was all right again. They were together. Here, where they'd sworn they would never return. And they were still okay. Better than okay. The dress design didn't matter. Grant didn't matter. Even Amanda's impending arrival didn't matter.

It had all worked out somehow. And the rest would too.

"I can't believe you're here," Cassie breathed when she pulled back, taking in Whitney's pretty face, with the bright blue eyes and auburn hair that fell at her shoulders.

"*I* can't believe I'm here!" Whitney laughed.

She had the best laugh. It sounded like the windchimes that Willow always hung from their front porch, made from the sea glass she collected on the beach, the sound traveling up to Cassie's bedroom window on breezy summer nights.

Only unlike the wind chimes, Whitney's laugh was a sound that was often stifled. Reserved just for her.

And Amanda.

Cassie's stomach tightened when she thought of Amanda, and she felt her brow tug with worry lines. She broadened her smile, reminding herself that worrying wouldn't change anything and that it was too late to change anything now. Whitney was here. Amanda was on her way. And this was either going to be the much overdue reunion they all needed or a complete disaster.

But Cassie wouldn't have brought Whitney here if she didn't believe that it would all work out. That was the thing about worry; the only way to battle it was with hope.

All too aware now that they were being watched, Whitney's cheeks flamed as she turned to the man who was staring at them with an amused grin.

"Sorry," Whitney said. "Derek, this is Cassie. Cassie, this is Derek. He owns the place."

Cassie glanced from Whitney to Derek and then extended her hand to the undeniably handsome man even if she doubted Whitney would ever admit it. "We spoke on the phone."

"You called just in time," he replied. "I had no less than five calls from people wanting this rental within an hour of speaking to you."

"Guess it was meant to be," Cassie said, giving Whitney a grin. She knew what her friend thought of these types of sentiments, but what could she say? She was her mother's daughter, no matter how she might try to deny it.

"Well, I should be going and let you two get settled." Derek inched toward the Jeep with the local plates, and it was obvious that Whitney was watching him go. He stopped as he reached for the door handle. "Remember to call if you need anything."

Once Derek was safely tucked inside his car, Cassie murmured, "Or even if you don't."

Whitney swatted her. "Please. He's our landlord. Besides, he's a townie. Or at least he is now."

"What's wrong with that?" Cassie asked.

Whitney gave her a long look. "Everything."

Cassie sighed, knowing that perhaps this was true. When they left Starlight Beach, each at different times, the reasons were still the same. And any connection to this town and everything that had happened here was severed.

Only the bond that they shared remained.

Until, that was, the bond between Amanda and Whitney broke.

Cassie swallowed uneasily, feeling that same flutter of nerves in her stomach that used to creep up every time Willow announced she had a new "idea." Those bursts of inspiration were frequent, always short-lived, and included things like offering to read people's palms down at the shore, even though she'd only gleaned some knowledge on the subject from a book she skimmed at the library. Cassie could still hear the snickers some of the kids gave her, the dirty looks that lingered long after she hurried away. The names they had for her, that they said within earshot, even though she pretended never to hear.

"Help me get my bags," Cassie said, knowing that if she didn't, she might just turn around and leave—not just to flee the memories but to get back to the life she'd left behind in New York. The closest thing she'd gotten to everything she'd always wanted. Maybe, it was enough.

Maybe, it was all she could have hoped for.

Whitney walked with her to the car and grabbed a duffel bag from the back seat. Cassie slung her tote over her shoulder and pulled her suitcase from the trunk. After unloading Whitney's car and dropping everything in the hallway, they decided a toast was in order. Whitney had come prepared with a few good bottles of wine that she pulled from a grocery bag.

"Unless we should wait for Amanda," Whitney stopped mid-reach for the wineglasses that were housed behind the glass-paned cabinet.

"Oh." Cassie felt her mouth go dry.

"Do you know what time she's arriving?" Whitney's expression bore the same trepidation that Cassie felt, only she did her best to disguise it.

This would be, of course, the perfect time to mention that Amanda wasn't aware that Whitney would be joining them. But to admit that now would risk Whitney getting in her car and driving back to Boston. It would only further damage their already fractured relationship.

No, a reunion was in order here. If not now, then when? And Cassie had learned a long time ago that sometimes it was easier to ask for forgiveness than permission, even if it was another one of Willow's philosophies.

"I don't know exactly," she managed as she inspected her manicured nails, painted a pale shade of blue. She resisted the urge to bite one—another habit she'd left behind in this town. "But I'm sure she won't mind if we get a head start."

Whitney poured the wine and Cassie drank her first glass in three gulps, vowing to slow down when she poured herself a refill and followed Whitney onto the covered porch that spanned the width of the house and gave a stunning view of the ocean. The waves were big today, crashing and foaming against the sand. The sound washed away her worries, calming her in a way that only it could, and always did.

"I've missed this," she admitted, closing her eyes briefly to let the breeze wash over her, filling her lungs with salty air and rustling her hair.

Realizing that Whitney hadn't replied, she glanced at her friend. But Whitney seemed to be lost in the moment, too, her eyes on the water but her mind somewhere else, somewhere far away, in the distant past.

"It still hasn't lost its power in all this time," Whitney finally said.

Cassie nodded. It had the power to calm her when fear gripped her like a vice, to bring them all joy even in the darkest times. Maybe, it still could.

"About Amanda," Cassie started to say, but Whitney whipped

her face to her, her blue eyes filled with a look that Cassie recognized all too well: pity.

"I feel terrible about what happened the last time we were all together," Whitney blurted.

Cassie felt her shoulders relax as she set her wineglass down on the porch railing.

"I'm usually so careful with what I say," Whitney went on, shaking her head. "I...shouldn't have said what I did."

Cassie studied her friend closely. Whitney shouldn't have said it, but did she actually mean it?

"Probably not," she said lightly, reaching for the glass once more. She took a slow sip, fighting the urge to ask Whitney for clarification.

To ask could result in relief, but it could also confirm her worst fear, that their problems were not behind them at all, but that they'd remained right here, in Starlight Beach, where they'd first taken place.

"To be honest, I'm kind of worried about seeing her again," Whitney admitted with a tense smile.

You and me both, sister. Cassie drained her glass.

"Well, I'll take it as a good sign that she didn't put up a fight about me coming." Whitney sighed and looked out over the water.

Cassie's heart was positively pounding now, and she opened her mouth and then closed it again, trying to work up the courage to say something, but failing to find the words. Her grand plan had stopped here. But then, who was she kidding? She didn't have a grand plan. Maybe she never did. Maybe she'd been silly to ever think that she could make a better life for herself. That things wouldn't always end up messy for her.

"Maybe we've tempted fate by coming back here," Whitney said before Cassie could come up with a reasonable explanation for why she hadn't mentioned to Amanda that she'd invited Whitney along on this trip.

"How so?" Cassie asked warily.

"I ran into my brother," Whitney said. "He was the first person I saw when I crossed the town line."

Now Cassie's pulse started to race for a different reason, and she fought back the smile curving her mouth.

Tripp Palmer was, at least Cassie had once believed, the best-looking guy in all of Starlight Beach. Probably the best-looking guy in the state of Rhode Island. Or on the entire Eastern Seaboard. His eyes held a perpetual gleam, as mischievous as his grin, and every time his mouth parted to smile at her, she fell in love with him just a little bit more.

It was ridiculous that she still got excited at the sound of his name. She hadn't seen him in…eighteen years! Last she knew, he was married! Not to mention that she was settled into a serious relationship with a man that, up until a few days ago, she had every intention of marrying—if he'd ever planned to propose.

"Tripp is…here?"

"You sound as surprised as I was," Whitney said with a frown. "No one in the family has heard from him in years, not since the divorce."

Darn it if her heart didn't soar on hearing that. She remembered hearing from Whitney that he was marrying someone he'd met at a bar somewhere in Vermont, and Cassie had assumed he'd live happily ever after, enjoying an easy life like he always had, like all the Palmers did.

"He's divorced?" Realizing the glee in her voice, she said more gravely, "I mean…that's too bad."

"Has been for years!"

"But you never mentioned it," Cassie said.

"Oh, why burden you with Tripp's mess? Besides, are you really surprised?" Whitney raised an eyebrow and pursed her mouth. "He was always a flirt."

Except with her, Cassie thought with a sigh. Being four years his junior and best friends with Whitney had put her firmly into the "friend of the little sister" bucket.

"I am surprised, actually," Cassie said honestly. "More than anything else, because you never mentioned it before."

"You know I don't like talking about Tripp."

Whitney's statement wasn't just a fact, but also a reminder to Cassie that the topic wasn't an open door. As much as she always longed to hear news or glean information or insight into Whitney's older brother's life, Whitney remained stubbornly closed off to the subject, usually rolling her eyes or shutting down completely, falling quiet, or abruptly changing the topic.

As an only child, Cassie didn't quite understand the nuisance that an older brother could be, but over the years Whitney's complaints had gone from petty to larger in scale, especially when Tripp dropped out of Harvard, something that Cassie did understand to be a huge slap in the face to the Palmer family, who had passed through its iron gates for generations, and later, refused to work for the investment firm his grandfather had started from nothing.

But now Tripp was here. And better yet, he was single. And as far as Cassie saw it, that made the topic fair game.

"Where…did you see him?" She twirled a lock of her hair, waiting for details.

"In town," Whitney abruptly walked back into the house, a signal that the topic was over.

Cassie took another deep breath of the salty breeze and then followed her friend inside, wanting to ask more about Tripp but knowing better. When Whitney didn't want to talk about something, nothing could make her. Her love life was a perfect example, and her brother was another.

Cassie couldn't help but stare at her friend and remember when things were different. When they'd stand out on that very beach and tell each other everything. When had it all changed? But of course, the answer was simple. When had everything changed? The day that Shelby died.

Her phone pinged, and Cassie gave a little jump.

"It's a text from Amanda," she said, glancing at the screen. Her hands started shaking, and she wasn't sure if she might have felt better hearing from Grant—or even her demanding client.

She read the text, feeling only slightly better. "She said she's going to stop by the lawyer's office first and get some of the paper-work out of the way so she can relax when she joins me. I mean us!" Cassie added quickly. "Us. When she joins us."

Her eyes went to her wineglass, which was empty. Pouring another wouldn't help her predicament.

"It's a nice day," Whitney commented. "Why don't we put on our suits and go down to the water?"

A swim did sound nice, and there was no reason to sit around the house, waiting. Amanda would show up soon enough. But if Amanda thought she was going to be able to relax when she arrived, she was in for a surprise.

The question was whether it would be a good surprise or a very bad one.

chapter seven

AMANDA

WHO WOULD YOU *be without Ryan?*
Three years after Whitney had asked that question,
the words stung sharper than ever because now, like
then, Amanda didn't have a good answer. She'd built her world
around her husband, working at his practice, raising his child,
hoping to grow their family. Throwing herself into that relationship
full force wasn't just an escape from her past, it had felt like her
only chance to have a different life, the life she'd always wanted.

She knew that there was context to Whitney's accusation.
They'd argued, over life choices, over her not understanding
Whitney's devotion to the family business and Whitney not
understanding that she enjoyed domesticity. But Whitney had
hit a nerve, deeper than Amanda could have ever cut.

Who was she without Ryan? The question repeated itself in
Amanda's head for the first half of her short drive to Starlight
Beach. She'd run straight from her childhood home and into his
arms at the age of eighteen. All her life, she'd been defined by the
roles she'd played: daughter, sister, wife. She'd failed at all three.

And now, she was hanging on to her most important role by her fingertips: mother.

Until Amanda stopped at that rest stop to text Cassie, she didn't even realize how hard she'd been clutching the steering wheel of her "mom" car, as Whitney always teased because Whitney was happily childless and unmarried by choice. Amanda could only imagine what her former friend would have to say about her current circumstances, but luckily she'd never have to know. There was only Cassie to tell now—but even though Amanda knew that Cassie was already at the cottage, waiting for her, she also knew that once she saw her friend, the floodgates would open, the tears would start and might never stop. But worse, the truth would be out. And once it was out, it would feel all too real.

Ryan. Leaving her. For his receptionist!

It was so cliché, so obvious, that she should have seen it coming. Should have taken one look at those perky dimples when Katie came in for the interview two and a half years ago and sent her packing. Should have hired someone with more experience, and a full head of grey hair to boot.

Should have been more focused on her marriage and homelife all this time instead of trying to make things right with a woman who would only ever see her as a painful disappointment.

Should have held on to those who did love her instead of trying to earn love from someone who never would.

Amanda reached for a donut in the box she'd picked up before her drive and chewed through salty tears as she started to recognize the homes that lined either side of the road. She was closing in on town now, just a few minutes away, and even though it had been years since she'd been here, it still held a strange sense of familiarity.

She took a deep breath, trying to steady her nerves. She wasn't sure exactly how she'd feel coming back here after all this time, or if she'd even be able to do it. But as she pressed on down the road, she felt a strange sense of numbness wash over her.

Objectively, the road was pretty, and seagulls swooped in the clear blue sky ahead. Before she had time to consider turning around, she was cresting the hill into town, and there it was, all the pretty little buildings in cedar shingles and white trim, flowerpots flanking front doors, practically overflowing with pink blooms. The sidewalks were crowded, filled with families licking ice cream cones or women carrying shopping bags. But the thing that Amanda noticed more than anything else, even more than the strange feeling that she knew this place, and yet she somehow didn't, was how happy everyone looked.

No dark clouds were hanging over the rooftops, but rather, a blazing sun. She could hear children laughing as they chased each other down the sidewalk, and for a moment, she smiled.

These were the sounds of her childhood. Of summer. The time when she was free to wander and roam. To be with her best friends. To live.

There was nothing sinister about the place. No one frowning at her through the car window. And the heaviness in her heart that she expected to feel was instead replaced with surprise.

This was a happy place, despite everything that had happened to her here. And maybe, it could be again, for this week at least. Maybe she too could be one of those women carrying a pink shopping bag and strolling down Main Street, her hair rustling in the ocean breeze. She was a tourist now. This wasn't her home anymore. And maybe, for this week, that was what she needed.

To be away from her home with Ryan. To lick an ice cream cone and worry about the calories later.

To worry about everything later.

At the intersection, she double-checked the address of the lawyer her mother had used years back when she set up her will, the same who had drawn up a contract for the property management company to maintain the basic upkeep of the house these past couple of years. Starlight Beach might only be a bit over an hour's drive from her safe suburban life, close enough for her or, once, Ryan to pop over and check on the house, but it was worth the small fee to have someone take over that task. To ensure she never had to go back inside—until now.

The law office was in the center of town, in a corner building with crisp white trim and inviting pots of blue hydrangeas flanking the front door. Maybe they were put there by the lawyer's cute, young receptionist, Amanda thought as she pulled into a parking spot nearby and turned off the engine. Maybe this attorney was having his fun at the office, and his poor wife was none the wiser.

His poor wife. Was that what people back in her small town would call her?

Maybe, they already did. Maybe the neighbors, when they went in for their biannual teeth cleaning, had noticed the little glances that passed between Katie and Ryan, and maybe their radar went up, and when they opened wide, instead of worrying about a potential cavity, they were thinking "Poor Amanda."

None the wiser.

Amanda quickly brushed the back of her hand over her mouth, hoping there weren't any remnants of the powdered sugar treats she'd enjoyed as much as one could enjoy anything after one's spouse had impregnated his size zero assistant.

A woman in her sixties sat at the front desk with a smile. "Welcome to our office! Can I help you?"

"I have an appointment with Mr. Mitchell," Amanda told her. She glanced at her watch, seeing that she was thirty-five minutes early, meaning she must have been going over the speed limit the entire drive here, a sign of her mental state if ever there was one.

"Ah, yes." The woman's expression was tentative when she looked up from her computer screen. "I'm very sorry for your loss. Your mother was such a kind soul."

Amanda was fully aware that her emotions were at a tipping point, but even she had the strength to refrain from bursting out laughing. It was an opinion she had heard many times—from strangers, from observers, from those who only knew her mother from a distance. Yes, her mother had appeared kind, and sometimes she even was, until Shelby died.

"Mr. Mitchell will be back in a moment."

Amanda nodded. "I don't mind waiting."

"Why don't I show you into his office?" The woman stood and Amanda followed her through the door beside the front desk, grateful when it was closed behind her, leaving her alone to face a large, paned window behind the wide, walnut desk and executive chair.

Across the cobblestone street, three girls who looked to be about eleven chased each other on bikes, their ponytails flying behind them in the wind, their beach towels tucked into their baskets, promising a day of fun ahead.

For a moment, Amanda smiled, thinking back to a time when she wasn't much different until she remembered that she and Whitney and Cassie weren't those girls anymore and that they hadn't been for a very long time.

Spotting a candy dish on the attorney's desk, her spirits rose when she saw that it was filled with the salt water taffy that she'd loved as a kid, even if she only ever got to enjoy it when she was with Cassie. Her mother had a lot to say about her weight back then and, well, always. Plucking a piece, Amanda unwrapped it and popped it into her mouth, closing her eyes as she slowly chewed the soft sweetness. She didn't wait to swallow before grabbing another, this one orange-flavored, and then another, cherry, she guessed. One of her hands held the sticky wrappers, the other four more candies, and she was just about to dig for what she knew was a watermelon taffy at the bottom of the dish when the sound of the door opening behind her made her freeze mid-task.

"Sorry to keep you waiting," a deep voice said as footsteps quickly approached on the polished wood floor.

For lack of another option, Amanda quickly shoved the handful of wrapped candy into her handbag and managed a polite, close-lipped smiled through a mouthful of taffy, but as she extended her hand, her eyes widened to see not the grey-haired gentleman she expected, but a younger one in his place.

And a very handsome one at that.

The lawyer took her hand, giving it a professional shake, but there was nothing professional about the way that Amanda's stomach fluttered at the feeling of his warm skin pressed against hers. She stared into his eyes, a deep blue as dark as the ocean itself, but it was the laugh lines around them that got her heart pounding. His grin was wide, genuine, and it wasn't until she saw the slight shift in his features, and the little worry line appear between his eyebrows that she realized she was still holding his hand, well past the shaking part.

She started to apologize, but the candy made it impossible, forcing her instead to smile a little wider through tight lips. The lawyer, mercifully, turned his back to her as he opened a file cabinet, talking about the weather to keep things light, while she frantically chewed the stubbornly chewy candy in her mouth.

He turned, looking at her questioningly, and she realized that he had asked her a question. "Your drive?" he repeated.

She had no choice but to swallow the candy and pray that she didn't choke. Not that she wouldn't mind a little mouth-to-mouth from this handsome stranger if it came down to it.

Her cheeks flamed at that thought. Really! What had gotten into her? She cleared her throat and sat a little straighter. "The drive was wonderful."

She smiled properly now, feeling downright giddy, and suddenly the drive did feel wonderful, even if it did include white knuckles, cramped hands, four bouts of wailing and sobbing when she pictured Katie and Ryan decorating a nursery, and three pit stops where she had to talk herself out of turning around and going back home, where she might somehow manage to convince her husband to leave his new family for his old one. And then, of course, there had been the donuts, meant to be shared with Cassie the next morning. Four perfect donuts in different flavors from the bakery in her town that she knew Cassie liked so much from the few times she'd visited over the years. And the stomachache that followed after she'd consumed every one and shamelessly licked each finger.

Now, as the lawyer settled into his chair and opened her file, she felt her skin pressing against the unforgiving button of her jeans. What was she thinking, eyeing this man, caring what he thought? She'd let herself go—why would he take a second glance at her if even her husband wouldn't?

And then there was that jolting reminder. Technically—legally—Ryan was still her husband. The only man she'd ever loved. The only man who had ever loved her.

How was she even thinking of another man in this way, even if he did have a twinkle in those eyes when he gave her that warm grin?

Even if her husband had no problem thinking of other women in that way. And acting on it.

She smoothed her blouse, hoping it covered the evidence of her muffin top.

"So, Mr. Mitchell," she started, but he held up a hand.

"Please, call me Mark." There was that smile again.

And there was that swooping sensation, one she hadn't felt in so many years, she hardly recognized it. When Ryan walked through the door each day, it wasn't a tingle or a flutter that she felt anymore—and maybe, she realized, it never had been.

The real emotion, the strongest pull she'd always had when she saw Ryan each day was overwhelming relief. Relief that he loved her. Relief that he'd stood by her. That he was kind. That he was steady.

That he wasn't going anywhere.

Well, so much for that!

"Thank you for meeting with me on a Saturday," she started.

He brushed his hand through the air. "My pleasure. We often meet with clients on Saturdays. It's one of the things I love about this town. You don't find this kind of community everywhere."

No, you certainly didn't, but right now, Amanda was more unsettled by the reminder than encouraged.

"I meant to call sooner, but..." But where to start? She'd planned the funeral herself, just like she'd had to tend to all of her mother's medical needs by herself.

"This is a delicate matter, and everyone needs to decide when they're ready to handle the final affairs of their loved ones." Mark tented his fingers on the desk and gave her a kind smile. "It's all fairly straightforward," he said, starting to explain her mother's possessions, which amounted to a car, the house, and the items in the house.

He slid her a set of keys. "In case you don't have a copy."

"I'll be selling the house," she said, thoughtfully turning the keys in her hand. "That's why I'm here."

"It's yours to do with as you please," he said, nodding, seeing nothing wrong with her decision.

She felt her shoulders relax a bit. He wasn't here to judge her, but only to help her. And oh, she needed help, even if she never asked for it.

"In terms of her finances, there wasn't much. Your mother's will is dated," he admitted. "She handled it with my grandfather long before my time. She names two daughters in it."

Amanda felt like she had another wad of taffy in her mouth to swallow as the lump in her throat seemed to close up.

The Dodson name was as infamous in town as the story behind it. Amanda had run and changed her name, but she couldn't change who she was. Or what she'd done.

"Shelby was my sister." She stared at him, wondering what he knew, what the town had told him since he'd moved here because she'd never seen him before, and she doubted her mother ever had either. "She...she died when she was ten."

Died was a kind word for it. Shelby had been taken from them. One minute she was there, smiling and laughing, giggling through a mouthful of lemonade, and the next, she was gone.

And it was all Amanda's fault.

"I'm so sorry for your loss," Mark replied, again not giving away whether he knew the story or not.

"She was riding her bike," Amanda explained. She never discussed it; she didn't even like to think about it even though she did, still to this day, far too often. Maybe it was his kind eyes or his calm demeanor, or maybe it was because she was back here, in Starlight Beach, where it had all happened, or maybe she was closer to a nervous breakdown than she thought she was, but for some reason, she felt the need to put it out there. The truth. No matter how ugly it was. "It was a hit and run. They never found the driver."

I was watching her. I got distracted. The dog got loose. She went off to find him on her bike. And I stayed behind. With my friends.

She closed her eyes, taking a steadying breath.

When she opened her eyes again, she saw Mark shaking his head, his mouth a thin line of regret. "Again. I'm so very sorry."

How many times had she heard those words? They fell empty every time, just like when she said them to her mother.

I'm sorry. She'd said it over and over, waiting first for the comfort to come, and later, for the forgiveness. Neither ever had.

"I have a ten-year-old daughter myself," Mark continued.

And it was then that Amanda looked at his desk and saw the framed photo of two little girls, sitting side by side on the sand, their eyes the exact color of the deepest part of the ocean.

Mark followed her gaze and smiled. "My pride and joy."

"They're beautiful," Amanda managed because it was true. She tightened her grip on her handbag straps, suddenly eager to get away. She'd said too much. Let her guard down. "Well, I should get going. I'm staying with a friend in town for a week and she's probably waiting for me. Thank you again for your time."

"Please," Mark said, taking her hand in his once more. "Don't hesitate to call if you need anything."

His gaze was steady on hers, his smile still kind, but now she saw it for what it was. Professional, nothing more.

She removed her hand quickly and gave another tight smile. Mark was a family man, of course he was.

And she...was on her own.

IT WAS ONLY THE PROMISE of seeing Cassie that kept Amanda from digging the remaining taffies from her purse the moment she got back to the car. Cassie, with her long, golden hair and bright smile, with her sympathetic eyes and quiet understanding.

Cassie knew every detail of her life—except the latest turn. Amanda was now aching to tell her, to release the words, the fear, the shame, and every other emotion that had been twisting and turning inside her head and heart since Ryan had dropped the bomb on her. Cassie wouldn't judge her, or question Amanda's part in it. She wouldn't comment on the extra fifteen pounds that Amanda had put on since they'd last seen each other, three years ago. She probably wouldn't even notice! But more than that; she wouldn't care.

Cassie had her back. She always had. Amanda had always sensed it, but now, as she pulled into what appeared to be the only free parking spot on a crowded residential street, she stopped to think of something her friend had said years ago, when they were just young girls, really, but already carrying so much of the world: "I'm on your side."

Amanda sighed at that not-so-small comfort. Right now, it felt like Cassie was the only person in the world on her side. And luckily for her, she was only a couple hundred feet away.

Locating the number of the cottage Cassie had rented, Amanda was pleased to see the big hydrangeas wrapped around the house, which was even prettier than she'd imagined, not that she'd dared to picture it. Coming back here had felt too surreal to even think about until she was actually here, and even as she stepped out of the car, somehow it still didn't feel real. It felt like a dream, though not a particularly bad one, more of a strange one, where she couldn't quite find her bearings or understand her purpose.

Amanda grabbed her bags from the trunk and lumbered them along the flagstone path and up the stairs, grunting at their weight, but telling herself it offset all the donuts she'd consumed.

She had only barely turned the knob when the door flung open and Cassie stood there, her face so familiar, so comforting, that Amanda almost fell into her arms and wept on the doorstep.

But as the bags dropped from her shoulders along with the stress of the past few weeks, she realized she couldn't do anything of the sort.

Because there, at the end of the hallway, was Whitney.

"What are you doing here?" Amanda stared at the other woman whom she once knew so well, whom once she would have been equally relieved to see, but not now. Definitely not now. Whitney's smile turned to a look of confusion, and a shadow of hurt seemed to pass over her blue gaze.

Amanda looked sharply at Cassie, who was visibly wincing.

"I can explain—"

"You *knew*?" But then it hit her. Of course Cassie knew. Whitney hadn't magically appeared. This wasn't a coincidence. Meaning, Cassie had invited her. "Why didn't you tell me?" Amanda demanded.

"You didn't tell her?" Whitney cried, stepping forward.

Cassie's eyes were wide as they darted to Whitney and back to Amanda. "I was trying to find the right time…"

Amanda stared at her friend, trying to make sense of the situation she had put her in. "You invited her without asking me first?"

"I knew this trip would be hard for you," Cassie began, looking desperately from Amanda to Whitney and back again.

"Damn straight!" Amanda blinked back tears as the betrayal set in. Cassie had planned this, without telling her, after offering to join her here, insisting that they'd find a way to enjoy themselves.

Cassie knew how Amanda felt about Whitney! Better yet—she said that she understood. Just like she said she understood how Amanda felt about her mother's death, and why she kept the service small and private. Why coming back here didn't just stir up ghosts, it stirred up thoughts and feelings that only these two women knew about.

But only one understood. Whitney had made that much clear three years ago. So why would Cassie make this trip more difficult than it was supposed to be?

"I didn't want to upset you," Cassie whispered urgently.

"I can't believe you didn't tell her," Whitney pressed. She looked at Amanda, who struggled to meet her eyes. "I didn't want to upset you either."

For a moment, Amanda felt her heart soften, thinking that this was true, that Whitney knew what it would be like for her to be back here, especially under the circumstances. But just as quickly, she remembered what Whitney had said to her the last time they'd spoken. *Who would you be without Ryan?*

She hadn't exactly cared how Amanda felt then, had she? And she certainly wouldn't care now. The only thing that Whitney cared about were the very things she claimed to loathe as a child. Money. Success. Work. All the spoils that working for the family business could buy her.

"Cassie told me about your mother..." Whitney's face was somber, and her hesitation underscored her understanding of the complicated situation. "If I'd known—"

"What? You would have called? Written?" Amanda shook her head. "It doesn't undo anything, Whitney. You told me exactly what you thought of me the last time I saw you. You see me as someone who lives to serve others. And that's exactly what I've been doing for my mother since the last time we spoke."

"Amanda." Now Whitney's voice was firm, in that insistent way only an entitled Palmer could possess. A voice that she'd only adopted as an adult, and one that she probably used daily in the corporate boardroom. "Can we talk?"

Talk. That was exactly what she had been hoping to do—but with Cassie, not Whitney. And now, she realized that she couldn't unburden herself on Cassie after all. That there would be no long chat over glasses of wine, no laughter to replace the tears.

Not with Whitney here. She could only imagine how Whitney would react to finding out that she'd been right all along. That Amanda had defined her life by her relationships, and where did that leave her when they were gone?

"I'm going to unpack," Amanda said. It wasn't like she had the option of leaving, after all, not when she had her mother's house to deal with, along with all the possessions it contained.

Memories it housed.

She picked up her luggage and made for the stairs, glancing back at Cassie to see the worry lining her friend's forehead, and she knew that she'd been wrong to think that coming back here could end up being a fun time.

The bad parts of this town always won out in the end.

chapter eight
CASSIE

WELL, THAT HADN'T gone as she'd hoped. Cassie cast a wary glance in Whitney's direction and saw the dismay in her friend's expression. She waited for the lecture, knowing she didn't have a good explanation, at least not one that would be good enough for Whitney. She'd withheld the facts from her friends. Worst, she'd deceived them.

"Why don't I go to the store and get some food for dinner," she offered. She was aching to get out of the cottage now, out of fear of what might happen if she stayed, but she wasn't going to leave until she was sure that Whitney intended to stay.

Her friends might both be upset with her right now, even still upset with each other, too, but Cassie still firmly believed that this was exactly what they all needed. To be together. Especially here in Starlight Beach. None of them were tough enough to brave returning here alone.

Whitney paused long enough for Cassie to wonder if she intended to pack up her car and leave, but eventually, and with obvious reluctance, she said, "I'm going to take a shower."

Cassie didn't release her pent-up breath until she was standing on the front step of the house, the door firmly closed behind her. She hurried to the car and sank into the front seat, grateful for the opportunity to be alone and collect her thoughts.

Space, she thought, as she headed back into town. It was what they all needed to recover from the shock. And maybe some margaritas.

Cassie didn't know if it was a good idea to leave her two friends alone in the house together, but right now, she didn't exactly see how things could possibly get worse. Besides, that little voice said to her, as she pulled her car into the parking lot of the small market where her mother used to talk up the produce man for any hookups on things he was about to toss, maybe this was exactly what they needed. Maybe, without her around to target, Amanda and Whitney would be forced to talk with each other. Maybe, by the time Cassie returned with the groceries, they'd be sitting on the back porch, laughing, like old times.

They'd even thank her for making this trip exactly what it was: a long, overdue reunion. The first of many more to come.

She managed to almost convince herself of this as she took a cart and walked the aisles, loading it with practical items like milk and coffee and not-so-necessary things like chocolate, wine, fixings for margaritas, and fresh crabcakes.

The last time she'd been in this market, she was hunting in the bargain bins. The sense of knowing that now she could afford to buy whatever she wanted filled her with a sense of not exactly pride, but more like relief. A reminder that those hard times were behind her, that she wasn't the same anxious, scrawny kid anymore. She had a beautiful city loft, a career she'd salvage, and a relationship that she'd get back on track.

But by the time she started unloading the items on the conveyor belt, her stress returned. There, one person behind her in line, was none other than Missy Cutler, a classmate through high school. Missy, who, like so many other kids in town, used to whisper and giggle anytime Willow actually showed up for a school event or they crossed paths around town. Missy, whose mom baked cupcakes for class parties and used to help sew the costumes for the holiday play.

Cassie fumbled in her bag for her wallet, hoping to keep her face down and conversation to a minimum, mentally cursing herself for leaving her sunglasses in the car.

"Cassie?"

Shoot. Cassie momentarily wondered if she could pretend she had no idea what Missy meant, but there was no denying it. She might have moved to New York, snagged a handsome boyfriend, and made a name for herself in the wedding fashion industry, but the hard truth of the matter was that she hadn't changed that much, had she?

She was still living life in hope, even when it was starting to feel very bleak.

"Missy?" Cassie pretended to only now recognize the woman standing before her.

"I thought that was you!" Missy's gaze raked over her, her eyes were wide. "What are you doing back in Starlight Beach? Your mother moved away years ago, didn't she?"

Cassie tensed at the mention of her mother, but when she looked for judgment in the other woman's eyes, she didn't detect any. "Right after I graduated high school. She lives in Arizona now," she added, just to confirm that Willow was still alive and well. She eyed the cashier, willing her to scan her items quicker.

"What brings you back to our little beach town then?" Missy tipped her head, her eyes still soaking in every inch of Cassie's face, hair, and clothing, which was at least a step up from the rags she used to run around in.

"Oh…" Cassie wondered if she should blow Amanda and Whitney's cover, but then she figured that the word was probably out now—or would be by tomorrow.

That was if Amanda and Whitney even stayed until morning.

"And what have you been up to all these years? Where do you live now?" Missy pressed without bothering to wait for an answer.

"New York City," Cassie said, opting for the easier of the two questions. She glanced at the counter, wishing she wasn't buying so much so she could pay, give a polite goodbye, and dash out the door to the safety of her car.

"New York City!" Missy looked impressed, or maybe, just curious. "Married?"

Cassie's smile froze. "Not yet," she managed tightly.

Maybe, not ever. For reasons beyond a need to stop this conversation before it became even more uncomfortable, she pulled her cell phone from her back pocket and checked the screen. No messages. No missed calls.

Grant hadn't tried to reach her. But then, neither had Amanda nor Whitney.

Wondering what to make of that, she dropped her phone in her bag and dug for her wallet.

"And how about you?" she asked as she pulled out her credit card and hurried to pay for her items.

"Oh, married for three years now. I'm a teacher at the school." Missy sounded content with her life, but then, why shouldn't she?

She lived in this beautiful town, one that she didn't feel run out of, one that she got to enjoy.

"That sounds really nice," Cassie managed, because it did. It really, really did.

She didn't even realize that she was on the verge of tears until she felt the lump form in her throat as she reached for a paper bag by the handles.

"Well, I should be going," she said, motioning to the line that was forming behind her. "It was nice seeing you again, Missy."

Except that it wasn't. She may be walking out of the store as Cassie, a woman who had turned her life around despite her rough start, but somehow, through Missy's eyes, she knew that she could never outrun the girl she was here. And oh, how hard she had tried.

THE HOUSE WAS QUIET WHEN Cassie pushed through the front door ten minutes later, and the only sign that anyone was still here was that the door had been left unlocked. Cassie carried the heavy bags down the hall to the kitchen and hoisted each one on the counter. She looked around the open space, then out onto the porch, and then farther beyond, to the sandy beach where children played in the waves and couples walked hand in hand along the surf.

"Ladies!" She tried to keep her voice more chipper than she felt. Her stomach was starting to hurt in that old familiar way, when she knew something bad was about to happen and she could only brace herself for it.

Only this time, she couldn't blame Willow. No, she could only be mad at herself.

"Amanda!" Then, after a deliberate pause, and somewhat more weakly, she called, "Whit?"

A door opened, and Cassie heard footsteps on the stairs as she began unpacking the food, setting everything out on the counter for now. Amanda appeared quickly, her eyes red from crying, and Cassie felt an overwhelming sense of guilt.

"Amanda," she said urgently. "I'm sorry. I thought…" She didn't know what she'd been thinking anymore. She couldn't trust her judgment—not with her friends, not with her boyfriend, not even with her designs.

Her jaw clenched when she thought of that dress she still had to sketch. Of the blank page waiting for her.

"I just wanted it to be like old times," she finished lamely.

"It can never be like old times," Amanda said firmly.

"And why is that?" came Whitney's voice as she entered the room, arms crossed defensively against her chest. "I'm sorry for upsetting you, Amanda. I told you then. I'm saying it again now."

"Sorry for upsetting me, but not for what you said," Amanda said, shaking her head. "Can't you see that they're two different things?"

Cassie gave Whitney a hard, long look that she hoped conveyed the desperation that she felt. But Whitney was rigid—something that grew more prominent with each passing year. And even though this steely side of her was something that had been drilled into her from a young age, Cassie still wanted to shake her sometimes.

"Why don't we all have dinner on the porch?" Cassie suggested, sensing that this conversation was getting off track quickly. "I bought crabcakes! And margarita fixings!"

But neither Whitney nor Amanda seemed tempted by the offer. Instead, they stared each other down, their silence speaking more than any words could.

"Whitney wanted to be here for you," Cassie tried, but the flash of Amanda's eyes told her it was probably best not to say anything. Still, she had brought them both here, and she couldn't help but feel like it was her job to fix things. "We're here to support you, Amanda. Honestly. You know we would never lie to you."

She glanced at Whitney, whose gaze had dropped to the floor.

"We all have a lot of history in this town," Cassie continued. "But can't some things be left in the past? Can't we move on? We need each other, Amanda. All of us."

Cassie realized from the tightness in her throat that she was on the verge of tears, and not just because of the mess she'd made of this trip. She did need Amanda. And Whitney. More than ever. Her business was tanking, her relationship was at a breaking point, and she didn't even know what she'd be returning to when she got back to New York.

She needed advice. Laughter. Support. But more than anything, she needed the one thing that only these two women could give her: confidence. If they could just tell her that everything would be okay, then she could almost believe it herself.

She looked at Amanda, whose expression was bleaker than her own.

Now wouldn't be the time to mention her troubles, even though she ached to share them, to voice her fears, instead of harboring them in her heart until the panic felt like it would consume her.

She was here for Amanda. Just like she'd said.

She looked at Whitney, who was still staring at the floor. They both were, right? After all, what other reason did Whitney have for coming back here? It wasn't like she'd known that Tripp was in town when she agreed to come—not that she seemed pleased to have found him.

"I'm going to bed," Amanda announced.

"Me too," Whitney said firmly.

"But—" But so many things! It was only five thirty, for starters. The sun wouldn't set for hours. And it was their first night here, together, after so many years apart. Weren't there stories to be told, memories to be shared, drinks to be poured, and laughter to be heard?

She wanted to say all this, and so much more, but from the looks that both of her friends gave her, Cassie decided that she wasn't in a position to protest.

"I'll put away the food," she offered with a resigned sigh. Neither of them protested, and she had to bite her bottom lip from pointing out that this was the second thing they'd agreed on for tonight.

Whitney seemed to hesitate, and for a moment Cassie thought she at least might stay downstairs, but then Cassie saw that she was only giving Amanda a head start, letting her tuck herself away in the privacy of her guest room, alone.

Cassie knew she could use the time to work. That's how she *should* use the time.

Because something told her that none of them were going to be finding any sleep tonight.

THE NEXT MORNING, CASSIE WOKE to the sound of the waves crashing against the sand, but there was no smell of percolating coffee inviting her downstairs, no buzz of conversation from the kitchen either.

Normally on these trips, Amanda insisted on doing most of the cooking, and Whitney and Cassie were all too happy to let her.

But this morning, Cassie decided to take on the task herself, not just because she didn't think it was right to impose on Amanda today, but because unless she lured her friends out of bed with the food and coffee, she wasn't sure what could.

She went to work in the kitchen, toasting bread, breaking eggs into a bowl, and whisking them with a splash of cream, a dash of salt, and a sprinkle of pepper. The coffee maker percolated, the smell rich and inviting. It was a smell she'd come to love over the years. The start of a new day. Hopefully, a better one.

Amanda was the first one down, her long brown hair tied up in a messy bun, dressed in a terry cloth robe over her pajamas, even though the circles under her eyes suggested she hadn't slept.

"You made breakfast," she said, half comment, half question.

"I figured it was the least I could do," Cassie said. Then, because she had to make this point clear: "I didn't invite Whitney to upset you. But coming back here wouldn't have felt right if we didn't all do it together, you know?"

Amanda hesitated and then gave a small nod. "I know. A part of me felt sad, knowing that she wouldn't be here. *But*," she added, with growing emotion. "That doesn't excuse what she said to me the last time we were all together. What she thinks of me."

"Whitney grew up in a different world than we did," Cassie reminded Amanda, even though she often felt that Amanda did too. Sure, her mother was cold, critical, and downright cruel at times, but at least Amanda's basic needs were always met.

Shaking away those thoughts, Cassie went back to the issue at hand. "Whitney loves you," she said gently. "You have to believe that."

"I want to believe it," Amanda said. She grew silent and then shook her head. "But what she thinks of me... She thinks she's better than us. Or at least, better than me."

"She didn't say that," Cassie pointed out, even though at times Cassie wondered if she thought it. Whitney had never given her weird looks like the other kids in town, but what would have kept her from silently judging or pitying Cassie, especially from behind that tall hedge that divided the Palmer house from the rest of the town?

Amanda tipped her chin, giving her a hard stare. "That's what she implied. I guess I shouldn't be so surprised. I never had much in common with Whitney. We were the townies, living on the outskirts, and she was a summer girl, living right here on the beach."

Cassie opened her mouth to point out that her life was very different from Amanda's. Yes, Amanda's life was far from perfect, and her childhood home was modest, nothing like Whitney's oceanfront estate, but at least she had lights that never randomly turned off. A homecooked meal every night of the week. Groceries that were fresh and purchased at the sticker price. At least she'd known her father, for a little while.

"I suppose it was inevitable that our different backgrounds would drive us apart at some point," Amanda said. "Whitney can't understand my world."

"I do understand," came Whitney's voice from the base of the stairs, causing Cassie to startle. She dumped the eggs into the pan that was already warming over the burner, replacing the sudden silence with a sizzling sound.

"I know what you went through, growing up. Even if I didn't live it, I saw how it affected you," Whitney said, coming to stand at the kitchen island. "And maybe I don't understand what your life is like now because it is so different from my own. If what I said came out as an insult, that's not how I intended it."

Amanda stood silently, but the look on her face told Cassie that she wanted to believe her.

"I don't even know how the argument started," Cassie dared to cut in, hoping that if they could rehash that day, they might be able to move forward.

They had a habit, the three of them, of not revisiting the past, even when it was necessary.

"You guys were trying to convince me to join a dating site," Whitney said matter-of-factly.

Cassie frowned a little, trying to remember the details. "Oh, that's right. I found a site for career-oriented men. I thought it might be a good match for you."

"And what you both failed to understand then and now is that I don't need a match. I have everything I need."

She said it with such conviction and so little emotion that Cassie wondered if she even believed it anymore or if she had just gotten used to saying it to herself.

"That wasn't fair of us," Cassie replied. "We just want to see you happy."

"And I just want the same for both of you!" Whitney's voice rose. "Look, my career is my life. It's what I do. It's who I am. And what I said to you, Amanda, was meant to challenge you the same way you challenged me. And I see now that being a wife and mother isn't just what you do but it's also who you are. And I shouldn't have questioned it."

"No, you shouldn't have," Amanda said quietly.

"Look, I've never been a wife or a mother," Whitney went on. "You can't expect me to understand your life."

"But I can expect you not to judge," Amanda replied.

Whitney nodded. "I wasn't judging. I just..."

Cassie flashed her a warning glance. Really! They were finally speaking again, why push it?

"I always wanted what was best for you, Amanda," Whitney finally said. "I just wanted to make sure that you were happy. And you made your point. Being a wife and a mother is what's most important to you, even if that's not what is most important to me. I'm happy for you, Amanda. I'm happy you got the life you always wanted."

Amanda's eyes were wide now, brimming with tears, and she took a moment to collect herself, her hands shaking as she went to the cabinet in search of a mug.

"Yes, I did," she finally said. "I guess…we all did."

Cassie wasn't so sure about that, but she said nothing, almost not daring to breathe for fear of disrupting this newfound peace.

The coffee finished brewing and they each poured a mug, navigating in awkward silence, until Whitney suddenly lunged her neck toward the back windows. "Oh no, it's Tripp!" she all but shouted.

Tripp? Cassie set her coffee mug on the counter before she did something silly like drop it. Tripp was here? At the house?

"Tripp's in Starlight Beach?" Amanda asked in confusion, the earlier tension momentarily forgotten.

Whitney's face seemed to pale as she stepped back from the window. "I really can't deal with this right now."

Cassie looked at Amanda for help, who seemed as bewildered as Cassie felt. "I'll cover for you if you want. I…don't mind talking to Tripp."

The truth was that she felt as panicked as Whitney, only for very different reasons. Unlike her friends, she was dressed for the day, her hair washed and pulled back into a low ponytail, the toes on her bare feet painted. She was presentable, but still, that did little to quell the nerves that were building in her stomach at the thought of seeing her teenage crush again. Tripp Palmer.

Their friendship problem momentarily abandoned, the three women fell silent as they stared out the window, where sure enough, Tripp was walking along the beach, his legs tanned, his feet bare, his hair ruffling in the breeze.

Cassie's breath caught as she watched him, wondering if he'd pass by the house or stop and come inside. If he even knew they were here.

A phone rang, causing them to all jump and quickly back away from the window.

"It's Trevor," Amanda said, looking at the screen. "I have to take this."

Without further explanation, she took her coffee and slipped upstairs.

"Times like this I wish I had a kid," Whitney said wryly. "They'll get you out of anything."

Cassie looked at her for a moment. It was the first time that Whitney had ever mentioned children, and her comment left Cassie wondering if Whitney ever doubted her so-called perfect corporate life.

"Tripp's coming up the steps!" Whitney blurted, and without another word, she too dashed out of the room.

Cassie stood alone in the kitchen, her heart pounding, Tripp's form visible through the glass doors that led to the back patio. She had about two seconds to either crouch down and hide behind the island or open the door and speak to the first guy she'd ever loved. Or at least, adored from afar.

Because certainly what she felt for Tripp could never have been love. Love was pragmatic and sensible, stable and safe. It was everything she'd yearned for and found in the two women who were now upstairs, not speaking to each other. It was what she had with Grant—or she thought it had been, at least.

She took a steadying breath, reminded herself that she was an accomplished grown woman, and opened the door.

"Tripp Palmer," she said, unable to fight her growing smile.

He stood before her looking not much different than he had eighteen years ago, with his tousled chestnut hair and blazing blue eyes. He looked at her for a moment, his brow furrowed until it relaxed along with his other handsome features. "Cassie? Little Cassie?"

Little Cassie. She gave an internal eye roll.

"Not so little anymore," she said lightly.

He grinned, and she realized that his laugh lines only made him more attractive with age. She wondered if the same could be said for herself.

"You look…"

She swallowed hard, waiting for it. Old? Haggard? The worry and anxiety from the past few days couldn't be doing her many favors.

"Different than I remember," he said, his mouth flinching at the corners.

She raised an eyebrow. "Well, I'm not fourteen anymore," she replied pertly.

His gaze was appraising, and dammit if she didn't bask in it for a moment.

"I heard you were back in town," she said, standing up straighter and reminding herself that she had a boyfriend and that this man's sister, her best friend, was possibly eavesdropping on this conversation from a short distance. She couldn't flirt. Even if she sort of couldn't help it.

"Ah, so Whitney has blown the whistle?" Oh, how those baby blues glimmered with mischief.

Cassie tried to fight her grin. "Well, Whitney and I do tell each other everything."

For a moment, Tripp's expression darkened, and his brow pinched as he stared at her. Unnerved, Cassie shifted on her feet, eager to get the conversation back to lighthearted banter. She didn't need this man thinking that she held his sister's lowly opinion. Quite the opposite!

Tripp had always been nice to her, friendly, but not friendly enough to think that he'd ever really look at her in the way she'd hoped. There was no reason to have any ill will toward him then or now.

"How did you know where we were staying?" she asked. "I mean…Did Whitney tell you?" From Whitney's reaction to seeing him, she highly doubted it.

"I was taking a walk on the beach yesterday and I saw you and my sister taking a swim. This is a popular rental house, so it didn't take long to figure it out."

He'd watched them swim. Cassie tried not to flatter herself. He had probably been focused on his sister. Still, she tried to recall which suit she'd worn…

"So, how long have you been in town?" she asked.

Tripp seemed to consider his answer. "Over a year. It suits me, strangely enough."

Cassie didn't see a reason for why it wouldn't. Unlike herself or Amanda or even Whitney, Tripp had no reason to take issue with this seaside town. Her memories of him were intertwined with him loading up his Jeep and laughing with his friends as he cruised through town.

Flirting with the summer girls.

"I can only imagine what else Whitney has told you," Tripp remarked.

Cassie wasn't about to feed into sibling rivalries. "Oh, plenty of stories over the years," she said coyly.

Wait. Was she flirting with this man?

She felt suddenly guilty, thinking of Grant. Grant who was probably drinking his third cup of coffee, sitting on the sofa they'd picked out together, in the apartment they co-owned. Grant who was still her boyfriend, her person. At least for now, if not forever.

"Whitney just stepped out," she said, forcing herself to think clearly.

"I was out for a walk, thought I'd check..." Tripp glanced at his watch and frowned. "I need to be at work in an hour."

Cassie wanted to ask what work was. She wanted to ask him to come inside, have a cup of coffee, and catch up with her. To have the conversation she'd wanted to have all those years ago when she didn't have the courage, and she was just on the periphery of Tripp's life.

But Whitney wouldn't want that.

And Grant wouldn't either.

And Cassie didn't know what she wanted anymore.

"Well, tell Whitney I stopped by, will you?" he said, as he started backing down the steps.

Cassie waved him off and then closed the door, wishing she could have walked with him, not just because she longed to continue the conversation but because she also wanted to run from this house. From her life.

For just a little bit.

chapter nine
WHITNEY

WHITNEY HAD A headache, and it wasn't due to caffeine withdrawal because she'd carelessly left her mug downstairs. Tripp was here. Not just in town, but now at the house?

For years he hadn't bothered to keep in touch and now he was seeking her out. She wasn't sure why; she just knew that it couldn't be good.

She finished drying her hair, hoping that the sound of the blow dryer, much like the shower, would drown out any of the conversation coming from downstairs. When she finished, she strained for any sound of voices, and, hearing nothing, crept over to her closed bedroom door. She pressed her ear to it and, still hearing nothing, she slowly turned the knob.

Amanda's door across the hall was closed; presumably, she was still inside her room. There was no sound of movement from downstairs, but Whitney all but tiptoed down the stairs, craning her neck at first view to see if Cassie was out on the porch with Tripp. She didn't see either of them.

Had they left together? And did that mean that they'd return together too?

But no, Cassie seemed to understand her task, and that was to get rid of Tripp. Even if she couldn't understand the reasons behind it.

Deciding the coast was clear, and with the pull of coffee too strong to resist, Whitney walked quickly into the kitchen, retrieved her mug, and reheated it in the microwave. It was too nice of a day to be cooped up inside, especially when that's exactly how she spent the majority of her waking hours, confined to an office with only windows to remind her that the outside world existed. Telling herself that she was, technically, on vacation for the next week, she opened the door onto the porch and sat on the top step.

Clutching the mug in her hand, she took her first sip, enjoying the jolt of caffeine as she closed her eyes, feeling the salty breeze wash over her face, bringing her back to one of the first summers she could remember, when she was about five and building a sandcastle along the shore. The tide was coming in and the water kept washing over her efforts, frustrating her each time one of her perfect turrets was destroyed. Even then she'd been hard on herself, expecting just as much as was expected.

A little girl with brown braids and a friendly smile approached her, admiring her work and asking her if she wanted to make another castle with her, farther off shore. She was an expert, she said, because she'd lived here all her life.

Whitney and Amanda had played for hours, their teamwork turning into a summer friendship, one that had extended to Cassie. One that had lasted...until three years ago.

Amanda had been right to be mad at her. Whitney knew she deserved her friend's anger, just like she knew she was powerless to stop it. She'd wronged her. However unintentionally, she'd hurt her in the worst way.

Which just meant that she'd have to be more careful with her words on this trip. Much more careful, especially with all the emotions that being back here stirred up for her—for all of them.

"Whitney?"

She snapped her eyes open at the deep voice, and the look on her face must have betrayed her inner alarm because Derek's eyebrows shot up.

"I didn't mean to startle you."

"Sorry," she said, relaxing a little. "I thought you were someone else."

She'd thought he was Tripp, and she was more than happy to see that he wasn't. Derek was a friendly guy, one that she felt comfortable with, even though she shouldn't get comfortable about anything right now. Coming back here was a bad idea. She'd known it, but she'd done it anyway because not returning would mean turning her back on Amanda for good. And she couldn't do that, even if it was what might be best for her friend, and even if she didn't deserve the friendship.

"I hope I didn't disappoint you," Derek said, giving her a small smile.

"Quite the opposite," Whitney said honestly. "I'm happy to see you!"

Immediately, she realized that her meaning could be misconstrued, that Derek might think she was coming on to him when nothing could be further from the truth. Derek was a handsome man, sure, and she'd be lying to herself if she said she wasn't attracted to him, but she'd gotten used to denying herself things that she wanted in life, focusing instead on practicalities. Giving in to whims and emotions only led to trouble from her experience, but putting her head down, doing the hard work, doing what she was supposed to do, and doing it well, well, that led to certainty, and she liked certainty.

Besides, for all she knew, the man was happily married with a bunch of towheaded kids who were busy building their own sandcastles at this very moment.

For some reason, the thought made her chest ache.

"Were you coming to check on the house?" she asked, hoping to backtrack. The last thing she needed was for him to think that she was suggesting he'd stopped by specifically to see her.

But what if he had? Her heart swooped for a second before she put it in check. She didn't date in general; as she liked to remind her friends, who had the time? She certainly didn't. And she didn't have the desire either. She'd never been comfortable with the inquisition that came with getting to know someone. How could she explain to someone things that she didn't even like to admit to herself? That she didn't love her career much less like it, but it was a priority to her because it had to be that way, just like so many other parts of her life. It came with being a Palmer.

Well, unless you were Tripp.

But flirting...that would be fine. It always was, so long as she kept things from getting too deep.

"I came to see you, actually," Derek said with a grin.

"Me?" She stiffened, wondering what he could have meant by that until she saw the way he was looking at her, his gaze unwavering.

So the attraction, if that's what she was calling it, might be mutual.

"I saw you sitting out here," he said.

Whitney tipped her head. "Were you taking a walk on the beach?"

"No, I was on my porch." He jutted his thumb over his shoulder. "I live next door."

"You live next door?" Whitney repeated. Well, now she felt like a fool again, flirting with this man when he lived next door, possibly with a wife and kids, or at least a girlfriend.

"I usually sit outside most mornings," Derek went on easily. "No reason to sit inside when this view is in my backyard. You don't seem as impressed by it," he observed. "The view."

"Oh, I guess I'm used to it," she said before she could stop herself. She gritted her teeth, angry at herself for giving away a clue to her past, angrier for the entitled brat that she sounded like. Who took this kind of view for granted, or grew so used to it that they never stopped to appreciate it again?

She did once. She certainly didn't now.

She glanced at Derek again, wondering just how much he had seen from his porch view, but his expression was a mix of confusion and interest.

"That came out wrong," Whitney said, shaking her head. "The truth was that I had other things on my mind this morning."

Like Tripp. And Amanda. Worries that had resurfaced since being back here. Memories that she'd tried to avoid and mostly could from afar. It was work that kept those thoughts of the past at bay, work that filled up her hours day after day, week after week until the years passed and the distance between now and that last summer here grew bigger. But somehow, every time she stopped and came up for air, there it was again. That awful day that Shelby had died. The day that had changed everything, for all of them.

Whitney stared at the water, so blue beyond the wide stretch of sand, and for a moment she dared to enjoy it, to see it the way she used to, as her happy place.

Her happiest.

Derek hesitated. "I'm not interrupting anything?"

"Quite the opposite," she said. "Seeing you was just what I needed."

She felt her cheeks grow hot. She was off her game, the words coming out wrong instead of directly as intended, like usual. She'd meant that she liked the distraction, that he stopped her from worrying about Tripp or thinking about Amanda, wondering how the rest of their time together was supposed to be spent when they were tiptoeing around each other and nothing she said seemed to come out right.

Even now.

But the gleam in Derek's gaze set her at ease and told her that maybe there wasn't a woman waiting for him back at the house next door.

She glanced over at it now. Like all of the homes on this stretch of the beach, its rear exterior was almost completely made up of windows, but instead of just having the single porch as this one did, there was another porch, stacked above, on the second floor.

"Why live next door when you could live here?"

"Good question but a long answer," Derek said mildly.

"I've got time," she said, not just because she enjoyed his company. She wasn't used to being idle, or to having her thoughts drift. The day stretched ahead of her without a purpose or a plan and that left her unsettled.

He hesitated for a moment, as if considering it, but then held up his mug and said, "Unfortunately, I don't. Once this cup of coffee is finished, I'm afraid I have to get to work."

Work. Right now, she craved it nearly as much as she dreaded the thought of returning. The soulless office, the nagging thought that each day would be spent exactly like the one before it.

But then she thought of the alternative. Who was she kidding? There was no alternative.

"I thought I was the only one guilty of working on weekends," Whitney said.

Derek shrugged. "What can I say? I may have left the big city, but I didn't completely change my ways."

"And what is work exactly?" she asked. She'd learned over the years that keeping conversation away from personal topics made it easier for her to spend time with people. And work—she could discuss that for hours.

"Rental properties," Derek explained. "It all started with this cottage until I spotted a good investment and snatched it up. Before I knew it, I had no reason to return to Boston."

"You own more than these two cottages?" She was impressed.

"A bit more," he said, giving her a modest grin that only made her opinion of him rise a few notches.

Careful there, she warned herself.

"Maybe you could help me out then," she said, seeing an opportunity to not only continue the conversation but better her current situation. "My friend—" Here she stopped herself. Was Amanda still her friend? In her heart, yes, but her head said otherwise. And she'd learned that listening to her head was the only option in life. But when it came to her friends, the emotions that she was usually able to keep at bay always fought their way to the surface. "She's going to be listing a property soon. A small one, on the edge of town—"

"Cassie?" he asked.

"No, the other woman staying with us. Amanda. Her mother was Martha Dodson?" Again, she gauged him for a reaction, to see how much he knew. If people still talked about the tragedy that shook this town all those years ago, when a little girl had been struck while riding her bike, and Whitney and Cassie and Amanda, who were supposed to be watching her, had been back at Amanda's house, lounging on folded lawn chairs covered in faded beach towels, working on their tans, talking about their celebrity crushes, and laughing without a care in the world.

It had been the last time Whitney had ever laughed so freely again. For years she'd wondered what might have happened if she'd stayed home like her mother asked her to instead, helping to set up the patio for another one of her parents' stuffy cocktail parties.

She wondered about so many things, but it never changed the facts, did it? It was as pointless as wishing for a different outcome.

Or wishing for anything at all.

Whitney studied Derek's face, his warm brown eyes, the faint lines around his mouth that gave the impression he smiled a lot. The name didn't seem to register in his expression. But like he'd said, he hadn't moved here until recently and only visited occasionally as a kid. And that story, that awful story that had ripped apart the town and put a dark cloud over the bright summer skies, was old news now.

Even though it still felt like yesterday to her.

"I'll stop by and talk to her this week," Derek offered.

"I'd like that," Whitney said. Then, catching herself, she added, "I mean. That would be great. Amanda will be grateful."

Whitney felt a small glimmer of hope, that maybe she could deliver some good news to Amanda for a change.

"And maybe next time I see you, you can tell me about your work," he said with a smile that crinkled his eyes.

"I can do that," Whitney said honestly, because she could; that topic was safe.

"I look forward to it," Derek said, taking a step back in the sand, giving her one last glance over his shoulder before he disappeared into his cottage.

So did she, Whitney realized. Maybe, more than she should.

chapter ten
AMANDA

AMANDA HADN'T BEEN telling the truth.

It hadn't been Trevor who called—only who she wished had called. Instead, a telemarketer had spared her from a conversation she didn't want to have, not when she didn't trust herself from bursting into tears and admitting that her husband was leaving her and that Whitney was right: Who was she if she wasn't a wife, if she didn't have her routine, her house and her role that had been so comfortable that she'd dared to take it for granted?

Amanda hadn't just lost out on the dream of a bigger family. She'd also lost the one she had.

First her sister. Then her father. Her mother. And now…her husband.

What she would have given to be in Whitney's position this morning, watching as someone who was supposed to love her came walking up the steps, toward her. How could Amanda expect Whitney to understand how important family was to Amanda when Whitney didn't even want to speak to her only brother? Sure, Tripp could be annoying at times when they were kids, and everyone knew he'd let the Palmers down when he dropped out of Harvard, but was that worth holding a grudge for all these years?

Amanda might be Whitney's friend, and she might know her better than anyone in the world, but she had a soft spot for Tripp that she knew was just one more thing that Whitney wouldn't understand—or, in this case, tolerate. Amanda knew what it was like to be the family disappointment, and deep down, she always felt a little sorry for Tripp.

Not everyone could be as perfect as Whitney.

Sitting in the privacy of her bedroom that looked out over the long stretch of beach, Amanda texted her son to wish him a good morning. Whitney used to comment on the way that Amanda could never fully relax during their annual reunion, and she was right, Amanda couldn't. Neither, however, could Whitney, who was forever checking work emails, but pointing that out led to their big argument. Whitney didn't understand that you couldn't clock out of parenthood like you would an office. You couldn't close the laptop or wait to return a call. Amanda's responsibilities didn't end just because of distance or space.

She would always worry and wonder, because how could she not? And Whitney—even Whitney, who had been with her that awful day that Shelby died—couldn't understand that. And no matter what Whitney had said this morning, and no matter how sorry she said she was, Amanda knew that Whitney still didn't understand.

They weren't young girls with shared hopes and dreams anymore. They'd been fractured, first by circumstance, and later by life. They'd each fallen onto the path that had been predetermined for them, even if they hadn't realized it.

It took Amanda three unanswered texts and two calls that went to voicemail before she managed to get a response from her son.

By then, she was panicking, like the palm-sweating, room-pacing, heart-pounding anxiety that had only gotten worse when she'd become a mother. Every scenario, however ordinary, held potentially disastrous possibilities. Every outing, however routine, could be the day when something unexpected happened, and by unexpected, Amanda meant bad, because in her life, surprises weren't often of the good variety.

This trip was a perfect example.

"Trev?"

"Hey, Mom." He sounded distracted. She'd probably interrupted him in the middle of a video game. She didn't care. What mattered was that he was safe. He was healthy.

"Just checking in," she said, trying to keep her tone light rather than desperate. "Did you get the food I left in the fridge?" She'd been sure to label the prepared meals, down to the heating instructions.

"Dad and I went out for pizza last night," Trevor replied.

"Oh." Amanda swallowed hard at the mere mention of her husband. Had Ryan enjoyed her absence, or had he guiltily choked down each slice, staring into the face of his son, knowing that he was about to shatter his entire world when Amanda returned to town and they sat Trevor down for the big talk?

Sadly, Amanda knew that this, like the scenario she'd entertained of Katie revealing that the baby's father was actually her gym trainer, was a mere fantasy.

"I gotta go, Mom," Trevor said. "Dad and I are heading out."

"Anything special planned?" she dared to ask.

"Just guy stuff," her son replied.

"Okay." She managed to keep her tone bright. "Have fun, honey."

She pressed the phone to her ear long after Trevor had already disconnected the call, telling herself that this was the way of the world. Her boy was growing up. He didn't need her as much. And maybe that was just as well, seeing that soon, she'd be forced to split her time with him.

Knowing that her son was oh, so fine without her, she flopped back on the bed, fighting back tears. Her son was out with Ryan, doing "guy stuff," which she supposed was better than helping to set up the crib for their new family member or having lunch at Katie's condo on the other side of town, which was where Ryan would be living soon.

How was Trevor going to adjust to all the changes? Was the disappointment of the divorce going to be overshadowed by the excitement of having a new sibling?

It was just what she'd wanted for him. But nothing at all like she'd envisioned it.

All her plans. All her hopes. All her dreams. Up in smoke!

She fumbled around in her handbag for the taffies she'd taken from the kind attorney's office, but then remembered she'd consumed them last night after the shock of seeing Whitney. Instead, she cried, because what else could she do in light of Ryan's transgressions, other than say, slash his mistress's tires or perhaps add a few laxatives to his morning coffee? Not that she would, but sometimes the passing thought did make her smile. She rolled off the bed and walked into the small, connecting bathroom, where she muffled the sound of her sobs in a towel, turning on the faucet as extra insurance. The last thing she needed (well, maybe not the last, because the very last thing she needed was her husband starting a new family with another woman!) was for Whitney to ask what was wrong.

Whitney with her corner office and problems that could be solved by her numerous staff. Problems that were contained to business, not her personal life.

With a pounding headache, Amanda lay back down on the bed, fatigue finally getting the better of her until she was abruptly startled by the sound of a knock on her door. She must have dozed off, because she felt disoriented by the sound when she opened her eyes, blinking against the light that was filling the room, unsure of what time it was or how long she'd been asleep.

With relief, but not surprise, she saw Cassie in the hallway when she opened the door.

"How about lunch?" her friend suggested.

Amanda stared at her warily, her head wanting to say no nearly as much as her stomach wanted to say yes. She'd skipped breakfast, even though it had looked delicious, and slept away the better part of the morning.

And as for her heart… Staring at Cassie, with her hopeful smile and big eyes, she wanted nothing more than to settle in for a long chat and forget that Cassie had let her down too, even if her intentions had been in the right place.

Before Amanda could ask exactly what this lunch entailed, Cassie said, "We could all use a break from this house. It will do us good. What do you say? The Wharf?"

The Wharf was as much an institution in the town as the lighthouse at the edge of town. It made her think of summer afternoons, when she'd be gone from sunup to sundown, mostly at the beach, or the library on rainy days, sometimes grabbing candy on Main Street, standing to the side when Whitney stopped by the Wharf to collect money from her mother, who was always lunching on the big porch with other summer wives. She always treated them to ice cream, even though Amanda sometimes had the money. Cassie never did.

Now, thinking of Whitney as a young girl with a generous spirit, her heart softened a little.

"Did Whitney say she was going?"

Cassie nodded but then explained, "She said she'd go, but only if you went." Then, after a beat, she added, "She also said that if you didn't want her to go, she'd stay back. She isn't here to upset you."

Amanda wanted to believe that, but then, where had believing in people gotten her in life?

Warily, she nodded, if only because she was still tired, still a little tearful, and because the idea of getting out of this house, nice as it was, did sound tempting. She'd only ever been to the Wharf once, that last summer, shortly after Whitney had returned from Boston. The warm days seemed to stretch ahead of them indefinitely, full of possibility and fun, and they'd celebrated with pink lemonades on the dock, wearing their fanciest sundresses, feeling very grown up at fourteen years of age, their final summer before high school. Before everything changed—more than they could have imagined.

She longed to go back to that perfect day when they were so happy to be back together after a long winter that they'd talked over one another, catching up, making plans, striking that fragile, messy balance between childhood and adulthood, from girls who weren't quite ready to grow up but eager to all the same.

To imagine, for a few minutes at least, like they had that day, that she didn't have a care in the world.

"Okay," she said. If Ryan could have some guy time, then she deserved a little girl time.

Cassie's eyes sprung open in surprise. "Okay? You'll go? We'll all go?"

Amanda nodded again, but if Cassie expected her to match her enthusiasm, she'd be sorely disappointed.

THE WHARF WAS ONE OF the more popular places in town, set waterside like most establishments, and, like those lucky enough to have secured such prime real estate, a legend, passed down through the generations to protect not only the land but also the authenticity of the town, which could all too easily succumb to corporate chains like some of the neighboring areas.

Amanda followed her friends to a table on the outdoor patio, with a sweeping view of the beachfront to one side and the vast, seemingly endless ocean to the other, and for the first time since she'd arrived in Starlight Beach, all her troubles seemed to vanish.

"It's strange, isn't it?" she marveled as they tucked themselves into the table and reached for the menus. "I almost feel like I'm on vacation."

"You are on vacation," Whitney told her.

"I wish," Amanda said, as the reason for her being here resurfaced, causing her chest to tighten up. She pushed it away with a long sigh and trained her gaze on the ocean again. Whitney was right. For the moment, at least, she was somewhere beautiful, and she should enjoy it. "But it's strange, isn't it? I almost have to remind myself that I'm in Starlight Beach."

"Is that a good thing?" Cassie asked, looking a little nervous.

"Anything is better than remembering it like it was," Amanda said.

"It wasn't all bad, though," Cassie, ever the optimist, suggested. She glanced around the table. "We had a lot of good times here. And maybe we still can."

Amanda breathed in the salty sea air and gave her friend a nod of approval. She was sitting outside, with the sun warming her face, her closest friends whom she hadn't seen in years at her side. It wasn't perfect, but life rarely was.

And a week from now, it would all be a memory. This lunch.

Maybe even Starlight Beach.

She swallowed hard, wondering how she would be able to banish it from her mind again after coming back here and seeing it again. Even, almost, enjoying it.

"I'll drink to that," Whitney said, giving Amanda a small smile across the table. "Should we share a bottle of wine, or order those margaritas we never got to have last night?"

"Let's save the margaritas for one of the nights at the cottage!" Cassie looked at Amanda as if asking for permission. "Or more than one? Doesn't that sound like fun?"

Amanda stared at her friend, a part of her knowing that Cassie was simply doing what she had come here to do, to make this trip better than it would have been if Amanda had come on her own, back to the place that still haunted her dreams, crept up at times when she should be enjoying herself, holding her back from the life she'd always wanted. That Cassie was one of the good parts of living here, the best part of her childhood, really, the ray of sunshine in an otherwise dark time in her personal history.

Amanda thought of the house on the outside of town, the one filled with her childhood belongings, the one that would have to be dealt with, and soon.

But not today.

"A glass of wine does sound nice," she said, feeling a little thrill at the thought of having a drink in the middle of the afternoon instead of sitting in the stiff armchair in her mother's bedroom, or driving Trevor to a friend's house, or folding Ryan's laundry.

Across the table, Whitney closed the menu and flagged down a waiter. "We'll have a bottle of your best sauvignon blanc." Then, she looked at both of them, "Lunch is on me."

"No, we'll split it," Amanda insisted, feeling uncomfortable at the thought of Whitney buying her forgiveness. It would only complicate matters, and right now, she wanted to keep things simple, or at least not complicated.

"It's the least I can do," Whitney said, holding her gaze.

There was a long silence before Cassie finally said, "In that case, I think I will go for the lobster after all!"

Even Amanda managed to laugh, and for a moment, they were the Starlight Sisters again, able to giggle even under the most difficult of circumstances.

Three lobster rolls were ordered, the wine was poured, and no toast was made, because they all must have sensed that would be pushing things. And what could they toast to? Being back here, the place that had brought them together and eventually nearly tore them each apart? Cassie and Whitney might have their lives in perfect order now, but Amanda didn't have much cause for celebration these days.

A phone rang, and Amanda jumped, hoping it was Trevor, then worried it was Trevor until she realized it wasn't Trevor calling. It wasn't her phone ringing at all.

Pushing back the disappointment, she watched as Cassie glanced at the screen and, with a tap of her finger, sent the call directly to voicemail.

"Your bridezilla?" Amanda ventured a guess.

Cassie nodded miserably, reached for her wineglass, and took a heavy sip. "I have to finish her final sketch while I'm here. I've cleared my schedule just for her. It's crunch time now."

"I'd love to see what you have so far," Amanda said. Looking at wedding dresses was an old pastime, one that she'd shared with Cassie, all those years ago, when they used to lie on the beach, or Amanda's bed, flipping through magazines, imagining a better future. A fairy-tale ending. Of course, back then, Whitney had played along too, and they'd all known that Whitney would have the most beautiful wedding of them all, but that didn't stop Amanda and Cassie from hoping they'd find their happy ending, too.

Amanda looked at her friends. At Whitney, who had made it very clear for years that she was married to her work only. And inward, at herself, the only one of them to ever walk down the aisle and was now headed to divorce court.

Cassie busied herself with moving her silverware around the table. "I don't like to reveal my designs until they're finished. This one is still a work in progress."

"I'm sure she'll love whatever you come up with," Amanda assured her, thinking of the dress that Cassie had made for her all those years ago, as her wedding gift. It made her feel guilty that the marriage had failed—another reason, she supposed, to keep it to herself. "I loved the dress you made for me."

"Ah, well, yours was a labor of love," Cassie said wistfully.

Amanda smiled despite the hot tears that welled in her eyes, thinking back on that early summer day. It had been a simple affair, with just a few of their closest friends and family. Amanda's mother had been present, but she'd remained on the periphery, and the only people that Amanda remembered from that day were Ryan—and Whitney and Cassie.

"I didn't even know what I wanted my dress to look like," she reminded Cassie. "But somehow you created something that was exactly what I wanted, even if I didn't know it."

"That's because I know you," Cassie said with a warm smile. "Better than you know yourself, sometimes." She gave a happy sigh. "I loved making that dress and seeing you wearing it while you walked down the aisle. I'd never seen you so happy."

"It was the happiest day of my life," Amanda said softly, swallowing the lump in her throat. She could still remember the way she'd felt when she saw her reflection in the mirror, when she didn't notice the extra few inches around her waistline or even the nose that her mother had always said ruined her profile. When she saw the girl looking back at her, she saw someone with sparkling eyes and a smile that almost broke her face. She saw someone who was loved. And beautiful.

"Your dress was stunning," Whitney agreed. "Almost enough to make me consider getting married."

"I seem to remember a little girl who had visions of a twenty-foot satin train and a bouquet of pink roses." Cassie grinned.

"Peach," Amanda blurted, wondering where that had even come from. She'd buried so many memories of this town, but somewhere, they were all still there.

She smiled, thinking of the dreams they'd once shared, sacred wishes that they'd never told anyone else.

Whitney raised an eyebrow. "Peach. Huh. I guess I forget about that."

Amanda felt a pang, even though she was guilty of it herself. Forgetting the best parts of herself. And of her friends.

Of this town, she thought, looking out to the ocean once more.

"You don't think I could ever sway you with one of my designs?" Cassie cajoled her.

Whitney reached for her wineglass, giving a thin, tight-lipped smile. "If anyone could, it would be you, but... My work doesn't leave me much time for romance."

"But you do date," Cassie pointed out.

"Casually. It's tough to commit to anything more." Sensing that her answer wasn't enough, Whitney set her glass down and explained, "I'm always traveling or attending charity events. Entertaining clients at dinners."

"Sounds rough," Amanda commented, mildly sarcastically. Whitney was inarguably beautiful, and she could probably have her pick of handsome rich men in her circles.

Whitney's lips thinned. "My life is not as glamorous as you might think."

"I've never heard you complain about it before," Amanda commented, which was the truth. But Whitney had never bragged either, even though she'd grown up with more than either of the other women at this table could imagine.

"We all make our choices," Whitney replied. "That's all I'm saying."

Amanda felt the blood rise to her cheeks. She should have known better than to come to this lunch. To think that their differences could be shelved for one afternoon, much less an entire week. "I'm not judging your choices. So please don't judge mine."

"I told you—" Whitney paused to take a deep breath. "We took different paths, that's all. It doesn't mean one of us is right and the other is wrong. And I meant what I said, Amanda. All I ever wanted was to be sure that you were happy."

Amanda swallowed hard, but before she could reply, Whitney said simply, "And I know that you are. And that's a lot more than most people can say."

Cassie looked concerned. "But you're happy, Whitney, right? You're living the life you want, with your big career and glamorous dinners and travels."

Whitney hesitated for a beat and then nodded. "Of course." She cleared her throat. "I'm just saying that we all have different priorities. There isn't one right or wrong path. I'm most content with my career and Amanda is happiest taking care of a husband and son. That's all I ever meant." She gave Amanda an uncertain smile. "You got the life you always dreamed of."

"We all have the lives we dreamed of," Amanda said, because she did, for a little while at least. Swallowing against the ache in her throat, she said to Cassie, "Look at you. A famous designer. Clients on waiting lists for your custom gowns!"

"Most days it just feels like work," Cassie said with a sigh and then brushed a hand through the air. "I'll be happy when this client is behind me. I don't know what would be worse, not pleasing her or having her refer half her friends."

"Oh, but you may get more business from this!" Whitney urged in a tone that spoke from experience.

Cassie didn't look convinced. "I've never had a client wear me down so much, and I'm used to their demands. To be honest..." She hesitated and then shook her head. "To be honest, I can't be rid of her fast enough!"

"All the more reason to be sure she refers you to *all* her friends, and their friends, too," Whitney said firmly. "You could be booked for years off this one woman. Something good should come from something bad, shouldn't it?"

Cassie managed a watery smile. "Spoken like a true businesswoman."

"Speaking as a friend," Whitney said gently.

Amanda helped herself to another slice of bread, all too aware that she was the only one touching it, just like she was the only one who probably wouldn't be wearing a bikini at the beach later.

"It would be nice if something good came from something bad," she remarked. It had before, but she wasn't so sure she'd be lucky twice in her life.

"Well, one thing has," Cassie said. "We're all reunited, aren't we?"

They were. In Starlight Beach of all places. Amanda turned in her chair for a better view of the town, sitting up straighter when a familiar face at a nearby table caught her attention.

It was Mark, the lawyer with kind eyes and a friendly smile. The family man, with two beautiful daughters, she reminded herself.

Catching her eye, he grinned and waved. She did too, only this time her smile came easily, and lingered.

"You know him?" Cassie asked.

Amanda quickly turned her attention back to her table. "He's the attorney handling my mother's will. I met with him yesterday. He's a nice guy."

"Cute too." Cassie waggled her eyebrows at Whitney who dismissed that comment with a firm shake of her head.

Amanda didn't know why, but she felt her shoulders sag with relief.

"What?" Cassie chided Whitney. "You only have eyes for our landlord? Derek, that's his name, right?"

Whitney's cheeks grew blotchy, a telltale sign that she was caught, red-handed, or rather, red-cheeked, as they once liked to joke.

She could never tell a lie, or at least, she couldn't get away with it. They'd see right through it. They knew her too well. The only times she ever tried were when she was trying to convince her parents to let her do something she knew they wouldn't agree to without a little creative embellishment, and Amanda hadn't seen this reaction from her friend since they were young girls living in this beach town.

"Derek is a nice guy, but he's all wrong for me. For countless reasons," Whitney said briskly. "Besides, I'm not here to flirt with men. I'm here for some time with my two favorite ladies. My two favorite people."

Her gaze met Amanda's until Amanda looked away, stealing a glance back at the table where Mark was now seated with two other men, both older, probably related. Catching her eye, he grinned again, and she quickly looked away.

To Mark, she probably looked like a woman enjoying a casual lunch with her two friends, her hair blowing in the sea breeze, her smile not forced. Not a woman who couldn't look Whitney in the eye, or whose husband was already packing his bags, eager to move out of the home they'd shared the moment her car pulled into the driveway.

Maybe Mark saw what Cassie and Whitney saw. A woman who had gotten the life she'd dreamed of.

And who wasn't yet ready to admit that she'd lost it.

chapter eleven
CASSIE

THE NEXT MORNING, still full after a long, lazy lunch that had lasted nearly into the evening, Cassie showered and dressed and then made a quick cup of coffee before settling onto the back porch with her sketch pad. She couldn't avoid her work forever, even if being here, with her friends and the sounds of the waves, she wanted to do nothing but just that.

She thought back to what Amanda had said about her wedding dress as she sipped the hot beverage. There was a time when Cassie couldn't wait to sketch, when the designs just poured from her, and she felt a thrill with each new idea. Amanda's dress had been as joyful for her to create as it was for Amanda to wear. They'd been so young, just weeks out of college. The future had felt so bright, like it was stretching out in front of her, as vast and endless as the ocean.

She'd naively assumed that every dress she designed would be one she not just loved, but took pride in. One that was as much hers as the bride wearing it.

She squinted into the horizon, trying to force an image with the endless list of details her client had given her, but now, like before, her mind was blank. She couldn't see it. She certainly didn't like it.

She tried to keep her eyes on her sketch pad, but her attention kept flicking to her cell phone that sat on the wicker table beside her. She'd silenced it, thinking that would stop her from thinking about Grant, but that only resulted in her fighting the urge to pick it up and check the screen every two minutes.

No call. Two days and no communication at all from Grant, the longest they'd ever gone without speaking, even after what they now casually referred to as the "big fight" during Christmas three years ago, when they'd rented a cabin in Vermont for what was supposed to be a romantic weekend, only to discover that the place had next to no heat, soggy firewood, and was a mile trek to the slopes, not to mention that their rental car had neither four-wheel drive nor snow tires.

They'd laughed about it in the weeks following, and every Christmas afterwards. Grant liked to say it just proved they were city people, and Cassie had gone along with it, even as she questioned it.

But then, she'd gone along with a lot of things, hadn't she? The uptight dinners at restaurants that primarily served red meat when she only ate fish. The lofty apartment that she only really liked because the big windows allowed natural light when she would have preferred a balcony or easier access to Central Park. The vacations to places Grant's coworkers had suggested, so that he'd have something to discuss when he returned to the office. She sat through dinners with his parents, and skirted visits with her disapproving mother, which wasn't difficult since Willow bended with the breeze, as she liked to say. Followed where life took her without questioning it or striving for more. New York wasn't her speed, and she didn't think it was Cassie's either.

And as much as Cassie didn't want to admit it, not to her mother, and not even to herself, maybe Willow was right.

Maybe, no matter how hard she'd tried, she couldn't change herself from that little girl who had no other choice but to go with the flow rather than strive for anything more.

Couldn't change from that girl who had loved nothing more than running barefoot through the sand, feeling her hair whip around her face in the ocean breeze, and closing her eyes to hear the sound of the waves lapping against the shore.

She never saw a reason to return to Starlight Beach once Willow packed up and moved west; she thought that this place was just a part of her past, one that housed its share of bad times and painful memories.

But this beach...there was no denying that it was also a part of her. One that she'd forgotten, replaced with a new path, a new life, a future that was housed in concrete, one that couldn't be swept away with the next tide.

Without another thought, she picked up the phone and called Grant.

Voicemail. She tried not to read too far into that, telling herself there could be a dozen good reasons why he wasn't taking the call. She hadn't even considered that it was Monday morning and that he was at work, probably in a meeting. She hung up without leaving a message, deciding to try again this evening unless he beat her to it. He'd see that she'd tried to reach him. It was in his hands now.

Or maybe it was in hers. To use this time to decide what she wanted. And what would have to be good enough.

Her sketch pad remained blank, just like it had since she'd completed all the work for her other clients, and her chest started to pound the moment she brought her pencil to it.

With a slam, she closed the book and stood up, stretching her legs. A walk on the beach would clear her mind—it always had in the past, at least. And right now, she could only hope that some things hadn't changed in the years since she'd last been here.

Easing off her sandals, she left them beside her notebook and phone, then took the steps down the beach, walking straight to the shoreline before deciding to turn right, away from the direction of town. The water lapped at her toes, shimmering under the light of the sun and pulling every shade of blue from its reach, making her think of a palette for bridesmaid dresses that would be perfect for a seaside wedding.

The problem was that her client wasn't having a beach wedding—few of her clients did. They were mostly big city affairs, and this one was complete with a stuffy invitation list, but one that came with big names all the same. People with connections might ask the bride where she got her dress.

It was Cassie's big chance, but it was also her turning point. And even though the breeze off the ocean was cleaner than any air she'd ever find in Manhattan, she suddenly felt like she couldn't breathe.

She was just about to turn and head back to the cottage when she heard a voice calling in the distance.

"Cassie!"

It was deep, insistent, and her first thought was that it was Derek, in need of something to do with the house. But her eyes widened when she turned around and saw the handsome man jogging toward her.

"Tripp?"

At once, all thoughts of the dress and her career and her entire life in New York rolled out to sea. She waited for him to catch up with her, his grin broad and his blue eyes shining in the sunlight, matching the water beside him. Half the island had a crush on Tripp Palmer at some point in their lives, she reminded herself. He had money, charm, and a face that could get him out of any trouble—and into it as well, as she seemed to recall.

In the years before Whitney and her family moved away, Whitney was always telling them riveting stories about Tripp, ones that had seemed so titillating to Cassie and Amanda, who had no exposure to older boys. They'd sit eagerly, listening to Whitney complain about how Tripp had shown up at three in the morning, missing his midnight curfew, how he'd been to a party with college kids, down at some shore house they'd rented for the weekend, how there had been beer, and Tripp had come home smelling like it. How her father was always threatening to cut him out of the will. How her mother would plead with him to get it together, always reminding them that they had a name to uphold.

But now Tripp was walking toward her, and even though Cassie knew that he wasn't any more that rebellious teenage boy than she was a wide-eyed girl, she certainly felt like it right now.

"Hey," she said, smiling shyly up at him. All it took was her childhood crush to undo all the strides she'd made in life, she thought with a flicker of annoyance. Willow would for sure tsk her disapproval. A double tsk for him being a Palmer, even if he did walk away from that world in the end.

"Hey." He paused to catch his breath. His eyes locked with hers until she felt she should do the decent thing and look away, but she couldn't. And she didn't want to, either. "Did you mention to Whitney that I was looking for her yesterday?"

Cassie did look away then. So that was all it was. She was the messenger. Whitney's friend. Like always.

Yep, a college degree, a once-successful career, a coveted Manhattan apartment, and even a fairly stable relationship didn't change a damn thing.

"I…" She hesitated, unsure of what to say, not wanting to get Whitney in trouble or get caught up in their family drama. She was out of her element. She'd never had a sibling and she didn't know how these things worked. She just knew that her loyalty, as always, was to her friends.

Even if Amanda didn't seem to fully believe that right now.

"She's mad at me," Tripp confessed, blowing out a breath as he turned to face the ocean.

Even his profile was handsome, Cassie thought, taking a moment to gaze at his face. A strong nose and chin, and a hairline that didn't show any hint of receding, even though, four years older than her, he was already deep into his mid-thirties.

"Oh…" Cassie was torn between loyalty to her friend and the affection she felt toward this man and the boy he'd once been.

Tripp held up a hand and gave her a sheepish grin. "No need to deny it. I'm sort of the family screwup."

If dropping out of an Ivy League college and not joining the family's investment firm were grounds for being labeled the family screwup, she could only imagine how the Palmers had viewed Willow's life choices.

Whitney's parents had always been polite to Cassie, not exactly warm, but certainly welcoming. Unlike most people in town, they at least kept their opinions to themselves.

"You do know my reputation in this town," she reminded him with a conspiratorial smile. "My mother didn't exactly blend in with the crowd."

"Who could forget your mother?" Tripp said, making her shoulders tense up instinctively until she saw the easy grin on his face and the warmth in his eyes. "She was a free spirit. The older I get, the more I appreciate people who are willing to carve their own path."

Was that what he was doing? It would certainly seem so, not that it warranted approval from his family, his sister included.

"Well, I did carve my path, but I'm afraid that Willow doesn't exactly approve of my life choices," Cassie admitted. It wasn't something she'd ever even told Grant—having never met her mother, he wouldn't understand. But Tripp did know. And from the gentle slope of his eyes, he understood too.

"I'm not the only one from this town to disappoint their parents?" Tripp's grin broadened and Cassie felt her heart skip a beat. A group of kids chose that moment to rush past them, carrying pails and shovels, eager to make the most of their summer day. Tripp started walking in the direction of the cottage, and Cassie moved alongside him. They were both taking their time, in no rush, it would seem, to get back to their lives. Or to end the conversation. "So, what is it exactly that you do?"

"I'm a fashion designer." Saying it aloud made her think of that empty sketchbook waiting for her on the cottage porch, of the emails from her client waiting for a response in her inbox. Of the dress she didn't want to design. Couldn't design.

"I seem to recall your mother being artistic." Tripp looked at her in confusion. "She doesn't approve of your career?"

Cassie sighed. "She doesn't approve of how I've gone about it. Getting a degree that she claimed only stifled creativity. Putting a business plan in place. Designing for clients rather than for myself." She stopped to pick up a pale pink seashell and examined it in her hand, forever in awe that something so beautiful and perfect and unique could be created by nature. "Maybe she's right."

She couldn't remember the last time she'd sketched for the sheer fun of it when once she couldn't wait to get her hands on some paper or fabric, to give life to the ideas in her head. Now she designed for other people, sketched to their vision rather than her own.

Or didn't sketch at all.

"I for one hate to think that maybe our parents were right." Tripp's eyes gleamed. "But sometimes, they are, and we don't realize it until it's too damn late."

She studied him, wondering just what part of his life he regretted, but then figured it was probably the obvious. He'd dropped out of college; joining the family business was likely no longer an option. Or maybe that's what he was so eager to talk to Whitney about—maybe he was hoping she'd offer him a job.

"What made you come back to Starlight Beach?" she asked. Whitney hadn't offered this information. She was determined to be tight-lipped about her brother, just as she was determined to avoid him.

Tripp was quiet for a moment. "I always liked it here, and when my marriage ended, I found myself sort of at a loss for a while. I thought of the last place where I was really happy, and it was right here."

"This beach always brought out the best in me, no matter how rough things might have been back at my house." Cassie smiled at a memory. "Amanda, Whitney, and I used to come out here when the sun set and make a wish on the first star we could see." She glanced at him, suddenly feeling like that twelve-year-old girl again. "It probably sounds silly."

"Not at all," he said, holding her gaze. "Did your wish ever come true?"

Cassie held her breath, unsure of exactly how to answer that question. She shifted her feet in the sand, feeling uneasy as her mind drifted to Grant.

Changing the topic, she said, "So, what is that you're doing back in Starlight Beach? I mean, do you work here?"

Tripp let out a bark of laughter. "Yes. Tripp Palmer works, and for his own money, too. No handouts from Daddy for me, not that he's offering any."

So that wasn't what he was so eager to talk to Whitney about then. Cassie winced, sensing she'd hit a nerve. "Sorry, I didn't mean it like that."

He shook his head. "No, I'm the one who should apologize. You asked a simple question and I…well, I get touchy about things from my past, you could say."

Cassie nodded. "So you broke away from it." Oh, she understood. So very well. They had both run from their upbringings, from the life that they hadn't chosen.

"I work at a youth center on the edge of town. They run a camp during the summer months. It's for troubled kids, not the privileged ones who learn to sail while their parents golf and sip iced tea at the yacht club like I did."

"Wow." Cassie was surprised. And impressed. Did Whitney know any of this? She had to assume her friend didn't, or she wouldn't be so hard on her brother. "That sounds…rewarding."

"It is. And it's damn hard work, too. Harder than sitting behind an office in a necktie but try telling my family that." His eyes darkened for a moment.

Was this why he wanted to talk to Whitney? To explain? Or to get her approval?

Cassie thought of Willow, and her wish that her mother could be proud of her accomplishments, even if they didn't feel like much these days.

"Sometimes you just have to follow your heart," she said out loud, remembering something that Willow always used to say to justify her choices, however bad they had seemed at the moment.

Tripp gave a genuine, wide smile that made the corners of his eyes crinkle in a way that made her stomach turn over.

She could stay out here all day, talking to him, but he had a job to get to, and so did she.

And she had a boyfriend, too. And a phone that probably contained a message from him by now.

"Well," she said, moving a foot to the side, creating a little distance between them as they walked. The cottage was just ahead now, there was no reason to linger. "I should probably get back. It's a working vacation for me, and I have a long day ahead."

One that wasn't rewarding, to use her own words.

"I'll walk you back," he offered, and even though she knew that Whitney would prefer if she came up with some polite excuse, and even though she knew she had a boyfriend waiting for her back in New York, one that had once seemed like her wish come true, Cassie couldn't think of a reason to say no.

chapter twelve
WHITNEY

WHITNEY WAS STRETCHING for her usual morning run when she saw Cassie's unmistakable figure a few hundred yards in the distance. Even now, after all these years, her gate was still recognizable: long, carefree strides, her curly hair blowing in the ocean breeze, her chin tilted upward, toward the sun. She walked like she lived, without a care in the world.

And now, even more than back then, Whitney envied her for it.

She knew what people said about Cassie's mother, of course. Whitney's father especially had opinions about Willow. He called her work "crafts" and said she was indulging herself rather than taking responsibility, especially for her child. But Cassie never complained about her homelife, and when Whitney had to sit down to yet another stuffy dinner at the country club while her mother cleared her throat in a less-than-subtle reminder that Whitney hadn't used the proper fork, or when she had to present her report card each term to her father in his study, her knees always a little weak if she slipped down to a B in science, she thought of how her friend never had to worry about any of this. Every day of Cassie's life was spent doing as she pleased, eating what she wanted, and wearing what was comfortable. There were no expectations, and each day stretched before her, as free as the ocean itself.

It was a life that Whitney had never known and never would.

And the part that Whitney envied the most was that Cassie got to spend every one of those days in Starlight Beach, long after Whitney and her family had returned to Boston for the school year.

As Cassie grew closer to the cottage, Whitney raised her hand in an energetic wave, dropping it just as enthusiastically when she saw that Cassie wasn't alone.

Too late. Cassie—and Tripp!—both waved back and, after what seemed like a brief discussion, began approaching the porch where Whitney stood, her heart pounding as if she'd just done a five-mile sprint, not barely laced up her running shoes.

Tripp wasn't going to let up, which only gave the bad feeling in the pit of her stomach merit. Tripp being back in this town wasn't a random choice, and it wasn't because he loved it as much as she once had.

He was here for a reason. And no reason could be good enough.

As they approached and sensed her disapproval, the smiles dropped from Cassie's and Tripp's faces, and Cassie's expression was wary as she climbed the wooden steps to the porch.

"I'll give you guys some privacy," Cassie said, giving Whitney a nervous glance and—if Whitney didn't know better—what appeared to be a conciliatory smile over her shoulder for Tripp.

Whitney waited until the glass door was firmly closed before turning to face her brother.

"So you go for years without any contact and now you're stalking me?"

"Just trying to talk," he said mildly.

"Now? Why now?" Her hands dug into her hips as she glared at him.

"Because you're here." He said it like a question, and one that she should know the answer to.

"More like because *you're* here," she snapped. She glanced to the door, which Cassie had drawn shut behind her. Still, she lowered her voice. "What are you doing here, Tripp? You didn't exactly explain that when I saw you at the bar."

"Getting my life in order," he replied. "And I told you. I wasn't drinking. I haven't had a drink in years."

She frowned at him, wondering if that were true and wishing that it were. Thinking, automatically, of their mother, and how happy that would make her.

Well, aside from the whole being in Starlight Beach bit. Her parents never discussed their sprawling beach home just down the shore from here, instead replacing it with a bigger one on the Cape, where Tripp never made trouble because he never visited.

"Yes, but why *here*?" she asked. Surely, he remembered how they'd all left, under strict orders never to even mention this town. Shelby's accident had cast a spotlight on the family, one that didn't serve their reputation. But then, when did Tripp ever care about such things?

"Why not here?" Tripp shrugged. "This place meant a lot to me once. To both of us." He sighed and heavily dropped onto the top step. After a brief hesitation, Whitney joined him.

"Don't you remember all our summers here?" His eyes, the same shade of blue as her own, searched hers. "I couldn't wait for school to let out. This was the one place I felt free."

"The one place you caused a lot of trouble," she said pointedly. Surely, he couldn't argue that.

But then, she supposed, in the end, she was just as guilty. Then and now, seeing as she too had returned against the promise she'd made to their parents.

She sighed, trying to let go of the resentment she held for Tripp, but one glance at the ocean, at the place that had meant so much to her, just like he'd said, only reminded her of how she'd have to leave it again, to go back to Boston, and her office, and all the responsibilities that awaited her, while Tripp would remain here. Doing as he pleased. Doing what served him best, like always.

"I've made a lot of mistakes in my life," Tripp said after a long pause. His jaw clenched as he looked out at the ocean.

Whitney nodded, then followed his gaze, keeping her eyes fixed on the sea this time. The waves were big today, crashing steadily against the sand, rolling in from as far as the eye could see.

"You've hurt a lot of people," she told him, thinking of their mother, and how quiet she'd been at her birthday dinner. Of their father, who never said it but clearly saw Whitney as a consolation prize, and his last chance to pass down the family legacy. Of Tripp's wife, who had tried so hard to stand by him, even when he went out on benders, leaving her to wonder where he was, just like Whitney had wondered for so many years. "Myself included," she said quietly.

But not just because he stopped calling or because she worried even when she didn't want to. Because of everything she'd had to give up to pay the price of his mistakes.

"I'm sorry for that," he said. "It was never my intention to hurt anyone."

She turned to glare at him. "Are you sorry, Tripp? Because words don't change anything without action."

"I told you," he insisted as he turned to her. "I'm a changed person."

She stared at him, wanting to believe that as much as she was waiting for him to disappoint her again.

"I've been sober for over two years," he said, surprising her. "Vanessa leaving me was my wake-up call."

She widened her eyes. "*That* was your wake-up call?"

She wanted to point out all the other people he'd hurt or lost or betrayed along the way, but her friends were inside, and she didn't want them to overhear. Besides, what did it change?

Her life was what it was. She couldn't go back. They couldn't undo anything. All she could do was atone for the past and make damn sure that she never made another mistake or took another careless risk.

"Vanessa was the last person in my corner," Tripp said. "The last person I hadn't pushed away. And after she left…there was no one."

"That's not true," Whitney said, her voice rising with emotion. "You could have reached out to Mom or Dad."

"Oh, please," Tripp scoffed. "You know that even if I did it wouldn't change a damn thing. Mom just sides with Dad in the end and he's made it clear that I'm no longer a part of that family and never will be. He'll never see me as anything more than a screwup."

Whitney closed her mouth, filled with momentary shame. Tripp was right about their father; even she knew there would never be a second chance or hope of reconciliation. He was stubborn, and earning a place in his life meant falling in line and living on his terms.

"Mom misses you," she said softly.

"All she ever did was try to push me into compliance." Tripp gave her a pointed look. She tried to ignore it, even though she knew what he was saying. The same was true for her.

"She wanted the best for you," Whitney told him, wanting to believe that for herself as much as for him. But she couldn't, not completely, not when she thought of how much she'd given up, the heartache she'd felt when they'd boarded up the house here and driven back to Boston, leaving her friends behind. Not when she thought of how much she'd given up for a life she didn't want. One that was planned for her, without consulting her.

"Mom wants what Dad wants," Tripp continued. "To save face. To have something to boast about at the country club. For me to be the son of Walter Palmer, not to be Tripp Palmer. Not to be the real me."

Whitney sighed. There was no sense in arguing that point, for either of them.

"Believe it or not, I'm just as mad at her as she is at me," Tripp went on.

"She's not mad at you," Whitney corrected. "Besides, what do you have to be mad at her for?"

"For starters, she was the one who pushed to leave here," Tripp told her. Seeing her blank expression, he said, "You didn't know?"

Whitney blinked, trying to digest this information, to rewrite the only story she'd ever known. "I thought…"

"You thought it was Dad?" Tripp's laugh was bitter. "All Mom could think of were appearances. All Dad could think about was how dare I not become a mini version of him. He never wanted me to be my own person. He never would have allowed it. He hasn't allowed it."

Whitney swallowed hard, knowing that Tripp was right, that her father didn't know her, her wishes, her dreams, her true feelings about Tripp or Starlight Beach, or the company she worked for against her will.

That if he did, he wouldn't tolerate it. Just like he hadn't tolerated Tripp.

That her mother wouldn't either.

"I don't know how you do it," Tripp commented. "You've done everything they told you to."

"I didn't have a choice," she said, growing angry.

He gave her a look that showed he wasn't convinced. One that was so very Tripp, one that showed that even now, no matter what he said, his rebellious spirit had never waned. "We all have a choice, Whit."

She clenched her jaw, wanting to punch her fists against the wooden porch beneath her, wanting to scream and shout at Tripp. At her parents. At herself.

"It isn't that simple," she insisted, and there was no sense in wishing that it were.

"Of course it is," her brother replied in that breezy way of his. "I'm doing my own thing. Living my life, not the one they chose for me. I'll never be rich again, but I don't care about money. You know I never did."

"And you're saying that I do?" Whitney asked, growing hot with indignation. One thing was for certain, her choices had never been about money or success. They were about protecting the people she cared about.

But that wasn't entirely true, she knew. It was also about protecting herself.

And Tripp knew it.

Tripp shrugged. "You're working for Dad, aren't you?"

Now, Whitney struggled to hold back her temper. "I'm working for Dad because you wouldn't. Just like I went to Harvard, because you wouldn't. I show up every damn day because you don't, Tripp."

"No, you're doing it because that's what's expected of you," he replied.

It was true, she knew, because she'd learned the hard way what happened when she didn't do what was expected. When she didn't toe the line but instead dared to dream and laugh and let her guard down.

Mistakes were made. People got hurt.

And Tripp should understand that firsthand.

"You could have called me," Whitney said in a voice so low she wasn't sure that he had heard. "After the divorce. You could have kept in touch. Instead, you disappeared."

Tripp's jaw set as he stared out onto the water. "I wasn't proud of the way I'd handled things. I'm still not. But I'm working on it."

Whitney nodded because, despite everything, she understood.

"I want to get my life back on track," Tripp said. "I've been giving back, helping struggling kids get on the right path. Giving them the kind of guidance and hope that they need to see that their lives don't have to be defined by their mistakes."

Whitney could only nod because wasn't that what had happened to Tripp? To her even? She could blame her brother all she wanted, but she was to blame too, and her mistake, her involvement in that awful day that Amanda's sister had died had changed everything. She wondered now what her life might have been if someone had told her that she didn't have to bear that burden, that she didn't have to let one mistake follow her every step into her future.

She shook away that thought. Some mistakes were too big to overcome. And some wrongs could never be made right.

"I should get back inside," she said, pushing to her feet, even though she didn't have anywhere to be. She'd lost the desire to take her jog; not when she no longer felt free from bumping into people she'd rather not. Not when the memories of that last summer here were rushing back and she knew she'd never outrun them, not here.

"Come on," Tripp said, opening his arms as he stood. "You're my only sister, Whitney. You're...all I have left."

She stared at him, knowing from the look in his eyes that it was true. That in some ways, they'd only ever had each other, even if they had chosen not to look at it that way.

Whitney felt the heavy reminder of her family responsibilities, not just to her parents, but to her brother. Of needing to be more than she was; of needing to give more than she could. Of having to hold everything together when she felt like falling apart.

She pulled in a breath, wanting to push her brother away the way she had Amanda, only to live to regret it and feel even worse about herself than she already did. Against her better judgment and all the defenses she'd built up over the years, reluctantly and stiffly she let Tripp pull her into his arms. She closed her eyes briefly, breathing in his familiar scent, feeling the soft cotton of his shirt under her cheek, remembering for a moment what it felt like to be whole again. How family, however long you went without seeing them, could fill a part of you that you hadn't even known you'd been missing.

Maybe she had missed Tripp all this time. She just hadn't been willing to admit that to herself.

It wasn't until she pulled back that she realized they weren't alone outside like she'd thought. Derek stood on the sand, looking straight into her eyes, a funny smile on his lips turning to one of brief confusion when Tripp turned around.

"Tripp," Derek said pleasantly, and Whitney felt her stomach lurch.

So they did know each other. Of course they did. Everyone knew everyone in Starlight Beach unless you were just a visitor, one of the summer people who rented a house like this one for a week of fun and escape.

Everyone knew everyone. And everyone's business too.

"Good to see you, Derek," Tripp said. He gave Whitney one of his hundred-watt smiles—the kind that used to make their mother shake her head, but always with a suppressed grin. The kind that won him the hearts of every girl who lived in Starlight Beach, and even some who were just passing through.

The kind of smile that got him anything he wanted. Including trouble.

"I'll see you later?" Tripp asked her, hope lifting the end of his words.

Whitney wasn't about to make any promises. She gave a brief nod. "Sure."

The seagulls squawked overhead while Whitney and Derek watched Tripp trek across the sand in the direction of town, his figure growing smaller with each step.

Finally, Derek gave a stilted smile at Whitney. "I was coming by to see if your friend was free. You mentioned that she might want to sell her childhood home?"

"Yes!" Whitney nodded firmly, but her mind was still spinning, thinking about Tripp, fighting against the emotions that their conversation had stirred up. "She's inside." However, Whitney wasn't sure if she was yet off the phone with her son, whom she'd heard her talking to through her closed bedroom door before she'd stepped outside.

Now, she wished that she'd stayed inside. Or better yet—back in Boston. In the safety of her office.

"So, how do you know Tripp?" she blurted, even though part of her didn't want to know. What if they were best friends? The kind that told each other everything? What would Derek think of her then?

And why did Whitney even care?

She licked her lower lip, knowing the answer to that because it was the same way she felt about Cassie and Amanda. She didn't like being misunderstood. And no one in this town—heck, no one in her life—understood her.

"I'm in the real estate market," Derek said with a shrug. "I tend to make it my business to get to know everyone. Helps with word of mouth."

She nodded, realizing that friendliness wasn't just in his nature, but it was also part of his business. That he chatted up everyone.

That she wasn't an exception but just one of the crowd.

She should feel relieved. She was off the hook. He wouldn't expect anything from her. But for some reason, she didn't.

"How do *you* know Tripp?" Derek surprised her by asking.

She blinked at him. He didn't know? Her heart sped up, knowing she had an opportunity to lie, or at least deny the truth, something that she'd mastered over the years. But she was tired of pretending her life was something so very different than it was.

And she liked Derek. She couldn't help it. She liked him a lot.

"Tripp's my brother," she said grimly.

"Brother." Derek nodded thoughtfully as if trying to make sense of this revelation.

Then, he looked her straight in the eyes and said, "You're a Palmer." It felt like an accusation instead of an observation.

"The secret's out," Whitney said jokingly, but still, her stomach tightened. Not every secret was out. And never would be, not if she had anything to do with it.

"I guess I can see it now," Derek said, looking at her carefully. "The resemblance. In the eyes."

"Oh?" Whitney felt her cheeks turn warm as Derek stared at her. He wasn't just looking at her eyes; he had noticed them.

She cleared her throat quickly and said, "Amanda's in the house. If you wanted to talk to her."

Derek nodded. "Right. Yes. Before that, though, there's…a thing tonight. A bonfire. Lots of people go. It's right here on the beach. If you aren't busy…"

Busy? Whitney was so busy she usually didn't have time to even think of how she might want to use her time, and right now, this was an invitation she couldn't imagine turning down.

"I'll talk to my friends," she said, even though she knew that she would go, and they'd want to, too. Anything to break up the tension that still hung heavy in the silence between their conversations. Anything to keep her from saying things she shouldn't.

"Great!" Derek's eyes brightened and Whitney's heart sped up, no matter how hard she tried to steady herself.

They were interrupted by Amanda, pushing through the porch door, pausing when she spotted them.

"Amanda," Whitney said quickly, happy for the opportunity to press the pause button on this conversation with Derek. "Have you met Derek yet? He owns the cottage."

"Oh." Amanda smiled at him and extended her hand as she walked down the stairs. "It's nice to meet you."

"I hear you may be selling a house in town," Derek said. Then, when Amanda frowned, he added, "I'm a real estate investor. I can take a look if it will help."

"Oh. Oh, yes, sure, if it's not a problem?" Amanda looked so relieved that Whitney did too.

"Not a problem at all. Any friend of Whitney's is a friend of mine." Derek smiled warmly. "She asked me to do anything I could to help you with this process."

Amanda glanced at Whitney. "I didn't realize...thank you."

Whitney couldn't bring herself to give the standard response. Who was she to make Amanda feel indebted to her for anything, much less grateful?

"I'm happy to help," she said instead, holding Amanda's gaze, hoping that her words weren't just heard, but also believed.

The moment stretched until Derek clapped his hands. "So, what do you say? I have time now if you want to drive over?"

Whitney saw Amanda hesitate, meaning that she hadn't gone to the house yet, and still wasn't ready. Just like Whitney couldn't bear to walk far enough down to the beach to where her former summer house was visible.

"Maybe I could give you the keys? And the address?" Amanda looked tense.

Derek gave a casual shrug. "Even easier. I can swing by in between appointments this week and stop by once I've crunched some numbers. You want to sell, right?"

"Oh, yes," Amanda said firmly, nodding her head over and over again. "There's nothing for me to hold on to here."

Derek's eyes slid to Whitney's, and she looked down at her bare feet, at her perfectly pedicured toes, and she knew that she could say the same, that she should say the same, should think it. But right now, she couldn't help but feel that she might have found something good in Starlight Beach after all.

Or, at least, someone.

chapter thirteen

AMANDA

"I STILL CAN'T BELIEVE you dragged me to this," Amanda said under her breath as she joined Cassie on the back patio later that evening. It had been an uneventful day, one she'd spent reviewing her mother's paperwork, having a brief chat with Trevor after his day at sports camp, and trying not to imagine Ryan in his office, sneaking off with his bride-to-be during the lunch hour while his wife sat in this oceanfront cottage avoiding the women who were supposed to know her best.

She suspected they'd done the same—each using work as their excuse until Cassie approached her with an invitation to the bonfire. Lunch yesterday had been a good distraction from Amanda's troubles, but there was no denying that there was still some lingering tension between them all, and being back here, in Starlight Beach, wasn't helping.

"It was Whitney's idea," Cassie said. "Don't blame me."

Amanda raised an eyebrow, and Cassie gave her an apologetic smile.

"Sorry," Cassie said, her expression turning worried, eager even. "For everything. And for what it's worth, I think it will be nice to get out tonight. It beats sitting around rehashing our issues, doesn't it? Or thinking about things we'd rather not?"

There was a lot that Amanda didn't want to think about, and it went well beyond the argument she and Whitney had had three years ago.

"You're not worried about who might be there?" Amanda asked. "From town?"

Cassie hesitated for a moment as if she hadn't considered this. They both knew how it felt in the months following Shelby's death, when they couldn't go anywhere, it seemed, without people staring at them and whispering. But Cassie took it in stride, and not just because Shelby hadn't been her sister. Cassie had gotten used to people in town talking about her because of her mother.

"Did anyone ever tell you that you worry too much?" Cassie said with a little smile. "Worrying doesn't change anything. But time does. And we're older now. We've changed. We can handle a little party on the beach. We might even enjoy it!"

"I guess that a party on the beach qualifies as a distraction," Amanda agreed slowly, and it would be better than sitting around the house just the three of them, trying to pretend that nothing was wrong when nothing was right—not with them, not with her marriage, not with her life in general. "But don't you worry we'll be the oldest people there?"

"What did I just say about worrying? Derek is older than us. And he invited us," Cassie pointed out. "Or...Whitney, I should say."

"He didn't invite me," Whitney said as she stepped through the door and closed it shut behind her. In a simple linen tank dress and leather sandals, she looked completely at ease. "He invited all of us."

It was already dusk, and the sun was low in the sky, casting a glow over the ocean and its soft, rippling waves. Amanda stared out onto the horizon, thinking of how this was usually the time they looked forward to gathering on the beach most. Just before the first star appeared, when they were still preparing their wishes, hoping that someday, somehow, they might come true.

"Seems to me that he was only talking to you," Cassie said, unable to fight off her smile as they moved down the porch steps, her long skirt billowing behind her.

Whitney batted away the comment, but it was clear she was smiling, too. Nervously, if Amanda didn't know better.

Since when did Whitney get nervous? She had the kind of confidence that Amanda had always lacked, the attitude that came with the assumption that everything always worked out for her, that she didn't have to worry about anything.

Even now, in her early thirties, Whitney looked young and refreshed, and even Amanda, who had lost sight of all the fashion trends by the time Trevor was a year old, could tell that she was dressed in the latest styles.

Amanda looked down at her fading sundress and unbuttoned her cardigan, even if it did reveal a bit of a stomach roll.

"You mean to tell me that you're not looking forward to seeing our handsome landlord tonight?" Cassie bantered. "Not even a little?"

Derek was handsome, and helpful too. Amanda's chat with him earlier today had been brief, but she'd tucked his card into the manila envelope that held her mother's important paperwork, knowing that when she was ready to face everything, he'd be the first person she'd call.

"Why are you so eager to see me settled into a relationship?" Whitney replied and then shook her head. "But then, I shouldn't be surprised. People who are madly in love just want to see everyone else end up the same."

Cassie's brow pinched for a moment but then she smiled broadly and said, "Busted. Can I help it if I want to see you happy?"

"Who said I'm not happy?" Whitney's tone was sharp, and she must have realized it because she said, "Not everyone needs to be in a relationship to be happy."

A week ago, Amanda would have taken offense to this, finding it to be a jab at her life choices, and a reminder of the argument at their last reunion. But Amanda wasn't in a relationship anymore. She was single. Single and over thirty.

"What if everyone there is in their twenties?" she said, her mood plummeting when she thought of Katie.

"So? We're only thirty-two," Whitney pointed out.

"Yes, but—" But her husband was already leaving her for a younger woman.

"But what?" Whitney said, giving her a steady look.

"But…I have a kid," Amanda said, bracing herself for Whitney to comment on this like she seemed to do all the other times motherhood had interfered with a night of fun. "The last time I stayed out past eight o'clock was on Halloween."

"You and Ryan must have date nights," Cassie said.

Amanda felt her pulse begin to race and she was grateful that they were walking side by side and no one could see the look on her face, one that she was sure was filled with panic and regret. And shame.

She supposed now could be the time to mention her so-called date night last Friday. The last date night she and Ryan would ever have. Tears stung the back of her eyes and she blinked quickly, staring out to the ocean, letting the wind blow her hair, and the salty air fill her lungs, willing it to give her the peace and sense of calmness that it always had.

"A lot of my time was consumed with my mother recently, and of course, Trevor."

"All the more reason for you to get out tonight," Cassie replied. "Besides, it's better than spending another night alone in that house with the two of you."

"Hey, you have only yourself to blame for that," Whitney said, giving her a playful jab with her elbow.

Amanda met Whitney's eye, and even though she wanted to fight it, she couldn't help but share in the camaraderie that Cassie's little setup had created.

Leave it to Cassie to always know how to make things a little better.

Still, Amanda's anxiety ratcheted when they approached the bonfire, where a group of people were already gathered. Whitney casually disappeared into the crowd, and Cassie, being Cassie, easily slid into conversation with a woman strumming a guitar near the bonfire, leaving Amanda to hover near a tented table that had been set up with drinks and snacks. She was pouring a glass of wine when she felt a tap on her shoulder.

She turned, expecting to see one of her friends, hoping that they'd suggest leaving, so she could get back to the house and change into pajamas and maybe indulge in some of the ice cream Cassie had bought at the store, but instead, she saw another familiar face. And not an unwelcome one.

"Mark," she said in surprise, blinking up at the handsome lawyer. Make that just a lawyer who was objectively handsome—like Derek, except that Derek didn't make her stumble over her words or feel suddenly hot in the cheeks. "I seem to be seeing you all over town."

"Well, it's a small town," he pointed out.

She felt her smile tighten, at once being brought back to those weeks and months after Shelby had died, when everywhere she went, it seemed that people were discussing it. They'd stop once they saw her, of course, their eyes full of pity, but something else, too, something close to judgment.

"Such a senseless tragedy," they'd whisper when they didn't think she could hear. "Her older sister was supposed to be watching her."

"Yes, it is," she managed to say to Mark. Then, remembering just how small, how any event could be made the talk of the town, she checked herself, determined not to be fodder for local gossip once more. This was a married man. A family man. "Is your wife here?"

"If she is, then that's my cue to leave." His grin turned wry. He held up his hand, and for the first time, Amanda noticed that his ring finger was bare. "Divorced. Two years now."

"Oh!" Then, realizing she'd spoken with a little too much enthusiasm, she said again, more regretfully this time. "I mean, *oh*. Oh, I'm sorry to hear that."

Mark shrugged. "It was a long time ago. And if it hadn't been for that, I probably wouldn't have moved to Starlight Beach. It took time but I've come to see that it was all for the best."

Amanda nodded thoughtfully and took a sip of her wine. "That's good to know. I mean, speaking for myself, not for you. I'm still sort of new at all of this."

He frowned in confusion and then motioned to the rings on her left finger when she brought her plastic cup to her mouth again.

"Like I said," she explained, reaching down to twist the modest solitaire engagement ring that had felt so grown-up and fancy when she was just twenty-one. "It's still fresh."

She darted her eyes around the crowd, relieved to see that both of her friends were well out of earshot.

"So you're part of the club?" Mark sounded surprised. When she didn't respond, he clarified, "Divorced?"

"No," she said automatically. "At least, not yet. Not…technically. But…my marriage is over."

Announcing this felt strange, but also, final. It snatched the last shreds of hope out from under her feet, quick enough to make her feel like she was losing her footing, and she set a hand on the table to steady herself.

Her marriage was over. Ryan had ended it for them. But that didn't mean that she hadn't contributed in some way, however small and however unintentional, over the months, even years, that had brought her to this moment.

"I bet my story beats yours," Mark said, giving her a grin that pulled her out of her waning spirits.

Amanda couldn't help but laugh out loud. She then thought of her circumstances, which were pretty bad if she said so herself, and decided to take on the challenge.

"Winner gets what?" she asked.

"Oh, a betting woman." Mark's laughter was deep and gravelly. She liked it.

"How about loser buys lunch this week," Mark said.

Lunch? Lunch sounded an awful lot like a date, and Mark might be single, but she was still technically married. She was still wearing her rings as he had pointed out. And right now, she couldn't imagine the day when she would be able to take them off.

"Or drinks," Mark quickly said. "I'm sure you're busy with your friends."

Friends. Of course, he'd seen her at the Wharf yesterday, looking as content as Whitney and Cassie assumed she was. That was another sob story that Mark probably couldn't understand, but this "divorce" stuff was something that they had in common. And right now, she needed to talk about it, especially since she couldn't with anyone else.

"Drinks would work," she said, feeling a flutter in her stomach. She nodded firmly. "Okay, you're on."

"That confident your story is so awful?" Mark raised an eyebrow.

"Yes," she said with a twinge of self-pity. It was truly awful.

They found a spot on a nearby dune, far enough away from the water that the waves didn't muffle their conversation but close enough to the bonfire that she could feel the heat on her bare arms.

She told the facts, saying them as if she were relaying some other woman's story. Some poor fool who had been so busy trying to win the love of her mother that she'd lost the love of her husband. She glossed over the details of that part, but there was nothing vague to be said about Ryan's transgressions.

"Ah, so you're one of those 'my husband ran off with his assistant' spouses?" Mark grinned, and despite her circumstances, Amanda laughed.

"It's so cliché, I'm almost embarrassed to admit this is my life."

The amusement left Mark's eyes. "He's the one that should be embarrassed. And unless you're living in a big city—"

"Quite the opposite," Amanda clarified. "We live in a small town. The kind where you run into your neighbors—"

"And clients?" Mark raised an eyebrow.

Amanda nodded. "Definitely. The kind of town where your neighbors *are* your clients."

Amanda had considered this possibility too many times since Ryan had dropped the news on her, going so far as to consider switching all of her shopping to the next town over. Now she saw it from Mark's point of view. If anyone should be worried about showing their face in the dry cleaners, it should be the woman who replaced her.

"The worst part of it is that I chose her," Amanda explained. "When I took time off…for my mother. I hired this woman to replace me at the office. I thought she seemed great! Little did I know she was great at more than answering the phone and scheduling appointments."

"Ouch."

Amanda swallowed the lump that had formed in her throat, replacing the lighthearted banter. That was the other thing that she couldn't get past. It wasn't just that her time was being pulled away from her husband and son, but that by devoting herself to care for her mother, she'd replaced herself with another woman. In every possible way.

"It's hard not to feel like I've lost everything," she said, fighting back tears. She was grateful that it was already dark and that the only light came from the bonfire and the moon overhead, reflecting off the water.

"It can feel that way at first," Mark said gently. "But eventually you realize that you're better off alone than with someone who'd be willing to treat you that way. I know that doesn't seem possible right now. It sounds like you really loved your husband."

"I did." She blinked. But did she still? It had been so long since they'd spent any real time together. She didn't open up to him about everything she'd gone through with her mother; she'd told herself it hurt too much, that after a long day caring for her mother and trying to ignore the woman's endless criticism on everything from her hair texture to the size of her thighs to the fact that she had her father's nose, she didn't want to think about it anymore. But was that all? Or was there a part of her, a teeny tiny part, that feared that Ryan, who had always been so loving and accepting of her, would agree?

"I pushed him away," she admitted. She hadn't wanted to, hadn't meant to, but she had all the same.

"But you didn't push him into the arms of another woman," Mark said firmly. "He did that all on his own."

Amanda sighed. She wished she could be so sure.

"Well, it looks like you're buying drinks then," Mark announced, happily taking a sip of his beer.

"What?" Amanda perked up again as she stared at him. Even in the darkness, she could see the gleam in his eyes, one that made her want to stay and chat a little longer. "You mean your story is worse than mine?" Right now, it didn't feel like anyone's story could be worse than hers.

"Five words," Mark said. "Left me for my brother."

"Ouch." Amanda hissed in a breath. "Okay, you win. Your story is worse."

"Well, now I'm not so sure," Mark said teasingly. He appraised her for a moment, and she shifted under the heat of his stare, feeling herself blush in the moonlight. "Your husband left you for his assistant. That you hired. To replace you while you tended to your dying mother."

So it was as bad as it felt.

But still not as bad as his story. She couldn't imagine a sibling betrayal like that.

Other than her own.

She looked at Mark, who was grinning at her, and once again, all the weight of the past seemed to slip off her shoulders.

"Well, seeing as she is pregnant…" My goodness, did she crack a smile as she delivered that line?

"What?" Mark's eyes popped and then he tossed his head back. His laughter was like a soft rumble of thunder, and despite the circumstance, he pulled a laugh from her too. "You didn't mention that part."

No, and she hadn't mentioned the other part, about how she was the one who wanted a baby—that she'd been comfortable enough to believe it would eventually happen.

Some things were just too painful to talk about.

Seeing her frown, Mark reached over and set a hand on hers, giving it a long, warm squeeze.

"I'm sorry," he said, not letting go.

His hand felt strange in hers, bigger than Ryan's, different, too. But it didn't feel bad. It just felt…new. And comforting.

"I'm sorry too," she said, looking into his eyes.

He held her gaze for a moment and then cleared his throat, letting go of her hand to reach for the beer that he'd propped in the sand. "Drinks then?"

"To drown our sorrows?" Amanda asked.

Mark grinned and held up his can to her plastic cup. "To toast to new beginnings."

New beginnings. Amanda hadn't even begun to consider that a new phase of her life was unfolding. All she'd thought up until this point was that everything she cherished, loved, and wanted was ending.

But as she toasted Mark, she felt a strange sense of excitement. Maybe her story wasn't over just yet.

chapter fourteen

WHITNEY

WHITNEY'S EYES FLICKED over the group of people, scanning them for anyone she might recognize, or worse, anyone who might recognize her, telling herself that she wasn't actively looking for Derek, even if he had invited her, and even if she had spent far too much time looking through the clothes she'd packed for this trip for just the right look: something casual, but not too revealing. Something flirty, but not too obvious. Something that said she was up for some fun, and nothing more.

Finally, not seeing him, she turned to find Cassie when her gaze locked on someone else instead. She sucked in a breath, her heart hammering, and hurried over to her friend who was standing at the drinks table.

"My brother's here," Whitney said.

"Is he?" Cassie's eyes darted over the small crowd.

Whitney supposed she should have expected to see him. This was Starlight Beach, where all the locals knew each other, and now Tripp was one of them.

For not the first time, a swell of anger bloomed inside her, one that she knew housed a different, bigger emotion. Envy.

How many times during the school years would she fantasize about coming back here? Sometimes, on those cold winter days in Boston, she could think of nothing else but the warm sand in between her toes and the sunshine on her face. Even when they sold the house, she still dreamed of the day she would return, knowing deep down that she never would.

That none of those wishes or dreams she'd made here on this beach would ever come true.

"I can keep him busy if you want a little alone time with Derek," Cassie offered pleasantly enough.

"I don't want a little alone time with Derek," Whitney replied, trying to cover her lack of honesty with annoyance. She glanced around, feeling another swell of disappointment that she tried not to let show in her expression. "Besides, he's not even here."

"Of course he is," Cassie said with a teasing smile. She jutted her chin toward the water, where sure enough, Derek was talking with a young couple, his sandy hair blowing in the breeze.

When he caught Whitney looking at him, he raised his beer and flashed her a smile, causing her stomach to do something funny.

"I can walk away now if you'd like," Cassie offered, grinning broadly now.

"Don't you dare," Whitney said, grabbing her arm. "I told you, I'm not here for Derek and certainly not alone time with him. It's supposed to be a party, meaning, lots of people, not one-on-one time anyway."

"Really? Because from the way he keeps looking over here at you, I'd say that alone time is exactly what he has on his mind." Cassie's expression was coy as she filled her cup, but it slipped when she turned around. "Who's that guy Amanda is talking to? Isn't he the guy from the restaurant yesterday?"

Whitney looked over to see Amanda sitting on the sand, a handsome man around their age beside her. They were shoulder to shoulder, the man's eyes deep-set and unwavering from their hold on Amanda's face, and Amanda looked...happy, Whitney realized.

She laughed as if to underscore Whitney's opinion, and it was a sound that pulled right at Whitney's heartstrings, bringing her back to a time when they were young and carefree. If she closed her eyes now, just listening to the sound of the sea and her friend's peal of joy, she could almost for a minute believe she was right back there again. That everything was going to be okay.

She opened her eyes again. Nothing would ever be okay again, and she knew it. Not with Amanda. Not with their friendship.

Definity not with Tripp.

"That looks like the guy," she said. "Her lawyer, right?"

"Looks like more than a professional conversation if you ask me," Cassie said, frowning.

"Please, Amanda is completely devoted to Ryan. He's her entire world."

Cassie flashed her a warning glance. "Don't let her hear you say that."

Whitney sighed. Were they still talking about the argument from their last reunion? "Cassie, you know what I meant then and now." They had both been at Amanda's wedding, helping her with her veil, and then watching her walk down the aisle of the small church with stars in her eyes. Whitney had stood beside Cassie, feeling strangely replaced by the way her best friend only had eyes for Ryan, maybe even a little jealous. She'd listened while

Amanda said her vows, pledging her love—her life—to this one person, and she'd wondered if she'd ever be able to do the same. She'd pledged herself to these women, the closest she'd ever come to finding a soulmate, and she'd still let them down. And even with them, she kept her distance. But Amanda wore her heart on her sleeve. She didn't hold back.

And maybe Whitney was a little jealous of that, too.

"All Amanda ever wanted was to be a wife and mother," Cassie reminded her.

"We made those wishes on this beach when we were kids," Whitney pointed out. "People change. We don't all want what we once did."

Cassie raised an eyebrow, and Whitney instantly regretted opening the door to this conversation. She shut it down quickly by adding, "But Amanda does, I get that. I just…I guess I wanted to be sure that she was living the life she truly wanted. Even if it didn't come out that way." Not everyone got the life they truly wanted or anything that they hoped for, but if anyone deserved to have that, it was Amanda.

Cassie nodded but then looked back at Amanda. "Amanda got everything she wished for."

Whitney swallowed back a sip of wine, but it didn't go down easily. She didn't want to think about that fight three years ago any more than she wanted to think about silly wishes they'd made as children.

Besides, she had bigger concerns. If she stood here much longer, Tripp was bound to come over.

"If you're offering to distract Tripp, I won't fight you on it," Whitney said to Cassie, who was still frowning in Amanda's direction. "But I owe you, big time."

"Oh, you don't owe me." Cassie turned her back to Amanda and swatted away Whitney's concern. "Tripp doesn't bother me."

"Well, you're not related to him," Whitney said as she walked away.

She was happy to see that Tripp was standing nowhere near Derek, and her mind all but drifted from her brother when she saw the man walking toward her.

"You came," Derek said, giving her a slow grin that made her stomach tighten up a little.

"You sound surprised," she commented, returning his smile, knowing that she was flirting, reminding herself that it was just fun. She deserved it, didn't she? Especially when this time next week she'd probably still be at the office, catching up on all the work she'd missed, paying for this trip, right down to this little bonfire.

Yes, even she deserved a little fun. Only, as she thought it, that old familiar ache tightened her gut, the same one that twisted and settled there every time she thought of Starlight Beach, every time she dared to long for it. The magic she felt here was replaced with a different emotion, one that stayed there and took root. Shame. Fear. Guilt.

"You're full of surprises," Derek remarked. "Were you ever going to mention that you were a Palmer?"

Whitney shrugged, but now the clench of her stomach was rooted in anxiety. "I didn't realize that the name still mattered in these parts."

More like she'd hoped it didn't. That their part in that awful day had been forgotten by now.

"Well, the Palmer house is pretty well known, even if it has traded hands three times in the past eighteen years," he said, then, probably seeing the look of confusion on her face, added, "I'm in the know about these types of things. I probably know the story behind every house on this stretch of the coast."

And that was exactly what Whitney was afraid of. Her story wasn't a good one; it didn't have a happy ending any more than Amanda's did, even if Cassie thought otherwise. Yes, Amanda might have gotten the husband and the kid, but how could she ever be completely happy after what had happened here? After the part Whitney had played in it?

"I wasn't keeping secrets, if that's what you're wondering," she said, as that familiar surge of guilt reared again. She pushed it back with a small sip of wine.

"Oh, but doesn't everyone have secrets?" Now Derek's eyes twinkled in the moonlight.

She raised an eyebrow, happy to see that they were back to flirting, knowing she'd have to tread lightly all the same. Lighter than before, now that he knew who she was.

"Is there more to your story then?" she countered, happy to shift the heat onto him, and also, a little curious. Derek seemed like a genuinely nice guy. Could the man really be harboring some dark past?

She realized it was entirely possible. The people she knew in Boston saw her as a well-dressed businesswoman, one without a hair out of place, must less an inner battle that she was destined to lose.

Derek gave her a knowing grin. "If you stick around long enough, you might just find out."

Intriguing, but all the same, he'd hit a nerve, reminding her where she was, and that she wouldn't be returning. And even though she hadn't been here in eighteen years and had resigned herself to never coming back at all, the thought of leaving again bothered her in ways it shouldn't.

"I'm leaving Saturday." Whitney cleared her throat.

"Oh, I know. I'm your landlord, remember?" Derek tipped his head. "But surely you'll be back?"

Whitney hesitated and then shook her head firmly. She had no reason to come back. Certainly no business. "I don't get much time away from the office."

She thought she detected disappointment in his gaze. "I thought with your brother being here that I might see more of you in the future."

"Tripp and I aren't what you would call close," Whitney said, forcing back a caustic tone. The last thing she wanted was to go airing the dirty family laundry.

All the same, Derek chided, "A story there? Or a secret?"

He was still flirting, keeping things light, but Whitney couldn't match his tone. Instead, she said, "It's too nice of a night to spend talking about family drama."

"Sorry if I've overstepped."

Whitney looked at him, realizing she'd been too harsh with her tone. "No, it's fine. If you must know, Tripp's always been the rebel. And I've always done everything I was supposed to."

But that wasn't true, was it? Standing here, on this beach, the one place she'd sworn her parents never to speak of again, proved that much.

"Such as?"

"Oh, like graduating from Harvard even though I wanted to go to school in California. And studying finance and business even though…" She shook her head. There was no sense in talking about what might have been when it never could have been anything other than what it was. Even if Tripp had been the perfect son, she'd still have been expected to be the golden girl.

"Ah, so you never misbehaved?" Derek once again looked at her with a devilish grin that said he was enjoying this conversation much more than she was.

She stared at him, thought about it for a moment, and finally huffed out a breath. "Never say never," she admitted, and they both laughed, even though she wasn't so sure it was completely funny.

"And you?" she asked, eager to get off the topic of her own life for a bit. "Did you always do everything that was expected of you?"

Derek's eyes shot up and he seemed to think about it for a long time before finally saying simply, "No."

Now Whitney did laugh. "I guess no one's perfect."

"We're all just doing our best," Derek agreed, then, catching her stealing a glance at Tripp, happily distracted by Cassie who could charm anyone, he said, "Even Tripp."

She eyed him sideways. "Just how well do you know my brother?"

"Well enough to see the good he's doing with those kids at the camp," Derek replied.

Whitney could only nod. She hadn't seen it for herself, but maybe she didn't want to. Maybe she wasn't able to believe that Tripp could be anyone else than the brother she'd always known. Selfish. Unaccountable.

"He's mentioned you before, you know," Derek commented.

Whitney felt her cheeks flame and she was grateful it was dark enough now that Derek wouldn't be able to see the panic in her eyes. "What...what did he have to say?"

"Whoa," Derek said, laughing. "Not much and all good things, I swear. Said you've got a big job in your family company." He gave her a playful look. "But keep reacting like that and I'll *really* start to wonder about your secrets."

Whitney took a sip of her drink, waiting for her heartbeat to resume a normal speed. "Trust me, they aren't worth sharing." Then, sensing that she'd only managed to intrigue him, she added, "My life is quite boring."

By design, she didn't add. Boring meant safe. Even if it was also lonely.

"I don't recall Boston being boring from the time I spent there," he said.

She couldn't argue with him. The city was full of parks where mothers chased young children. Couples strolled hand in hand on the busy sidewalks. There were restaurants on every corner that she mostly dined in for business meetings, reminding her that she wasn't truly enjoying life. She was just standing on the sidelines—or behind the window of her corner office.

"Well, it is for me," she said. "It's all work. At my father's firm of course." She didn't say it as a complaint, but rather as a fact.

Derek seemed to understand. But then, he'd walked away from the life she was living, hadn't he? "Ah, and Tripp not working there is a problem?"

"A big one," Whitney confirmed, deciding to leave it there.

"Well," Derek said, stepping closer to her. "You're not in Boston right now. You're here, on the beach. There's a clear sky, a bonfire, drinks, and…a guy who likes your company."

Now Whitney had the sense that it was Derek who might just be blushing in the moonlight.

She felt her pulse quicken. Derek was right. She was on the beach, Starlight Beach of all places, the one place she used to never have a care in the world, with a man whose company she was also starting to like. Quite a bit.

And that was just the problem.

chapter fifteen
CASSIE

CASSIE WOKE UP to the sound of her phone ringing, jolting her from her half-dream, half-memories of walking along the moonlit beach with Tripp, talking about the old days when life felt so carefree, contrasting it with their lives now, and stirring up all sorts of emotions she hadn't expected.

Attraction. Longing. And nostalgia.

But now her phone was ringing, and she sat up with a jolt. Grant! He had finally returned her call. Maybe he'd even tried her last night, while she was at the party, so distracted that she hadn't even thought to check her phone when they'd all stumbled in, slightly tipsy, each quietly happy, none of them sharing why.

She fumbled on the nightstand for the device, all thoughts of Tripp and their easy conversation vanishing. But as she blinked the sleep away, she saw that it wasn't Grant's name on her screen. That he hadn't tried to reach her at all.

The phone rang again, and she quickly answered it before the sound woke up Whitney or Amanda.

"Willow?" She knew better than to ever call her Mom. That was too conventional for her mother; too limiting. Willow didn't believe in being defined by a role. She was her own person. It was why she went by the name Willow instead of her given name, Karen.

"You sound like I woke you," Willow replied, her tone not in the least apologetic. "I didn't even check the time."

Cassie glanced at the small clock that sat on the nightstand. "It's eight. It's even earlier in Arizona."

"You know me," Willow replied airily.

Yes, Cassie did. She knew that her mother liked to rise with the sun. And she also knew that her mother didn't call very often.

She had the uneasy feeling that she'd been caught, that somehow, Willow knew she was here, that all her talk of having psychic intuition wasn't just a story she'd made up during her brief tarot card reading phase.

And what would her mother think of her being here? She knew how Cassie felt after Shelby's death, and she'd assured her that it wasn't her fault, to ignore the talk in town. But that was something Cassie had never fully been able to do long before the accident, and she couldn't bring herself to explain that to Willow. To admit what people said about her. How they clucked their tongues and shook their heads.

Willow started talking about her latest artwork, some blown glass pieces she was planning to sell at a craft fair this upcoming weekend.

"Is that why you called?" Cassie asked, fighting back that anxious dread that always seemed to appear when she heard from her mother. She couldn't help it, even now, when she was a grown adult and her mother was on the other side of the country and had managed to live just fine by her unconventional means without

Cassie there to pick up the pieces of every mess she eventually made, Cassie worried.

"Is it so strange to call my daughter?" Willow gave a laugh that sounded like the chimes she used to hang from their porch roof. Cassie snuggled back against the pillow, smiling, until Willow said, "I had a dream about you. I woke with you on my mind."

"Oh?" So Cassie was right. Willow had picked up on something. Maybe it was a psychic ability or maybe it was simply mother's intuition.

"I had a dream about you flying that old kite we found that one summer."

Cassie's eyelids drooped. "We didn't find it," she said, the memory suddenly all too clear. "We swiped it from an unsuspecting family having lunch at the hot dog stand."

"Oh, they'd already had their fun for the day," Willow said breezily. "And you deserved a little."

Cassie bit back a sigh. Her definition of "fun" had never matched Willow's; they didn't have that in common and never would. But they had other things in common. Time, experiences that she sometimes didn't want to remember, and of course, their creative spirit. There was no denying that, even if Cassie didn't especially feel like she had any left.

"Actually, I'm in Starlight Beach right now," she admitted.

"After all this time?" Willow sounded, understandably, surprised, but far from displeased.

"It has been a long time," Cassie said, relaxing. "But somehow, nothing has changed."

"I know you had some problems there, but my years at Starlight Beach will always be some of my happiest." Willow's tone was fond if not a little nostalgic. "There was something so special about that ocean breeze. I always felt like I could be my true self there. Like I was free, you know what I mean?"

Cassie nodded, then, swallowing the lump in her throat, found her voice. "Sure," she said because it was easier than telling the truth.

Willow didn't know about the things Cassie's peers said to her at school or the way they looked at her when she and her mother walked through town. Willow kept her head high, seeming to exist in her own world, immune to the pain others could bring with a laugh or a point of the finger, but Cassie—Cassie saw it all and felt it all, and it only made her want to protect her mother more.

And never, ever end up like her.

No, she couldn't ever tell Willow any of this. It would be too cruel.

But Willow was right about one thing. She had been her true self here, and so had Cassie. When she was with Amanda and Whitney, all the worries she had vanished. That was when she was able to feel what Willow had felt every day of her life—free. Free to enjoy this beautiful beach, the salty air, and the quaint town.

Something that Cassie was determined to do. Today.

When their call ended, she set the phone back on the end table and then, after a second, snatched it back. She scrolled through her missed calls, and her texts, even dared to check her email, only to have her heart sink with dread when she thought of that dress she still had to design. The one that would look nothing like something she would create. She was merely a sketch artist and a seamstress at this point, she thought with a groan.

Knowing that she couldn't put it off any longer, she sent off a breezy, upbeat response to her client's multiple emails, promising her the dress that she'd always dreamed of.

Even if it wasn't one that Cassie ever would have.

Desperate for a distraction, she pulled a sweatshirt over her head and went downstairs, the smell of coffee lifting her spirits with each step. The kitchen was quiet, however, but through the glass doors, Cassie spotted Whitney sitting on one of the Adirondack chairs a few yards from the porch, her auburn hair blowing in the morning breeze, her bare feet resting in the sand beside her running shoes. Even on vacation, she couldn't stop.

Thinking of her workload, Cassie supposed she was guilty of the same. The difference was that Cassie wanted to take in the moment, soak up the present, and notice everything around her, whereas Whitney couldn't slow down, and she certainly didn't want to either.

Ever since college, it was clear that Whitney had thrown herself into her father's footsteps, acing every course at Harvard, setting herself up for a high-powered job, a busy life that fulfilled her in ways that Cassie could no longer understand. A life that was nothing like the one she used to long for when they were younger, back when that kind of life seemed to be one that she almost resented.

Clutching a mug of warm coffee, Cassie joined her a moment later, grateful that Amanda hadn't come downstairs just yet. She wanted to be alone with Whitney. She was concerned for Amanda, and not just because of her purpose for this trip.

"Beautiful morning," Cassie said, dropping onto the chair beside Whitney. "Nice night, too."

She spotted a hint of color darken Whitney's otherwise pale cheeks. "It was a nice night. And I have you to thank for that. I don't think I could have taken another night of Tripp's drama."

"Oh, it was no trouble," Cassie said, hiding a smile by taking a sip of her coffee. Really, it had been very nice. She could speak freely to

Tripp without worrying that she might upset Whitney, and talk they did. About the present and their pasts, and about all the little parts of this town that she'd almost forgotten, but now couldn't forget, like the old soda fountain at the pharmacy, or the warm nights when all the kids would go clamming, pails in hand. Tripp was easy to talk to—someone who listened and didn't judge. Someone who'd witnessed firsthand the girl she'd once been. Someone who, like herself, had wanted a second chance, a reinvention.

She couldn't talk about any of this with Whitney, of course. For starters, she had a boyfriend. A boyfriend! But did she? She frowned when she thought of the call that Grant still hadn't returned, of the way they'd left things, of a future that no longer felt so certain.

"But, speaking of trouble…" She turned her mind to what she'd come out here to discuss. "Amanda and that guy certainly talked the night away."

"Maybe it was her way of avoiding me," Whitney replied with a hint of hurt in her tone. She took another sip of her coffee. "Besides, you were busy babysitting Tripp, and I was talking to our landlord, so she was probably just happy to see a familiar face."

Cassie wasn't so sure it was just that, especially when Amanda had gravitated to the man before either she or Whitney had even noticed Tripp was there. But Whitney did have a point about Amanda seeking an opportunity to avoid them, and that stung.

Still, when they went back to the kitchen to start making breakfast and she saw Amanda at the counter cracking eggs into a bowl, Cassie couldn't resist getting to the truth.

"So," Cassie said, her tone forcefully light as she poured a second cup of coffee while Amanda added three teaspoons of sugar to hers. "Who was that handsome guy you were talking to all night?"

"I wasn't talking to him all night." Amanda's cheeks grew pink and she set the spoon down with a clank. "And I wouldn't exactly call him handsome."

Now Cassie knew something was up. The man in question was inarguably attractive; it wasn't a matter of opinion, it was fact. And what reason did Amanda have to deny the obvious unless…

Her stomach felt a little funny as she stared at her friend, who was now trying to distract herself from the conversation by buttering her toast, a little heavily.

It was another of Amanda's tells. When she got stressed, she ate. Like so many other little and not-so-little things that Cassie knew about this woman, she could not believe that she could be oblivious to something so big, so glaring, as a marriage in trouble.

"He's my attorney. The one we saw at lunch," Amanda said through a mouthful of toast. She gave Cassie a firm look, one that said, drop it.

But for some reason, maybe because of the way Amanda was plowing through her toast stack like she hadn't eaten in a week, or maybe simply because Cassie knew her, knew her better than anyone, even her mother, maybe even herself, she couldn't do what Amanda was asking.

"If that's all it is," she said.

It was, she realized as soon as she'd said it, the wrong thing to say.

"Of course that's all it is!" Amanda all but shouted, but then dumped the remains of her coffee down the sink. "I'm heading out," Amanda said, stuffing her empty plate into the dishwasher, the bowl of eggs forgotten. "It's about time I remembered the real reason I came back here."

Cassie tensed up, wanting to make things right. "Are you going to the house? I can come with you."

Amanda hesitated for a moment but then shook her head. Her eyes softened when she gave a little smile. "Thanks, though. For offering."

"Of course," Cassie said gently. "You know I'm here for you. For anything."

Amanda didn't say anything when she walked upstairs to get her things. A few minutes later, the front door opened and closed.

"Well, that went well," Whitney said sarcastically.

Cassie released a pent-up breath. "Getting out of the house would probably do me some good as well."

"I'm game," Whitney said. "Let me just shower and change out of this running gear."

Cassie wondered why Whitney hadn't done that directly after her morning jog. If Cassie didn't know better, she'd think that Whitney had been sitting outside in the hopes that Derek might walk by.

But then, what did she know about either of her friends anymore?

THIRTY MINUTES LATER, AND CHANGED into a flowing sundress, and still with no call from Grant, Cassie found Whitney sitting on an armchair, bent over her cell phone.

"Let me guess. Work?" she asked, even though she felt the familiar guilt build, reminding her that she should perhaps take a page from her friend's book, and use this time more wisely. Instead, she said, "Shopping or coffee?"

"Both?" Whitney pocketed her phone and met her at the front door.

"Town it is then," Cassie said decisively. Yes, there was a strong chance that she'd run into Missy again, or other old classmates, women who had once teased her, looked down on her, and made her feel worse about her circumstances.

She realized that Whitney was hesitating, possibly with the same shared worries. Seeing people they knew stirred up the past.

"That is…unless you're worried about running into Tripp."

It wasn't Cassie's motivation for walking into town, but she certainly wouldn't mind seeing his friendly face again either.

Whitney didn't meet her eyes as she pulled open the door and stepped outside. "It will be fine. Tripp's probably working anyway."

"He told you about his new job then," Cassie said, pleased, waiting as Whitney locked the door behind them.

"As did Derek," Whitney replied.

"It seems like he's thought of pretty highly in town," Cassie hedged.

Whitney pursed her lips, saying nothing to that, which was probably for the best. Cassie didn't want to dig up old hurts, and nothing stung more than the memory of how they'd all felt that last summer they were together here, when everywhere they went, people seemed to whisper and stare.

Cassie had to quicken her pace to keep up with Whitney. Even though she was a New Yorker now, she'd never quite been able to walk at an urban speed. She preferred to move slowly and soak in her surroundings. "So, what about you and Derek?"

"What about me and Derek?" Whitney kept her eyes straight ahead on the road, but her cheeks had turned pink.

"You two seemed pretty chummy last night," Cassie comment- ed, estimating that at this clip, they'd reach Main Street in five minutes. It helped that Whitney was tall and that her legs were a good four inches longer than Cassie's.

"I could say the same about you and Tripp," Whitney turned to remark.

Now it was Cassie's face that flamed. "We're just old friends."

"Really? Because I don't recall you two ever being friends. You were my friend, and he barely tolerated me much less anyone I hung out with," Whitney said.

It was true, but somehow it still bothered her.

"Besides, I'm in a serious relationship," Cassie replied, hoping to get Whitney off the topic and remind herself of why Tripp was off-limits. But even as the plausible excuse slipped from her lips, she questioned it herself. Sure, she and Grant lived together, but could she continue to classify their relationship as serious if they didn't even want the same future?

"How could I forget that you're madly in love?" Whitney smiled as she shook her head.

Cassie swallowed back the doubt that was growing inside her, hoping that she kept it from showing. Whitney wouldn't under-stand—she didn't long for a traditional, picture-perfect family the way Cassie had all her life.

Why should she when she already had it? Sure, Tripp might have gone wayward, but there was no denying the perfection that came with being a Parker.

"You could be too if you wanted to be," Cassie replied. Then, feeling frustrated, she said, "Seriously, Whitney, why are you so determined to be alone?"

Whitney frowned deeply, looking so hurt that Cassie felt the need to reply.

"I didn't mean alone. I mean, you have us. I just mean…"

But Whitney's face had relaxed, and she shook her head as they continued walking. "No, I get it. I…haven't gotten close to anyone. Like I said, work keeps me busy."

"It's funny, isn't it?" Cassie said, even though nothing was amusing about it at all. She missed her old friend, the younger Whitney. "How you ended up working for the family business when you were once so opposed to doing just that?"

"Well, we were kids back then, Cass." Whitney shrugged as they neared town, the storefronts now visible down the road. "I always knew that I'd end up following the path my parents chose for me."

"But you had dreams. I remember." Cassie could see it now, the three of them, on the beach, staring at the stars as they burst into the sky, one by one. "You wanted to travel—"

"And I do travel. Extensively. We have clients all over that world." Whitney stared at her blankly for a moment and then turned away, stopping to admire a shop window.

"It wasn't just that," Cassie replied. She could hear Whitney's voice as clear now as she had back then, before the wish was taken away with the wind. "You wanted to live here. On Starlight Beach. Forever. Do you remember that?"

Whitney's expression turned stony, and she continued to stare in the window of the bookstore, the very one that Amanda loved to spend rainy afternoons inside, curled up in an armchair, flipping pages and transporting herself to another world.

Another life.

Cassie had usually joined her, oftentimes with the bridal magazines spread out on a table.

Were they so different now than the young girls they'd once

been? Cassie had thought so, but now she wasn't so sure—about herself. About any of them.

"That was a long time ago, and even then, I must have known that it was just a fantasy," Whitney said. "I didn't grow up like you, Cassie. I didn't have options."

Options. Those were the last things that Cassie ever felt she had as a kid, but what was the point in explaining that to Whitney now? Cassie had gotten her life on track. She was secure—or at least, she was for a while. She'd pulled herself from that rut, from the lack of stability, from the fear of never knowing when the lights would go out, where the next meal would come from, or what the kids would say the next time Willow floated through town in a beach towel with nothing underneath it because she wanted to skinny dip after dark?

She'd busted her butt to be as secure and certain and content as Whitney. And the way she saw it, she didn't have an option about that either.

"You're right," she said, hearing the hurt creep into her tone as they moved onto the next shop window, this one selling household items with a nautical theme. "You didn't grow up like me."

"I didn't mean it like that," Whitney protested.

"I know what you meant," Cassie said. And it was exactly the way that Cassie interpreted it. Whitney was told what she was having for dinner each night as a child, while Cassie was left guessing.

She kept walking, past a clothing boutique that mostly catered to tourists looking for tee shirts with summer slogans, finally stopping at the corner, where a prime storefront sat vacant. Cassie stared through the large, paned bay window, wondering what had once been displayed in the space, and then farther, into the shop itself, which boasted another window on the opposite wall, and a bright, big space that still felt cozy.

It looked abandoned, dusty even, but she could imagine it all painted a crisp white, the overhead lighting replaced with something more interesting, but not stuffy, not something that wouldn't be true to the sense of Starlight Beach.

She realized with a jolt that she could imagine dresses in the window. Her dresses.

That she was dreaming. Wishing even. That even now, this town still brought that hope out in her.

Her phone rang, bringing her back to reality, and she glanced down at the screen to see Grant's name flashing. She hesitated, knowing that she could easily excuse herself and take the call, but they were approaching town, Whitney would want to pop into the shops, and Cassie would like to, too.

She could call him back, tonight, when she was alone. When she wasn't distracted or searching for distraction.

When her head was clearer.

She let the phone ring until it stopped, and then waited for a text or voicemail notification, telling herself that it was for the best when neither came. That the strange sense of dread she'd felt when she saw his name hadn't meant anything.

That everything would be fine in time; they just needed a little space. That her wish had come true, she was living the life she'd always wanted—and she still could.

Only as she pushed into the gift shop around the corner, breathing a little easier in the cool air-conditioning, she wasn't sure if she hadn't taken his call because she was trying to make him miss her or because she didn't miss him.

chapter sixteen
AMANDA

AMANDA HAD BEEN driving around for nearly an hour, circling the streets near her mother's house, but never close enough to sneak a peek, when she finally headed back to town, feeling frustrated with more than her inability to deal with the task that had brought her back to this town.

Amanda was angry—but not at Cassie. She was mad at herself for lying to her friends, and mad that she felt she had to.

She could have just told them Ryan had left her. Could have blurted it all out right then and there, the same dirty details she'd given Mark last night. But Mark had lived through the same heartache she was now experiencing. Whereas Cassie was blissfully settled into a long-term relationship without any complaints, and Whitney was happily married to her career.

Amanda parked in the center of town, fed the meter with the change she scrounged from the glove compartment, and began walking down Main Street with the hope of distracting herself for a bit—heck, maybe even doing something really out of character and buying herself something. Starlight Beach was full of quaint shops selling everything from touristy souvenirs to tasteful clothing boutiques. Her favorite, though, had always been the bookstore, and that was where she intended to go first. She could get lost in the winding rooms for hours, along with the pages of the stories, blissfully unaware of the world around her—and its many problems. But she hadn't even made it half a block when she spotted Cassie and Whitney strolling up ahead, pausing only to look in a shop window.

She ducked into the nearest door, which turned out to be a restaurant, already starting to fill up with an early lunch crowd. She'd never been here before—but then, her mother wasn't one for dining out, and when she was out with Whitney and Cassie, this place, like most grown-up establishments, hadn't exactly been on their radar.

She could only hope the same held true today.

Warily, she kept watching them, backing up slowly so they wouldn't see her through the restaurant's glass door, until she slammed straight into something warm and hard.

Panicked, she turned, already uttering her apologies, when she saw that the person she'd crashed into was none other than Mark.

His face broke into a grin when he saw her.

"Mark." Her mouth felt dry, and she had the horrible realization that she had barely brushed her hair that morning and now it had probably gone all frizzy in the heat.

She set a hand to it now, unable to push her mother's voice from her head, the one that always told her she should cut her hair off, that the length just dragged down her face.

But Mark didn't seem to notice or care, and instead, he said, "It looked like you were hiding from someone."

Amanda gave a nervous laugh. "That obvious?"

"Someone I know?" he asked. "I do know most people in town, at least the locals."

Yes, he would. But he wouldn't know Cassie or Whitney, only Tripp.

"Visitors," she said.

He gave a little curl of his lip. "No wonder you were hiding then."

Amanda laughed again. It was typical of the locals to get tired of the tourists after a while, even if they were good for business.

"There's a quiet booth near the back of the bar." Mark raised his eyebrows.

Her cheeks grew warm when she realized that he was inviting her to join him. "When you said drinks, I didn't realize you meant today," she said.

"Well, you aren't in town for long," he pointed out.

Amanda nodded, feeling strangely sad about that, even though coming here—being here—wasn't easy.

Mark was certainly making it more pleasant.

"And you need an excuse to hide out. And I don't have a meeting for an hour."

"You've convinced me," Amanda said, even though she hadn't needed it. She liked Mark, and she quickly felt like he was becoming a friend.

More of a friend than Cassie and Whitney lately, she thought a little sadly as she followed Mark to the back of the room and settled into a booth that was hidden from the front of the restaurant.

"What'll it be?" he asked, scanning the menu.

Given the hour, and Mark's need to be back at work, not to mention Amanda's desire to keep a cool head, she said, "How about coffee?"

Mark grinned. "I like coffee."

They held smiles for a moment before Amanda felt her cheeks warm again. She cleared her throat, glancing over her shoulder just in case Cassie and Whitney had decided on a bite to eat. But then, Whitney would probably prefer something on the water, and Cassie would certainly prefer to be outside, taking in the ocean breeze.

"So," Mark said after their orders were placed and coffees delivered. "Are you going to tell me who you're hiding from?" Then, sensing her hesitation, he said, "Consider it confidential. As your attorney."

She gave him a skeptical look. "Does that apply in this case?"

He shrugged. "Not really, but I'm willing to bend the rules if you are."

"I'm not used to bending rules," Amanda told him. She had once—that awful day, when she was supposed to be minding Shelby—and she was still paying for it. "The truth is I've always followed them, or tried to anyway."

But where had that gotten her? It hadn't made a difference in her relationship with her mother, no matter how hard she'd tried. And as for her marriage, it seemed that rules didn't even apply to Ryan.

"Then we're both guilty of the same thing," Mark said. "Not that there's anything wrong with that."

No, Amanda thought, there wasn't. She was honest, at least she tried to be, even if she wasn't being honest with Cassie and Whitney right now.

Amanda's smile was wan. "If you must know, I was hiding from my friends."

He looked surprised. "The ones you were with at the party last night?"

Amanda nodded. "They joined me on my trip here. I've known them practically all my life."

"They're from here too?"

"At one point in time we all were," Amanda said. "That's why they came here with me this week."

Guilt weighed heavily on her when she considered their feelings about this town. How Cassie had always tried to ignore the way the kids talked about her mother, how Whitney had left so suddenly after Shelby's accident, the Palmer house quickly going on the market, confirming that their summers as the Starlight Sisters had come to an end.

But now, being back, Amanda realized that it hadn't. That they'd been given a second chance. One that was slipping out of her hands, like everything else these days.

"So why hide from them?" Mark asked.

Amanda sighed as she stirred creamer into her mug. "Oh, I guess because I haven't told them about my divorce." Saying it felt strange, like she was talking about another person.

But she also felt like another person, sitting here, with a man she'd just met a few days ago. A single man, a handsome man. A man who made her laugh and forget all about her troubles for a few minutes.

A man who made her feel like herself. Or a better version of it.

"Sometimes, it's easier to talk to a stranger," he said.

It was, but that wasn't the case here. Mark was beginning to feel more like a friend.

"You have nothing to feel ashamed of," he told her flatly. "Or so I tell myself about ten times a day."

Amanda saw the crinkle around the corner of his eyes and relaxed. "I wish that was true. The only upside to all of this is that my mother didn't live to see it, or I'd never hear the end of it."

"She was hard on you." Mark said it like a statement, not a question.

Amanda nodded. "But Whitney and Cassie were always there for me."

"Then what changed?" Mark seemed genuinely interested, and Amanda felt herself wanting to tell him, if she could even figure it out herself.

"After…my sister's accident, Whitney and her family moved away. It was a scandal, you see. There was a lot of talk in town about how I was busy with my friends. I wasn't keeping an eye on my sister."

"You must have been a kid yourself," Mark commented.

Amanda didn't respond to that. She hadn't been allowed to be a kid. How could she when she carried the weight of her family's problems on her back?

But with Cassie and Whitney, she could run free. Make wishes. Even believe they'd come true.

"The Palmers sold their house here," she continued. "Whitney and I kept in touch, and Cassie too. By the time we graduated from college, we even met for reunions every year or so. But…it was never quite the same."

"You went through a terrible experience together, but it was none of your fault."

"Try telling my mother that," Amanda said. She doubted that anyone ever did, and if they had, her mother wouldn't have listened. Someone was responsible for Shelby and that person was Amanda. "Being a mother has been the most important role of my life. And Whitney has never really understood that."

"So she wouldn't understand the divorce either," Mark concluded.

Amanda hesitated. "I don't think she ever understood my choices. She doesn't invest in people, she's even always been a little distant from me and Cassie, ever since her family left this town. But the last time I saw her, she made it clear that my life isn't the one she would have chosen."

Mark looked at her for a moment. "Would you have chosen her life?"

Amanda laughed just picturing herself in a corner office overlooking the Boston skyline, going home to an empty apartment each day, and waking up to silence instead of the domestic buzz of activity.

"No," Amanda said firmly. "Just thinking about it makes me feel sort of sad for her." But then, why should she, considering how happy Whitney was with her life? It was more than she could say for herself right now.

"You all looked like you were having a good time the other day at the Wharf." Mark sipped his coffee.

"We were," Amanda said. "It was a nice distraction from everything I'm dealing with. That's why they're here. They came to support me."

Mark leaned over the table, his eyes gleaming. "Then let them support you."

Amanda blew out a sigh. Her mother was one topic. Her marriage…that was another.

"My advice?" Mark tipped his head. "The truth always wins."

Amanda nodded slowly. Mark had a point. And right now, she had nothing else to lose.

CASSIE AND WHITNEY WERE SITTING on beach chairs when Amanda returned to the house later that afternoon, after visiting the bookshop and treating herself to a stack of books that she'd never have dared purchase in her little town in Connecticut. They were self-help books; specifically, they were about moving on with life after divorce.

It felt impossible. Unimaginable. Just buying them made her feel like she was a different person than the one she'd always been or hoped to be—but today, even the little bookshop with its winding rooms couldn't take her away from her problems. It was time to face them. And maybe, share them, too.

She slipped off her flip-flops the moment she stepped off the porch, smiling as her toes sank into the soft, warm sand.

"Hope I'm not interrupting," she said as she approached her friends.

"We were just talking about our old homes here and if we are going to visit them," Cassie said.

It hadn't even occurred to Amanda that her friends might be struggling with the same concerns she had about revisiting their childhood houses.

"But mine was torn down about a week after Willow moved out," Cassie said with a shrug. Even though she gave a knowing grin, her gaze was flat, and Amanda knew that it pained her to think about the place that Willow had inherited from her parents and had never been able to maintain.

"What about you?" Amanda regarded Whitney as she settled into the chair beside Cassie. "You jog every morning on this beach."

"Always in the opposite direction of the house." Whitney gave a small sigh. "It won't be the same seeing it now after all these years. It won't be that magical summer place that I couldn't wait to visit. Instead, it will just be the place that I hated to leave."

It was a rare glimpse of vulnerability, one that Whitney rarely shared, and Amanda felt something in her chest soften.

She stared at the ocean for a bit, watching the tide roll in, thinking of what Mark had said. He was good at advice, and not just the legal kind.

Good at making her feel better, too.

"I didn't go to my old house today," she admitted. "I know I have to at some point, but...not today."

"You have time," Cassie said gently. Then, with a little grin, she added, "Not *much* time, though."

Amanda couldn't help but smile. "Sorry for bursting out like that earlier," she said.

"I'm the one who should apologize!" Cassie protested. In her hand was a glass of white wine and in her lap was a sketchbook, open to a page of a stunning dress that billowed at the back, like the froth of the waves crashing against the wet sand.

Amanda pulled her eyes from it and said, "No. I overreacted. I mean. You were showing concern, that's what friends do."

"Wine?" Whitney asked, lifting a bottle from beside her chair. She offered a fresh glass, which Amanda took. It was still afternoon, but it was vacation after all, and what she was about to say might require a little liquid courage.

"I wasn't flirting with my mother's lawyer," Amanda clarified. She took a sip of her wine, but it did little to calm her down. "Besides, it wouldn't matter if I was."

"How can you say that?" Cassie looked aghast.

"Because I'm getting divorced." Amanda set down her wineglass on the wide armrest and looked at her friends, who were wide-eyed and silent. Given their earlier inquisition, she might have found this satisfying, but instead, she felt something much more powerful.

Relief. Fatigue. Sadness. And shame.

That was the part that she could never shake, even now, as a grown adult. It lingered there, deep within her, something that had planted itself and grown until there was no way she could ever undo it.

"A *divorce*?" Cassie was the first to speak as her eyes filled with sympathy. "But why didn't you tell me?"

"It just happened," Amanda replied. "Last Friday." Even though it had been going on much longer than that.

"But we've been here for days! You could have said something this morning!" Cassie looked so injured that Amanda knew she had to be completely honest, even if it hurt her friend more.

"I wanted to," Amanda admitted. "But then, with Whitney here…" She glanced at the third member of their group, who looked down at her lap. "I couldn't." She took another sip of wine, feeling it roll down her throat. "After a couple of days here, it got easier to say nothing. To pretend like it wasn't happening. Being away from home, I was almost able to believe that was true."

"Oh, honey," Cassie said, shaking her head.

Amanda felt the tears well in her eyes and she wished she hadn't left her sunglasses in the house. It had been a long time since she'd opened up like this about anything other than her mother. A long time since she'd had to. She'd been happy, just like she'd told Whitney. She'd gotten the life she'd always wanted.

And then she'd lost it.

"What…happened?" Cassie asked carefully.

Amanda sighed heavily, afraid to look in Cassie's direction, or worse, Whitney's. Afraid of what she'd see there. Lack of surprise? Pity? She didn't know which would be worse.

She just knew that Mark was right and that keeping this inside, hiding this secret from her best friends felt worse than almost anything.

"Ryan's leaving me. For another woman. Younger. Thinner, of course. Did I mention she works for him and that I hired her? I actually chose the woman who is replacing me, in every sense of the word." She let out a bitter laugh.

"The bastard," Whitney hissed, her eyes blazing when she looked up.

Amanda felt a slip of a grin behind her wineglass. She had forgotten the way Whitney could convey such emotion about people she cared about, how that usually cool and composed facade could be momentarily broken.

But did Whitney still care about her the way she claimed? Did she ever? She'd been distant for so long that it was impossible to know sometimes if they were friends or just two people with a shared history.

"You must not be surprised," Amanda told her. "I mean, this is what you always thought would happen, right? That I was crazy for thinking I had finally found my happy ending. That I was a fool for loving my life?"

Now a single tear slipped down her cheek and she quickly brushed it away.

"Amanda, all I ever wanted for you was to be happy," Whitney said quietly but forcefully. "That's all I still want."

Amanda swallowed back the lump in her throat. Maybe it was the revelation, maybe it was the exhaustion that came with not just sharing this news but finally accepting it, but she was all out of fight. She needed support. And she needed to believe that maybe, somehow, someone who was supposed to love her did.

"That's not the worst of it, though," she said, sniffing loudly as Cassie refilled her wineglass.

"I hardly see how it can get worse!" Cassie blurted and then, looking panicked, grimaced. "Sorry, I mean…"

"It's bad. I know it's bad." Amanda brushed tears from her cheeks as they fell. "And it does get worse because I wanted another baby and, instead, she's pregnant and they're getting married. He's already engaged!"

Cassie gasped.

"I'll get another bottle of wine," Whitney announced, pushing out of her chair.

"Better make it two," Cassie called after her.

When Whitney disappeared through the door into the kitchen, Cassie turned back to Amanda, taking her hand. "Why didn't you pull me aside and tell me sooner? We've always told each other everything!"

Amanda gave her a pointed look.

Cassie lowered her gaze. "I suppose not everything. I should have told you that Whitney was coming. Or I shouldn't have invited her."

"No," Amanda said softly, meaning it. "I'm glad you did."

"Really?" Once again, Cassie's voice was full of breathless hope, the way it always was when she was just a child. She always dared to think that tomorrow might be better than today. And right now, Amanda needed to believe that.

After talking with Mark, she almost did.

"Really." Amanda nodded. "My world is getting smaller by the day. I need all the friends I can get."

"Whitney feels awful, you know," Cassie said.

"I don't want anyone's pity," Amanda said, pulling her hand back.

"I have never pitied you," Whitney replied, returning with wine, a pint of ice cream, and three spoons. She sat down on her chair and opened the carton. "If anything, I always envied you."

"Envied *me*?" Amanda laughed again. Whitney was pushing it. She didn't need to go this far. Whitney was the one who'd lived in the oceanside mansion, who'd worn crisp white sundresses and later, designer swimsuits. The one who went to the best schools, and who now held a job that had been waiting for her all along, one that she loved, and wouldn't trade for anything. Or anyone.

Whereas Amanda had lived in a little three-bedroom house on the edge of town, and now lived in a house not much larger in a different small town. One without the glamour or chic restaurants and shops that a big city held. The only parties she went to were for children, and if she dared to wear a white dress, it would be stained within an hour. The closest thing she had to a designer anything was the knock-off handbag she'd bought with Cassie one of the times she'd taken Trevor into Manhattan at Christmastime.

But Whitney wasn't laughing, and there was no mirth in her steady blue gaze. "I mean it. You found happiness, despite everything. And you found love, at least for a little while. And you have Trevor, and that's never going away. But more than anything you knew what you wanted, and you went after it. And that's brave, Amanda."

Brave. Amanda had never thought of herself as brave.

"Well, I don't feel brave now," she admitted, taking the carton and a spoon and helping herself to a big spoonful of creamy vanilla ice cream before passing it to Cassie. "And I don't know if what I ever had was love."

Her chest squeezed so tight that it hurt when she thought of her wedding day. How young she'd been! How truly, genuinely happy! How all the pain and loneliness of her childhood felt like it was finally and truly behind her. That her future was bright. And her wish was finally coming true.

"No one has a perfect relationship," Cassie said softly.

"Or a perfect life," Whitney added.

Cassie and Amanda exchanged a glance that Whitney didn't catch as she plucked the cork from the wine bottle.

"I've never heard you complain about your life even once," Cassie replied. "Except for Tripp."

Whitney didn't speak as she topped off their glasses. "I'm just saying that appearances aren't everything. For all you know, this new woman in your husband's life isn't happy about the circumstances. Maybe she got pregnant by accident, and now she feels pressured into marriage."

Cassie was nodding along. "It was all exciting when he was the handsome boss, but it's about to get real. And fast. You know better than us what married life and motherhood are like."

Amanda did, and from the open expression on the other women's faces, it seemed that they were looking for her to explain it to them.

"It's far from glamorous, that's for sure," she said. "There were days when Trevor was little that I didn't even have an opportunity to shower unless he was taking a nap, and he was never much of a napper. Ryan would roll in after a long day at the office and I'd be torn between cooking dinner or finally getting a few minutes for myself."

Amanda saw Whitney wrinkle her nose but this time she couldn't even take offense.

"But it's also wonderful," she said as her voice broke and another tear slipped free. "I loved being married. I love being a mother." She stole a glance at Whitney, already knowing what her friend would have to say about this. "I even loved cooking dinner, because it was my way of taking care of the people I loved. I loved the consistent routine of family life. It wasn't exciting but it was…"

"Safe," Whitney finished. From her tone, it was clear she wasn't judging.

If anything, Amanda thought she detected another emotion in her voice. Something closer to understanding.

"Well, turns out that it wasn't," Amanda said, shaking her head. "You'd have thought that I'd have learned my lesson by now, wouldn't you? Just because you have a home and a family doesn't mean it can't all be gone in a second, when you least expect it. Just because you get comfortable and things stay the same, it doesn't mean that they can't change in an instant. You can't depend on anything in this world."

"Wrong." Cassie looked at her firmly. "Us. You can depend on us. The Starlight Sisters."

The Starlight Sisters. Amanda closed her eyes on that comforting thought. And then they all toasted to it.

chapter seventeen
WHITNEY

THE AFTERNOON TURNED quickly to evening, and Whitney hadn't even noticed the passing of time. It was like when she was a kid, sitting on this very beach, losing herself in the company of her friends while her days back in Boston seemed to tick away slowly.

They still did.

"Enough talk about Ryan," Amanda said, accepting a drink from the tray that Cassie carried out to the beach.

Margaritas had replaced the unopened second bottle of wine. Fun was in order, and Whitney wasn't the only one who needed it. Amanda and Ryan. She still couldn't believe it. Didn't want to believe it. Regardless of what Amanda had thought of what Whitney had said, all she ever wanted with all her heart was for her friend to be happy.

For all of them to be.

The sun was low, turning the sky shades of peach and purple, and a soft breeze blew in off the ocean. The beach had cleared out by now, and Whitney would have been content sipping her drink and waiting for the stars to appear in the night sky, but it was clear from the spark in Cassie's eyes that she had other ideas.

"How about a game?" she suggested.

"Cards?" Whitney was all too happy to fall back on their usual game of rummy, but Cassie only burst out laughing.

"I was thinking something a little more interesting than that." Leaning back in her chair to sip her margarita, she said, "How about…truth or dare?"

Whitney felt her back tense and she glanced at Amanda, hoping that her friend would disagree, knowing that Cassie would appease her. But Amanda seemed to consider it for a second before shrugging.

"I've already spilled all my news," she said with a sigh. "May as well double down."

Whitney's mouth felt dry, and it had nothing to do with the sour drink in her hand. She set her glass down carefully on her armrest, knowing that it was time to keep a clear head.

"It's only fair that you go first, Cassie," she said. "Seeing as this was your idea."

Cassie looked excited at the prospect, and wasted no time saying, "Dare!"

Of course she would. Truth was boring, but Amanda smiled slowly, clearly not willing to let Cassie off the hook so easily.

"Okay, then, why don't you skinny dip in the ocean? Before the sharks come out," she added, motioning to the waning light. Even Whitney smiled at the suggestion.

"That's all you've got?" Cassie brushed a hand through the air, unimpressed. "You're forgetting who raised me. Willow didn't believe in swimsuits half the time. Unless that was just an excuse for not being able to afford to buy one." Cassie was still smiling, but the light left her eyes for a moment.

"I have a better one then," Amanda said. "Call Grant and ask him to marry you. It's about time, isn't it?"

Now Cassie's smile left her face for good. She frowned as she took another sip from her drink. "Oh, no..."

"Why?" Whitney asked. "Surely you're not so conventional as to be waiting for the man to pop the question?" Manhattan hadn't changed her that much, had it?

"That's not the reason," Cassie shot back, because of course, it wouldn't be. Cassie didn't uphold traditional ideals because she'd never had to—something that Whitney had been fascinated by once, confused by, really, and now simply envied.

"Then why not?"

"Because..." Cassie blinked as if searching for an excuse. "Because...Grant and I are happy. Just as we are."

Whitney nodded. "Fair enough."

But something had shifted in Cassie. Her frown deepened as she stared down at the drink in her hands. Just as quickly, she shook her head, looked up, and gave Whitney a dazzling smile.

"I guess that means I'm going in!" She stood up and tossed her cardigan onto her chair.

Amanda, being Amanda, squealed and then darted her eyes down the empty stretch of beach. "You're not actually going to do it?"

"It's a dare," Cassie said.

But there was something she didn't say. Something that sounded to Whitney like it was the only choice.

"I'll grab you a towel," Amanda said, hurrying into the house where Whitney suspected she would remain until Cassie's naked rear end was out of sight.

"You don't have to do this," Whitney whispered to Cassie. "Amanda's probably hiding and counting to thirty. You can splash off and I'll keep your secret."

She took another sip of her drink. There were plenty of secrets she would be willing to keep to protect her friends.

"I want to do it," Cassie said. Her smile was radiant as she ran toward the water, stopping only to quickly shed her tee shirt and shorts. She dove into a wave and then resurfaced, laughing loud enough for Whitney to hear it all the way up near the cottage.

"Is it safe to come out?" Amanda called tentatively from the open door.

Whitney smiled. "It's safe. Hand me the towel and I'll bring it down to her." She stood and gathered the towel from Amanda, who was watching the water with an amused grin.

"Look at her," she murmured, and Whitney followed her gaze to the water where Cassie was diving into another wave, her silhouette visible in the growing dusk. "She's like a kid again."

"I think that was the point," Whitney said wistfully. She took the towel and walked it down to the water, politely shielding her eyes as she held it out to Cassie's wet hand.

"That was amazing!" Cassie exclaimed as she shook the water from her hair. "Seriously, Whitney, it was so…liberating! You should try it."

Whitney stiffened. "I don't think so."

Cassie just laughed and swatted her arm. "Oh, Whitney. You really haven't changed, have you?"

There was a gleam in her eye, and something else, too. Love, Whitney realized, with a lump in her throat.

"You haven't either," she remarked. And just like Cassie, she meant it in the best possible way.

They moved back to the chairs, then waited while Cassie ran into the house to change again, returning just as quickly as she'd left.

"Okay, your turn, Whitney," Cassie said breathlessly. "Truth or Dare?"

"Dare." Obviously. The last thing she needed was Cassie poking at her, trying to get her to reveal something she'd rather not discuss or even think about it.

"I thought for sure you'd say truth!" Amanda raised an eyebrow.

"What? I can't be fun anymore?" Whitney chided, making Amanda and Cassie laugh.

Whitney, however, frowned, thinking of the girl she'd once been, the laughter she'd shed, the way the sound would fill the air, and lift her chest.

She looked back down at her hands. She hadn't been that girl in a long time. None of them had.

Cassie's mouth was curved with mischief when Whitney looked up again. "Clothes off. Into the water you go."

"What? But I just told you—" Whitney cried. Instinctively, she glanced over at the house behind her, where a light was on in one of the back rooms of Derek's house.

"Too proper? Or too afraid Derek might see?" Cassie waggled both eyebrows now, clearly enjoying this. "Or afraid that Derek might *not* see?"

"Cassie!" But leave it to Cassie, Whitney was laughing now. Amanda was too.

"You work out every day," Amanda commented. "You have a figure I could only dream of having." Her expression turned sad for a moment before she said, "What's to hide?"

"I'm not hiding," Whitney insisted, even though that often felt like all she ever did. From problems. From people. From her truest self. "But I have never streaked in public, and I never will."

"Because you're a Palmer?" Cassie asked.

Whitney pinched her mouth, resenting that Cassie was right, partly, and that even now, in her thirties, Whitney was still worried about holding up the family name.

"My brother could walk by," she pointed out.

This, finally, silenced Cassie, who tipped her head and nodded once, and then craned her neck, searching the shoreline.

"That leaves truth," Amanda said.

Whitney's stomach rolled over. She steadied her breath, reminding herself that she could do this, she'd been doing it for years, putting on a face, whatever face it needed to be to get her through that day, to fulfill her family duty. This would be no different.

Only it was different because this wasn't a boardroom or a charity event. This was Starlight Beach. And these were her closest friends.

Once, her sisters.

"The question is…" Amanda paused dramatically. "Have you ever been in love?"

Whitney felt her shoulders drop in relief. The answer was simple, one that she could answer with one word, and honestly.

"No."

"*Never*?" Amanda gave her a look of heartfelt sadness.

"Wouldn't she have told us if she had been?" Cassie countered.

A strange silence answered that question. There was once a time when they did tell each other everything, but tonight it was revealed that this was no longer true.

"You know, it's funny," Amanda said. "You'd think right now that I'd regret ever meeting Ryan, ever marrying him, or ever loving him. But…I don't. And not just because he gave me Trevor. I had love. For a little while. And I wouldn't change that for anything."

Whitney looked up at the night sky and the stars that twinkled in the moonlight.

There was a lot she wished she could change, but that wasn't how life worked. And love, and the possibility of ever finding it or knowing it, was just one of the casualties that came with being a Palmer.

WHITNEY DIDN'T TAKE HER USUAL run the next morning, instead opting for a long, drawn-out walk on the shore. She needed to clear her head, needed to fight this feeling that was burning in her chest ever since she agreed to come back here, since she saw Tripp.

Since long before that.

She was both pleased and a little wary to see Derek sitting on his back porch as she began to head back to the cottage. But she wasn't ready to face her friends yet, and she didn't mind talking to Derek, either. In fact, with each conversation, she enjoyed herself a little more.

That, however, was just the problem.

"No run this morning?" he asked, pointing to her bare feet.

She wiggled her toes in the sand and stood at the base of his porch, waiting as he took the stairs to meet her at the bottom.

"I felt like mixing it up," she said, sitting beside him on the second to last step.

"Something tells me you're usually a creature of habit," he said, looking at her ruefully.

"Is it that obvious?" She smiled in spite of herself.

"I used to have one, back when I lived in Boston. Probably not much different from yours. Even started the day with a run before heading into the office, and I was still always the first one there and the last to leave. I had my takeout places for dinners. Saturday nights out to a restaurant. Sundays to catch up on housework, which wasn't much considering I was never at my apartment, and I certainly never used the kitchen."

Whitney cracked a wry grin. "That does sound familiar."

Derek gave a soft laugh. "Yeah. Probably for a lot of people. Don't get me wrong, I liked my life, I didn't really have any problems with it. It worked for me until it didn't."

"What do you mean? You grew bored?" Whitney could understand that, but she also relied on the consistency of it, even if it could be stifling at times.

"More like…uninspired," Derek said, his dark gaze searching hers. "I don't even know if I recognized it. I was too busy, well, going about my routine. Then my grandmother died, and I inherited the cottage. I started by coming out here on the weekends, and then I saw some investment opportunities. Eventually fixing up these properties became a full-time project. And the rest, as they say, is history."

"So you just walked away from your life?" she marveled, wondering if people actually did that. If they could quit the path they'd chosen, voluntarily or not, daring to believe that an entirely new one wouldn't just be different but better.

As many times as she'd dreamed of it, she knew that she'd never dare. What would she even do? Where would she go?

Who would she be without her career?

She almost had to smile at the irony of it.

"There wasn't much of a life to walk away from," Derek admitted. "I was working all the time. My friends were my coworkers. Relationships were fleeting. I guess you could say I was invested but at the same time I wasn't."

"No serious relationships then?" Whitney mentally kicked herself for asking—worse, for caring.

"Didn't have time." Derek shrugged. "Or didn't make the time. How about you?"

"Nothing serious," she replied, leaving him to assume that their reasons were the same. "You don't ever miss the city?"

"Oh, sure," Derek replied. "But Boston's not far and I can always visit, though I rarely do. My parents fought a lot when I was growing up, and getting to come to Starlight Beach was something I looked forward to all year. Work was my escape from the chaos at home for a while, starting when I was a teenager. It became a habit, I guess. But now I'm able to live here full-time, and I find that I no longer look backward anymore. No reason to."

"It's a wonderful place," Whitney said, meaning it. She could appreciate it now for what it was, while before she saw it for what it held. Magic. Laughter. Friendship. Starlight Beach was her favorite place at one time. And even after it was tainted, she'd never stopped longing for the way she once felt here, and only here.

"But of course, it's not for everyone." Derek tipped his head, studying her. "Do you ever think about walking away from it all?"

"No." The word came out fast, defensive in tone, and it was such a bald-faced lie that she felt her cheeks flame. She thought of the resignation letter, sitting on her hard drive, back in her office, where she'd be again in less than a week, hating every minute of her day and knowing that she had no other choice.

No other plan. And she relied on plans just as much as she counted on her routine. Tripp was a shining example of what happens when you deviate from the path you were meant to follow.

"You love working for the family company then?" Derek looked mildly surprised, but more than that, he looked interested. In her. In getting to know her.

And even though that was the last thing she wanted from him or anyone, he'd homed in on a part of her that no one else had. Or at least, no one had dared to question.

"I don't love working for the family business. Some days, I even loathe it. Most days."

It was the first time she'd admitted it out loud. Immediately, she wished she could take back the words, and she mentally kicked herself for stopping by his house—worse, for seeking him out.

Derek wasn't a friend. The only friends she had were Cassie and Amanda and even they didn't know the deepest parts of her. Not anymore. She'd made sure of that, knowing, like so many other things, that it was her only choice. That crying about the past or worrying about the future didn't change a damn thing. Some things just were what they were.

"Then why do it?" he asked. "Why not leave and do what you want to do?"

Why? There were a hundred reasons why, and all of them good ones, too. Why did she get good grades in high school? Because it was expected of her, and she'd always done what was expected of her because she couldn't imagine what would happen if she didn't—until it had happened.

She'd slipped, messed up, and paid the ultimate price.

"It's not that simple," she explained, growing defensive, even angry, but not at him. At herself. At her parents. At Tripp.

Tripp had also made a point, she knew, and one she hadn't wanted to admit to herself, just like so many other things. Her mother might miss Tripp and wish that he'd call or come back, but the cold hard truth was that she didn't want Tripp for the man he was, faults and all. She wanted the little boy he once was, the one who would eventually turn into the man he was expected to become.

"It would crush my father if I left the business," Whitney explained, knowing it was true and hating that it was. "It's not exactly like Tripp will ever step up and take over."

"Tripp's made his own life here and he seems pretty content with it." Derek gave her a small smile. "Shouldn't you be able to do the same?"

She wasn't sure if he was insinuating that she should build a life here, or one for herself, but since neither was remotely possible, she shook her head.

"It doesn't work that way," she replied, again wishing that she'd never brought it up. Her life was what it was, and there was no point in wishing for something else. It just made her feel agitated, resentful, and, if she was honest with herself, fearful.

She could long for a different path all she wanted but the plain truth of it was that she was scared of what would happen if she broke from the mold. Scared of what it would cost her. And where she'd end up. Her life might not be the one she had chosen but it was safe nonetheless, and that was something that all the money in the world couldn't buy—not even the Palmers.

"But wouldn't your parents want you to be happy? I mean, you're looking out for them. Wouldn't they do the same for you?"

It was the question she hadn't dared to ask herself, the possibility that she'd be met with Tripp's fate. In her family, love was conditional. And so far, she'd always earned it.

And she wasn't sure she could bear it if she didn't. She had no one else; she'd put her family above everyone and everything for as long as she could remember.

"If you did ever leave, what would you do?" Derek pressed.

Now he was sounding like Cassie, asking her the question she couldn't answer when her friend had posed it, unable to dare to dream the way she once had all those years ago.

"I just mean, how did you picture your life?" Derek was grinning at her. "You must have had dreams. Don't all kids?"

Starlight. Starbright. Whitney could also hear the whispered chant of those three girls, her voice full of hope, and maybe something more. Something closer to prayer.

"My family had plans for me," she said firmly. "I didn't even have to think about where I might like to go to college; it was decided before I was born."

Derek's expression was quizzical. "But you must have dreamed, wished. Wanted something?"

Her heart lifted and swooped and then stopped short of going there. She opened her mouth and then closed it.

"Like I said, that was a long time ago. I was a kid. All kids have silly thoughts about the future." Only it didn't feel silly at the time. It had felt...possible.

"As they should." Now it was Derek who looked nostalgic. "For me, it was a big family. I was a lonely only child and having a big, noisy household always appealed to me."

"You sound like my friend. Amanda." Whitney stopped herself, thinking that Amanda didn't have to end up being an only child, it had just ended up that way. Guilt rose and rested there, and she knew that it wouldn't fade as quickly as it came on. It never did. "She always wanted a family of her own. A big one, too. I guess I never understood that before, but to hear you say it, I think I understand her better."

"You never wanted that for yourself?"

Whitney hesitated. It wasn't that she hadn't wanted it—it was that somewhere along the way she'd stopped wishing for things that she couldn't have. And how could she ever have a family of her own when she was so consumed by the family she'd been born into?

"Amanda and I couldn't be more different. Well." Now she grinned. "Other than me and Cassie. Cassie and I grew up the most differently but somehow, as adults, we have more in common. We both have careers. We both live in big cities."

"And Amanda?"

Whitney sighed. There was no dodging the situation, and she welcomed the opportunity to discuss it, because as much as she could tiptoe around the subject with Cassie, she knew that Cassie was always going to play the peacemaker, always work to lighten the circumstances rather than deal with them head-on.

"Amanda and I had an argument. It was years ago, but I still don't know if she's truly forgiven me. Or if she ever will."

"Never?" Derek raised an eyebrow.

"Some things can't be forgiven," she said simply.

"That bad?" Derek asked.

Whitney hesitated but then nodded. Yes, it really was that bad.

"Well, maybe this week together will change that," Derek said.

Whitney thought about the conversation they'd had last night, what Amanda had shared, and what Whitney had, too.

And what she'd still kept inside.

"Did you get over to Amanda's house yet?" she asked.

"I plan to stop by today," he told her. "I'll leave a report on the doormat for her after I do. You know the house well?"

Whitney swallowed back a lump in her throat. "I spent a lot of time there as a kid. It's a family home. Probably better for locals rather than summer people. It's not near the water, but…it's nice. I used to like being there."

Until she was never allowed back.

He gave her a kind smile. "So, what's next for you today? You've already swapped out a run for a walk. What's next? Tea instead of coffee?"

She grinned back at him, her gaze holding his, noting the way his smile reached his eyes, crinkling the corners.

"Oh." She sighed. "I'll probably default to my usual routine. It's easier that way."

"People can change, though," Derek said. "If they want to."

She thought of Tripp, of his insistence that he was on a different path—a better one. "You believe that?"

He opened his arms wide, toward the ocean. "I'm proof of it. If someone had told me just five years ago that I'd be living here, I would have laughed. I'd gotten so wrapped up in my career that I'd forgotten there was any other way. That there was a better way."

"It's certainly a different pace," Whitney agreed.

"It's more than that. It's a different way of life. You get to know people here, and they get to know you. That was a concept I couldn't even consider back in the city."

Whitney felt uneasy at the reminder. It was true what Derek was saying. And it was the reason why her family had packed up and left, never to return. Until now.

"That's the funny thing about the city," Derek continued. "I moved there because I wanted to be around people, until one day I realized that I was surrounded by a bunch of strangers. Here, I'd like to think most of these people are my friends."

He gave her a slow smile, one that told her he was starting to consider her a friend.

"I guess people can change. I've changed," she acquiesced. Only not in the way she'd hoped. She'd gone from being the carefree girl who laughed away the days every summer to one who barely laughed at all. From the girl who'd dared to wish upon a star to a girl who didn't take any chances, and certainly didn't believe in happy endings.

She'd become more guarded, more private, more reluctant to let anyone get close to her the way that Cassie and Amanda once were.

She pushed people away.

Even the people she loved most.

chapter eighteen
CASSIE

CASSIE HAD SPENT the entire morning sitting on a beach chair, the breeze in her hair, the sand in her toes, sketching draft after draft of dresses that were nothing remotely like her client had requested.

For the first time in years, since she got her first client, and then her next, she was drawing for herself. From the heart. The one she'd set aside for too long. The one she'd tucked away and denied because somehow it wasn't convenient in this new world she was creating.

The trouble was that if she couldn't follow her heart when it came to her career, where did that leave her when it came to her personal life?

It was a thought that had come and gone, the questions building only once her mind got busy again, when she'd finished sketching and traded the imaginary world for the real one, only to lose herself in another vision, another burst of creativity that made all her problems seem to fade away, forgotten for at least a little while.

In a way, she couldn't blame Willow for preferring to stay in her dreamy little bubble. It was certainly easier sometimes than facing the hard stuff.

But unlike Willow, she knew that she couldn't hide from it forever, nor could she spend all her time sketching frothy skirts that billowed out from the waist in layers of tulle.

She had a dress she didn't want to design. A client waiting for her—as well as a man who may or may not still be her boyfriend in three days.

With a sigh, she closed her notebook and stood, pausing only to take one more glance at the ocean before she began the trek back to the house, the notebook at her side.

Whitney was in the house, her fingers tapping at her phone, her bare feet tucked under her on the armchair that faced the window. Amanda was in the kitchen, preparing lunch, seemingly, for the three of them.

"You don't have to do that," Cassie reminded her, as she did on every trip when Amanda took to playing mother hen, even though Cassie secretly loved it, and suspected that Amanda knew it.

"I like to," Amanda replied, so Cassie let it go. Amanda did like nurturing people, finding ways to make life nice for them, but now Cassie wondered if she'd ever stopped to make life nice for herself.

Cassie set the pencil on her sketch pad and poured a glass of iced tea, then a second when Whitney set down her phone to join them around the big marble-topped island.

"How's the sketching coming along?" Whitney asked.

Cassie bit back a sigh, wrestling with how much she wanted to admit—to her friends and herself. "I haven't felt this inspired in..." Months. Maybe even a year, she realized. Maybe, longer than that. "Too long," she settled on saying.

"So why the frown?" Whitney asked.

"Because nothing I've drawn will fit my client's vision." Cassie couldn't hide her frustration. "I'm beginning to think I never should have taken the job. But her wedding is in three months. It's too late to back out now."

"Why did you take the job then?" Amanda asked, looking up from her salad preparations.

"How could she not?" Whitney glanced at Cassie. "You said that this client could open doors. Sure, it's tough now, but think of what it could do for your business."

Leave it to Whitney to focus on the bottom line.

Cassie managed a weak smile behind her glass of tea. She wasn't so sure that the business she'd spent so much time building up, making so successful that she thought she'd never have to worry, would end up becoming something she'd dread. Something that didn't free her, as she'd once thought, but rather, held her back.

"Good point," Amanda said, though she didn't look convinced, but then, how could she? Amanda didn't have a career; she'd never wanted one. But now, with a child to support and Ryan leaving her, she'd have to find something, wouldn't she?

Cassie had thought she had her entire life figured out, her past put behind her for good, her future a sure thing.

If Amanda's situation taught her anything, it was that nothing in life was guaranteed. And that appearances could be deceiving.

Including her own.

While Amanda finished slicing the grilled chicken to add to the salad, Cassie began carrying plates and napkins out to the patio, longing for the fresh ocean breeze nearly as much as she longed for space. To clear her head. To think. To figure out what she wanted because for once, she didn't have a clue.

"You really should have let us do the cooking, Amanda. We're here for you, remember?" Whitney said once they'd all settled at the table.

"Says the woman who doesn't know how to boil an egg," Amanda replied.

Cassie burst out laughing. "Break an egg. Whitney didn't know how to crack it open."

Whitney pursed her lips. "I know how to crack an egg. I just didn't want to get my hands dirty."

Cassie laughed again at the memory of Whitney attempting to make breakfast. "When was that, the reunion before our last?"

"The one before that," Amanda said as she plated her food. "We were in Napa that time."

Of course! They'd rented a house with a view of the vineyards and spent days sampling wines without a care in the world.

But did she really not have a care in the world at that time? That would have been when her business was still in its early stages—her relationship too. Had so much changed in the last five years? Or had she?

Amanda started to take a big bite of food and then set the fork back down on her plate. She didn't need to say it for Cassie to know that Amanda's mother's voice was still loud and clear, if only in the back of her mind.

Cassie chewed her food angrily. She wanted to say right then and there that Amanda was beautiful, regardless of her size. Beautiful inside and out. That her mother had been cruel, and her husband had been a fool.

But she knew that she'd said half of this before, and Amanda always chalked it up to her just being a good friend, saying what she needed to hear.

Even if it was the truth.

"I like cooking," Amanda said. "Besides, it keeps my mind off everything else."

"Did you want to talk more?" Whitney asked. "About Ryan?"

"No," Amanda said firmly. "What's left to say? I thought I had this perfect life, and I was wrong. Or maybe I did have the perfect life and I blew it."

"How can you say that?" Cassie interjected.

"Because I neglected my marriage. I...took it for granted. And when I finally realized that it was too late."

Oh no. Cassie wasn't going to let her friend convince herself of this narrative. "He cheated on you, Amanda." She grimaced, realizing that this was harsh, even if it was the truth. "He neglected the marriage. Not you."

But Amanda just shook her head and poked at her food. "He tried. I see that, looking back. But I was always so worn out, the toll of the last couple of years...it changed me. He said it and now I see it. I wasn't the same person I used to be with him. I was, well, like my old self, I guess."

Cassie glanced at Whitney. They both knew what that meant. Self-critical, insecure, anxious. But they'd seen Amanda be her *real* self, content, and free, when she was on that beach, running alongside them, and later when she was with Ryan and Trevor.

"Looking back," Amanda said, "it had been over for a long time. I just couldn't see it. Maybe I didn't want to see it or believe it. Or maybe I was so focused on other things that I couldn't face the truth."

"The truth can hurt," Whitney said quietly. "Sometimes... sometimes it's better to avoid it, right?"

Amanda nodded thoughtfully. "Don't we all do that to some degree?"

Some more than others, Cassie thought as her mind went to her mother. She had a special ability to live in an alternate reality, one that suited her better than this world ever could.

But it was more than that, wasn't it? These years here were the best of Willow's life. They were the happiest. She'd said so herself. She wasn't bogged down by fear or worry or all the other anxieties that had triggered Cassie so much.

Here, she'd been free. She might have been avoiding reality but at the same time, she'd lived her truth.

And what was Cassie doing?

"You've been quiet," Whitney commented, turning to her.

"I've been thinking about Grant," she said, as her chest began to pound. "I...think it's over."

"Over?" Amanda frowned at her. "But—"

"But too many things," Cassie said, feeling a rush of relief as the words came out. She'd bottled up too much inside, for too long. Her worries and fears had been blanketed by a life that no longer gave her the comfort she longed for.

"You've never implied there were any problems in your relationship," Amanda remarked.

"I guess I didn't want to see them," Cassie said with a sigh. "I... didn't want to be honest with myself. The truth is that I've made a lot of compromises to live this life I wanted in Manhattan—or, thought I wanted. And somewhere along the way, I forgot who I was and what I really wanted."

"But isn't Grant everything you ever wanted?" Amanda pressed. "Reliable. Steady. Responsible. Kind. Loyal."

Cassie nodded, knowing that it was all true, but that somehow, it wasn't enough. "He's all those things. He is a great guy. And a part of me probably could keep going along, and I'd probably be happy enough. But…"

"And what about your career?" Whitney pointed out. "Surely you can't argue that you've achieved everything you set out to do?"

"I did," Cassie agreed. Her work gave her financial stability but it came with a cost—of her freedom. "But somewhere along the way, I stopped remembering why I started doing it. It's a job now. It's work." She gave Whitney a meaningful look. "And before you go saying that we're adults and work isn't all fun, that's not what I'm saying. I lost my vision. My passion. My creativity. But more than anything I lost the love for what I do. And I can't even list one good reason to keep doing it other than for money. Security."

"That's a good reason for working," Amanda said. "Practically speaking."

Whitney looked pensive. "I think I understand."

Cassie looked at her in surprise. "Really?"

"Well look at me," Whitney said, a little brusquely. "I have no husband or child. No relationship at all. I don't even have any friends other than the two of you. Not that I need more. I have my career. The family business. And it comes with a cost."

"I never knew you wanted more," Amanda said quietly.

"I didn't say that," Whitney said quickly, rolling back her shoulders, and sitting a little taller. She took a sip of her drink and then cleared her throat, once again setting her gaze on Cassie. "But you love Grant. What changed?"

"Maybe nothing changed," Cassie said wearily. "Maybe we're both the same people we were when we first met. And maybe that's the problem. Grant sees the woman I am now, not the person I used to be. Not the one who's sitting here now, with the two of you, on this beach."

"But surely he knows you by now," Amanda pressed. "The real you. The Cassie we know."

Cassie shook her head. "He knows what I show him. And tell him. What I haven't hidden from him. Or myself."

She stopped, thinking of the people she could be herself with. Amanda, of course. And Whitney, but only to a degree. Because there was still one thing holding her back from being completely honest with her friend.

"I like Tripp," Cassie said lightly, but Amanda's eyebrows rose, clearly picking up on something deeper. "I'm myself around him. I don't have to deny who I am, or what lifts me up, or who I used to be, here."

Whitney's eyes darted from Cassie to Amanda and back again, where they stared, lingering, disbelieving. "No. You can't like Tripp." Her tone was so firm, so angry, that even Cassie was momentarily taken aback.

"Why shouldn't I like him?" Cassie's voice rose with indignation. Really, what could possibly be so bad about Tripp that would cause Whitney to hold on to childish grudges into her thirties? "Besides, we're not in your boardroom right now, Whitney. I'm not one of your employees. I'm your friend."

"And as your friend, I'm telling you that Tripp is off limits." Whitney's voice was as steely as her gaze.

"Why?" Cassie stared Whitney down. "Because of Grant? Or because Tripp's your brother? Just because you have problems with him doesn't mean everyone else does."

"It's because you're my friend that I'm asking you to let this drop," Whitney said.

"Is this about loyalty?" Cassie asked in surprise.

"That's exactly what it's about," Whitney's voice was firm. Her expression didn't flinch. "What is it that you see in him?"

There was plenty that Cassie could say at that moment, but she settled on the one that drew her to him the most. "He's easy to talk to, and he's kind."

"He's a screwup," Whitney snapped. Her eyes were hard now, her jaw twitching behind her clenched teeth.

"Maybe," Cassie said. "But haven't we all messed up at some point in our lives?"

Silence fell over the table as the women looked down at their hands. It was the wrong thing to say, even if it was the truth.

"I still feel guilty about what happened with Shelby," Amanda finally spoke, her voice so quiet that it was barely above a whisper.

"I do too," Cassie said, reaching out to squeeze her friend's hand.

"And me," Whitney said heavily, closing her eyes against the memory of that awful day.

"But we've grown," Cassie said gently. They never talked about that day, just talked around it, and she knew she had to tread lightly. "We've changed. But maybe, we haven't grown or changed as much as we thought. Sometimes, especially here, I feel like I'm still that same girl I was the last summer we were here together."

"Crushing on Tripp," Amanda said with a slow grin.

That, but something else, too. Something...hopeful.

Whitney shifted in her seat, seeming agitated. "When you say you like Tripp—"

"I mean, I like him," Cassie said with a little smile. She paused and then decided, to heck with it. She was thirty-two years old. Her life was changing for the second time in a big way, and as scary as it was, it was also exciting. And if she couldn't share that with her friends, then who else was there? "I always liked him, Whitney."

"You have to admit he's a good-looking guy," Amanda told Whitney.

Still, Whitney looked baffled and even more pale than usual. "First of all, he's my brother, so no, I definitely won't admit to that. But I can't believe that I never picked up on your feelings, Cassie. Or that you never told me. I thought..."

She stopped talking, but Cassie knew what she was thinking. "That we told each other everything?" She shrugged, knowing that she always assumed the same—until this week. "I guess we have some secrets from each other after all."

Whitney's gaze shifted to her hands like she didn't want to be a part of this conversation anymore.

"I assumed you knew. You never noticed the way Cassie used to stare at Tripp every time he walked in the room? Or how she'd linger in the kitchen a little longer if he was grabbing a snack?" Amanda looked at Cassie and grinned. "You might not have admitted it to me, but it was obvious."

Cassie groaned into her hands as she covered her face. "If you noticed, then maybe Tripp did too!"

"I doubt that," Whitney scoffed, looking up at her again.

"Of course. He didn't notice me at all." Cassie could hear the hurt in her own voice.

"I don't mean that," Whitney said. "I mean...if I didn't pick up on it, then why would Tripp? We grew up together, we saw the way our parents interacted with each other...with us. Maybe that's why we're both still alone. Maybe neither of us could ever understand love because we'd never really experienced it."

Cassie glanced at Amanda, who was watching Whitney with a tenderness that they hadn't shared in years—since the last time they were all together.

"You experienced it with us. What's a lifelong friendship if not true love?"

Whitney looked like she might cry—something that none of them had seen her do since the day that she'd left Starlight Beach.

"I'm sorry, Amanda," Whitney said, and this time, the words seemed to hold a different meeting, one that went beyond an apology.

"I'm sorry, too," Amanda said. "For letting too much time be lost between us. We grew up together. We were in and out of each other's houses, worlds, lives. If anyone should understand the real meaning behind our actions or words, it's us. We know each other better than anyone else ever could."

Whitney grew silent, neither nodding nor agreeing. And Cassie, watching her, started to wonder if there was something that Whitney had been keeping from them too.

chapter nineteen

AMANDA

AMANDA SAT ON the porch, the lunch she'd spent the better part of an hour making long forgotten and mostly untouched, not that she cared. She hadn't made it to be eaten; she'd made it because that was what she did. She devoted her time to keeping busy, keeping the demons at bay, telling herself that if she kept moving, and kept taking care of the people who mattered to her in so many small ways, it would somehow ensure that she'd never lose them.

But loss snuck up on you, didn't it? Even to those you'd never suspect.

"Is it really over between you and Grant?" Amanda asked Cassie. She'd only met him twice when she'd taken Trevor to New York for the day, but she'd liked him. He was friendly and engaging, and he seemed like someone who could be counted on.

But then, she supposed she'd once thought the very same about Ryan.

"Not officially, but...yes. He's a good guy. He's just not the right guy for me." Cassie frowned deeply for the first time all week.

"I'm sorry, Cass." Amanda reached out to squeeze her hand.

"I'm sorry about you and Ryan." Cassie shook her head. "I still can't believe he'd do this to you. I thought…"

Cassie trailed off and Amanda knew that she was too polite to voice what she was really thinking, even though Amanda had thought the same thing. Still did, half the time.

"He was the safe choice?" They exchanged a long look of understanding, one that Amanda was sure made Cassie think of all those times they'd sit on the beach, gazing up at the stars, thinking of their future. Or a better life.

"I think that's what I thought about Grant, too. But maybe there is no safe choice." Cassie shrugged. "Or maybe there is but that doesn't make it right. My life has gone completely off track, even though I took every precaution to ensure that would never happen. Look at me. I'm single, or I will be the next time I talk to Grant again. My career is at a crossroads. For the second time in my life, I feel like I'm completely starting over."

"That makes two of us," Amanda said, only her options didn't seem as open as Cassie's. Cassie had a talent to fall back on, even if she changed course with her design business. And of course, there was Tripp…

She glanced across the table to Whitney, who was still frowning, no doubt none too happy about Cassie's announcement.

"It's kind of exciting though," Cassie said, her eyes lighting up the way they used to when they were little. "In a way."

"I wish I could see it that way." Amanda sighed and brought her knees up to her chair, hugging her legs against her chest. "But right now, all I can think about is being a part-time mother and finding a full-time job. I'm afraid that when I look at the future it feels like a long, lonely struggle."

"Hey." Cassie nudged her with her elbow. "How can you be lonely when you have Trevor? And me? And Whitney. And that lawyer of yours is pretty darn easy on the eye. I don't call looking at him a hardship."

Amanda laughed. "He's single, you know. Divorced. That's sort of what…bonded us, you could say."

Now Cassie's eyes gleamed. "I knew there was something between you too!"

"Oh…" Amanda bristled. "I don't think he sees me that way. I mean, look at me."

"I am looking at you," Cassie replied, her expression turning serious. "And what I see is a beautiful, loving woman who anyone would be lucky to know."

"It's true," Whitney said. "I think that Mark sees what we do. The real you."

Cassie nodded. "You light up when you're around him, the same way you do with us."

"It's not that simple," Amanda protested, shaking her head, even though she wished that it could be. That she could find love for the second time—a lasting one this time.

"Why not?" Cassie said simply.

"I'm not that young anymore," she started. "I never attracted boys back in high school. Ryan was the only guy I ever dated in college. I'm a single mother now, too. And…I've put on weight."

"That's not you talking," Whitney said gently.

No, Amanda thought. It wasn't. But that voice—her mother's voice—was in her head. And in her heart.

"Mark likes you for you," Cassie insisted. "Because he sees what we see. The real you. All of you."

"But what about all my flaws?" Amanda looked miserably at her friend.

But Cassie just smiled and said, "We don't love you despite your flaws. We love you because of them. Besides, how many times do I have to say you're too hard on yourself?"

"Only until I believe it," Amanda said with a little smile. And for a while, for a long time, she had believed it. She'd felt happy with Ryan and Trevor. And even beautiful.

And oh, it would be nice to feel that way again.

"So, what's the real reason you can't pursue anything with Mr. Handsome?" Cassie asked pertly.

Ah, Cassie, ever the optimist, ever the one to see the world as something that could be righted, or at least, made better.

"For starters, he lives here." Amanda looked out to the water now, to the long stretch of beach dotted with children building sandcastles, others flying kites, couples walking hand-in-hand. She'd never brought Trevor here, never wanted to taint him with this place. But now, with the bad parts nearly behind her, she began to wonder if she could. If he was still young enough to enjoy playing in the sand or splashing in the water. If they might be able to build new memories here, together.

"You have a house here," Cassie pointed out.

Amanda looked at her sharply. "You know how I feel about that house. It's full of nothing but bad memories and dark times."

Cassie's expression sobered. "You're right. I know. I'm just saying…now, well, now it might not be so difficult to return to Starlight Beach. Maybe you can leave the past in the past and see the good things about this town. Remember them too."

Maybe. But moving here was a different conversation. Moving at all was something she hadn't thought about, but now she considered that she might have no choice but to sell the house she and Ryan owned. All those details hadn't been discussed yet, even though she knew that they would be, and soon.

"I have to do what's best for Trevor," Amanda said.

"You only live an hour away without traffic," Cassie said. "You could make something work that wouldn't uproot Trevor too much."

It wasn't ideal, but then, what was? And wait, was Amanda even thinking of that, putting down roots in the one place she'd been so desperate to avoid for so many years?

But could she go back to the little suburban town that had been her haven, where she'd thought her world was safe and secure and stable, only to have it all snatched away?

She'd come back here to settle her past once and for all, and so far, all she'd done was avoid it. And now that the truth had come out, and she was armed with two friends who still loved her and stood by her, she knew that she could face it. The days were ticking away. She had no choice.

"You're right, Cassie. But not about Mark. Before I even think about my future, I first have to handle the past." She nodded, confirming her decision, resolving her strength. It would be scary, and painful even, but it would also be liberating. And it couldn't be avoided.

She stood, her decision made, even though she still felt a strange sickening feeling roll through her stomach.

"What did you have in mind for the rest of the day?" Cassie asked, following her into the house, Whitney coming along, slower, behind her.

Amanda paused at the kitchen sink. It was something she'd avoided for so long that most of the time, all she could do was think about how to avoid it while she was here. It was a part of her past, and of herself, that had never been addressed, just buried, along with the pain, but it still forced its way to the surface anyway.

"I think I need to visit the site of the accident," she said, watching as her friends stilled and slowly lifted their eyes to each other, and then to her.

"Do you think that's a good idea?" Whitney all but whispered. "It could be upsetting."

"It will be, I'm sure. But it also feels wrong not to visit it. I tried to forget that day instead, to put my past behind me and only focus on my future." Amanda felt a lump rising in her throat, fighting the words that needed to come out, the feelings that needed to be voiced. "It's like I tried to forget Shelby too. Like I tried to forget my sister."

Cassie rushed toward her with her arms extended, giving her a firm hug and then pulling back to look her fiercely in the eyes. "You have never forgotten Shelby. None of us have."

She looked to Whitney for confirmation, who closed her eyes and nodded once.

"If you want to do this, then I'll go with you," Cassie said, breaking the silence. "Unless you need to be alone."

"No, you can come," Amanda said, relieved that she didn't have to ask.

"I saw some bikes in the garage," Cassie said, then stopped herself. "Maybe we should drive."

"There probably won't be a place to park," Amanda said. The street was narrow, without a barrier. The road was remote and only used by locals coming and going through town when they wanted to avoid the bigger roads with heavier traffic. There wasn't another house for half a mile, and that was Amanda's childhood home.

"But biking…" Cassie looked worried. Whitney's jaw was clenched. She clearly thought this was a bad idea.

Amanda saw that she was trying—to make this friendship work, to show that she understood even when she didn't agree.

"It feels right, in a way," Amanda said, even though she was starting to get cold feet. She wondered if she could handle knowing that she'd be able to turn her bike around, come back to this house, and have a fun night with her friends—and that her sister never had that chance.

"Then we'll go," Cassie said with a smile.

And Amanda knew that, somehow, it would all be okay.

AFTER SHELBY'S ACCIDENT, SOME PEOPLE from town had installed a cross to mark the site, and for a while at least, it was surrounded by cards, stuffed animals, and flowers. Eventually, after a few months, the gifts stopped. By then Amanda had started avoiding the street altogether, taking different routes on her bike into town, afraid to meet the same fate nearly as much as she was afraid to see the last known spot where Shelby had been.

It had been years since Amanda had come down the narrow road in the woods, but she still knew exactly how to find it. With Cassie and Whitney behind her on their creaking bicycles, she led the way, dread growing with each push of the pedals until there, up ahead, was the marker.

"Stop!" she all but shouted, pulling hard on her handle brakes. She steadied the bike with her feet, staring at the large wooden cross that still bore her sister's name, and then, at what was beneath it.

Cassie, coming up from behind her, gasped.

Amanda climbed off her bike and began walking toward the memorial, where a bouquet of flowers rested on the grass.

"These flowers are fresh," she said, crouching to run her fingers along the soft pink petals. "It's been so many years. I'd assumed that people would have forgotten. Hoped they would have, even." She was ashamed to say it now. That the only way her part in that day would be forgotten was if the event was too.

"There's a card," Cassie said, pointing to the freshest bouquet of carnations.

Frowning, Amanda opened it, almost not believing what she saw. She stood slowly, her legs shaky. "It's from Tripp."

"Tripp?" Cassie and Whitney, who hadn't spoken since they left the house, repeated in unison.

Amanda stared at them. Whitney looked visibly pale. Cassie, however, seemed pleased. Tripp was no longer the shallow teenage boy who floated in and out of the Palmer house when the girls were over. He was a grown man. Living here in town. Dedicating his life to being a better person, and to making others better too.

"What does it say?" Cassie asked, stepping forward.

"Never forgotten," Amanda said, showing them the handwritten note. She looked up at Whitney, trying to make sense of this. "Why would he leave this?"

"Beats me," Whitney replied, frowning down at the card. "I've never been able to understand what motivates my brother."

"I think he was trying to be nice," Cassie said with a gentle smile. "He knew you were back in town. He probably knew this was difficult. Lots of people have moved on, but he knows the reason we all left and stayed away."

Amanda thought about it, finally nodding.

"I could stay," Cassie was saying to her, as Amanda continued to stare at the flowers, both puzzled and touched.

She looked at Whitney, whose expression was pained. "I wish I could stay, but I have this conference call. Work. You know how it is. I...I feel so bad, Amanda."

Cassie's mouth pinched and it was clear she was ready to push the topic, but Amanda cut in before an argument could break out.

"I understand," she said, even though she didn't. Not any more than Whitney could understand why she'd drop everything for her child, put him above everyone and everything else. Even her friends. Even herself.

She'd never had a career, never understood the responsibilities stacked into Whitney's days. To her, it might not be important, certainly not more than friends or family, but that was all that Whitney had, wasn't it?

Whitney was already climbing back on her bike, looking uncomfortable as she tried to find her balance.

"I'm sorry, Amanda," she said, pausing to reveal the angst in her eyes. "I'm so, so sorry."

Amanda watched as she pedaled away, quickly, as if she were running from something rather than to something, and Cassie started to lurch after her.

"Let her go," Amanda told Cassie, pulling her back. This wasn't Whitney's problem. It wasn't her story.

It was Amanda's past. And even though Cassie was there, holding her hand now just like she'd done all those years ago at this very spot, it was still Amanda's guilt to bear alone.

chapter twenty

CASSIE

CASSIE COULDN'T BELIEVE Whitney! Running off like that! This wasn't easy for any of them, but Whitney thought she could run away just like her family had done all those years ago. But then, maybe it was for the best that she'd taken an early exit. Maybe Amanda didn't want her here and Whitney had sensed that.

Or maybe, now, after all this time, it still was easier to run away than bear witness to what had happened. And accept the part they'd all played in it.

Amanda continued to stare at the memorial, lost in her thoughts. Cassie knew what this moment meant for her—even if she knew better than to say she fully understood it. Shelby had been Amanda's sister, her real sister, and she'd never recovered from what happened that day. Her mother had never let her.

"I could sit with you for a while if you'd like," Cassie said gently.

But Amanda shook her head. "You should go. I know you have work to do too."

She did. And two days to deliver something the client deemed wonderful.

"I should," Cassie reluctantly agreed. "But you're more important."

"Try telling that to Whitney," Amanda snorted. "She really became a Palmer, didn't she?"

"Maybe she was one all along," Cassie sighed, but her mind went to Tripp, who had fought against that path rather than taking it. "It's funny, because I thought I had changed. But being back here in this town, I realized that I haven't. But Whitney has changed."

And not for the better. Not that Cassie wanted to admit it. She'd tried not to see it, even after the last reunion, but now she knew it was one of those things she couldn't wish away, or hope might change.

She could sense that Amanda thought the same thing. "Maybe it's her career. Or the pressure from her family finally got to her. It probably didn't help that Tripp dropped out of college and then snubbed the family business."

No, but it was no excuse for the hard shell that Whitney now wore. One that she didn't possess all those years ago. It made Cassie sad to think of the way Whitney lost her spirit somewhere along the way.

And it made her all the more determined not to do the same for herself. Unless it was already too late.

"I shouldn't have invited her to come on this trip," Cassie said, angry at herself for daring to get caught up in some fantasy, one where they were all close again, laughing and connected. One where things went back to the way they used to be, the good parts at least.

She'd tried to ignore the bad parts—it was how she'd gotten through life. But right now, the worst of them was in plain sight. Her eyes drifted back to the flowers that Tripp had left. A kind gesture. Was that what had made Whitney uncomfortable? Did she finally feel bad for giving her brother such a hard time?

"You shouldn't have," Amanda admitted, looking at her side-long. "But maybe this was how it needed to be to put the past to rest. To be able to move forward."

Cassie stared at her friend, wondering what she meant by that. If by moving forward, it wouldn't be as the Starlight Sisters, but instead as a fragmented group forever divided by their past.

She clenched her teeth, not wanting to think of that. Distance hadn't pulled them apart, even after Whitney's family had moved away from here. They'd tried, maybe in vain, to keep their friend-ship tight over the years, glossing over the pain of their shared past, the strain that was always there, an undercurrent of their different experiences and choices.

Maybe, all that ever really bonded them was this one, horrible day. And now that they'd faced it again, there would be nothing left. Whitney would go back to her office in Boston, burying herself in work as she chose to do. Amanda would go back and make the most of her life with Trevor, and in time, that would probably be enough for her.

And Cassie...Cassie didn't want to think of a world without her friends in it. No matter what they'd shared. No matter what divided them. Something always brought them back together. Even if this time, it had been her.

Amanda was still looking at her. "Go, really. I'll be fine here on my own." Her tone was firmer, and Cassie knew that she needed to be alone.

All the same, Cassie hesitated, not sure if leaving her friend by herself was the best idea, but it was what Amanda wanted. What she needed.

With great reluctance, she walked back to her bike and toed the kickstand, pedaling slowly in case Amanda changed her mind. But when she glanced behind her, Amanda had already turned back to the flowers.

Cassie continued down the road, toward town. But she was not going back to the house to work on that miserable dress. She was going to see Tripp. A bright spot on this trip. And maybe a glimpse of her brighter future.

THE CAMP WHERE TRIPP WORKED wasn't hard to find once Cassie reached the center of town. She parked her bike near the marina, remembering what Tripp had mentioned at the bonfire about teaching the kids to sail, a skill he'd joked that he never thought he'd need in life but now served a purpose.

The sun was warm on her face as she slipped off her sandals once she reached the beach and began making her way toward the docks where a group of personal-sized sailboats were slowly making their way to shore. She shielded her eyes from the glare of the sun, recognizing Tripp's figure as they came closer, one by one, each sail a different pattern and color combination.

The older kids made it back first, laughing and splashing each other in the water as they climbed up the sandbank, dragging the small watercraft behind them.

Tripp helped one of the struggling girls with her boat and then did a double take in Cassie's direction.

Shyly, she held up a hand, her doubts about showing up uninvited like this put at ease when he flashed her one of those broad grins he used to do as a teenager, said something to the kids, and then began heading her way. In swim trunks and a water shirt that clung to his muscled chest, he looked completely relaxed and at ease, like he was in his element. Like he was happy.

Cassie found herself wishing that Whitney could see her brother now. That she could see once and for all that he wasn't the loser she thought he was, that he'd just chosen a different path, one that might not come with the same financial security that the family business did but one that brought him a better sense of fulfillment. One that let him be true to himself.

It was admirable. Freeing. And inspiring, really.

"I hope I didn't interrupt," she said as he grew closer. Her voice seemed to lock in her throat as her nerves got the better of her, but one look into those sea-blue eyes and she knew that she was right to come here. That this was the only place she wanted to be.

Tripp combed a hand through his wet hair and shook his head. "Not at all. We were just about to break for lunch. I can share my sandwich with you if you're hungry."

Cassie felt a smile slowly take over her face and her stomach fluttered at the invitation—not for the food, but for the company. "You must have worked up quite an appetite out there."

"You haven't seen the size of my sandwich." He waggled his eyebrows playfully and she laughed while he jogged and disappeared into one of the shingled buildings near the marina, reappearing a moment later with a small cooler.

They were flirting. He knew it. She knew it. But he didn't know that technically she still had a boyfriend, even if she and Grant both knew it was already over. And she still didn't know a lot about him either, but she wanted to. Badly.

Motioning to a spot on the sand, Tripp dropped down, and Cassie joined him, watching as he unpacked his lunch, which was admittedly enough to feed her for an entire day.

"You weren't lying!" she exclaimed as he pulled out the sub, which was about as large as an entire loaf of bread.

His face shadowed for a moment when he said, "I try never to lie."

Sensing a shift in mood, Cassie said, "Well, I already ate with the girls. And I probably only need about an eighth of that sandwich to be set until dinner. But that's just me. I don't need much."

Saying it out loud she realized just how true that was, that as a kid, she'd had nothing, but she'd never aspired for material things like Whitney had, only the stability that made it all possible for her. She was content keeping things simple, yet somehow, she'd gone and complicated her life, thinking that money could buy her happiness by the sheer security it provided, even when it came at the cost of what she wanted most. A family. A house. A roof over her head that she could fix if it ever leaked, instead of setting out pails like Willow always did. A connection. Not just to another person, but to herself.

And most of all, the freedom to be herself, without fear of being judged or pitied or thought less of. But Tripp hadn't felt that way back then, and he certainly didn't now.

She could be honest with him. And she sensed he could be with her too.

"I saw the flowers that you left for Shelby," Cassie said, searching his face which had morphed into a frown.

"You were there?" he asked, looking at her abruptly.

"Just now." She swallowed hard, uncertain of how he'd feel about that. He must have wanted Amanda to see that someone still cared. "We were all there. Amanda, Whitney, me. I think Amanda was touched to see that people still cared. That they hadn't forgotten about Shelby."

Tripp's jaw clenched as he set down his sandwich.

"It was nice of you to do that," she said.

"I didn't do it to be nice," he replied matter-of-factly. "I did it for the exact reasons you just said. What happened to that girl was tragic. It shouldn't be forgotten. By anyone."

His frown deepened when he stared out onto the water and Cassie followed his gaze for a moment, feeling strange discussing Shelby when for so many years she didn't dare bring it up, didn't want to. None of them did.

"If I'm being honest, sometimes that's what I wanted," Cassie admitted with a wave of shame. "Forgetting felt easier than facing the truth or living with it."

"I know all about trying to forget the past." He gave a hint of a wry smile. "But that's why I'm back here. To face it. To confront who I used to be head-on, learn from it, and hopefully, do some good with it."

"You do have a good thing going here," she told him. Then, because she sensed that he needed to hear it, especially when his own family wouldn't say it, she added, "You're a good guy, Tripp."

He barked out a bitter laugh and then shook his head.

"I'm not a good guy." Tripp's tone was clipped.

"But look at what you've done with these kids," Cassie stared at him, refusing to give in to his negative self-talk. She understood— Amanda got that way too. Being beaten down by the people who were supposed to love you the most could do that to a person.

But Tripp was packing up the cooler now, the sand clinging to his wet trunks as he stood.

"It's not enough," he said. "What I'm doing now doesn't erase anything."

Cassie stood, growing frustrated that she'd ruined their conversation. She couldn't say or do anything right these days—it was just like when she was younger, and everyone seemed committed to misunderstanding her just because she was different.

Everyone except Amanda and Whitney.

"Just because you didn't finish college and you didn't go to work for your father doesn't mean that you're a bad guy," she said calmly.

"I let people down," he said to her, his tone insistent.

She dropped her shoulders, suspecting he was referring to his sister. "You know how Whitney is. She loves her career. It's everything to her. That doesn't mean you have to love the same thing."

"I'm not just talking about Whitney," Tripp replied.

"Your ex-wife? Your parents?" Cassie stepped forward, wanting to take his hand, but worried that it would be overstepping. "For what it's worth, I'm pretty impressed with you."

Something in his eyes flashed, then darkened. "No." His tone was firm, and he was backing away. "You don't really know me, Cassie. You see who I want to be, but not who I am."

She blinked quickly, feeling the hot tears in her eyes. "I liked who you were then. And I like who you are now. And doesn't everyone deserve a second chance to become the person they always wanted to be, not defined by our past?"

"You can't outrun your past," he replied.

She hesitated, and then nodded, supposing that he was right. That maybe, people didn't even change that much, try as they might.

She certainly hadn't, had she?

"You deserve a second chance, Tripp," she told him. "Everyone does."

For a moment, his gaze softened. But all too quickly, he shook his head again. "Whitney was right about me. Right to keep away. I'm not a good guy. I'm not the person you see. As much as I wish I were, I'm not."

"Tripp—" She started to reach for him, but he took another big step backward, this time holding up a hand.

"It's never going to work between us, Cassie. I'm not who you think I am. I'm sorry. You have no idea how sorry I am, but I'll never be that guy. It's…impossible."

"Tripp!" She stared at him, indignant, hoping to convince him that she wasn't going to turn her back on him. That she'd meant every word that she'd said.

But the steel in his eyes when he turned and looked back at her confirmed something else: that he also meant every word that he'd said.

And believed it, too.

"If you know what's good for yourself then you'll stay away from me, Cassie. I was wrong to let myself get close to you." He paused and then shook his head. "I was wrong about so many things."

"Tripp—"

But her words were lost on the breeze, blowing in off the ocean, ruffling Tripp's shaggy hair as he walked away, one step after another, his broad shoulders slightly slacked, his pace never slowing.

Cassie stood in the sand, her heart heavy with defeat, knowing he wouldn't come back but wishing he would, wondering why Tripp felt just as lost as she did, but knowing better this time than trying to step in and fix things. She couldn't make everything right with everyone, try as she might.

Not when she had yet to make things right with herself.

chapter twenty-one

WHITNEY

WHITNEY KNEW SHE shouldn't have run off like that, making up an excuse that was only partly true. Work was always her go-to reason: for avoiding certain situations and conversations. For distracting herself from the guilt that she'd tried so hard to push aside.

Instead of going back inside the cottage, she went into town where she wouldn't risk having Cassie or Amanda show up when she was feeling so rattled that she might slip and say something she'd only live to regret.

She'd made that mistake once before and she wasn't about to do it again.

She had no appetite even though she'd only picked at lunch, but a boost of caffeine would hopefully clear her head, and the little coffee shop on the corner of Main and Dune offered sidewalk tables. She'd sit and people watch, she decided. She'd watch tourists window shop and kids lick ice cream cones and focus on the simple tasks of their day rather than the heaviness of her own.

Ownership didn't appear to have changed since she was last here, and the framed watercolors from local artists brought a sudden wave of nostalgia as she stepped inside. She'd always loved those paintings, not just for the colors, which seemed so bright and cheerful, but because each one captured a different scene from town.

Her happy place.

That's what it had once been. And she could see now that if that awful day had never happened, maybe it still would be. She'd traveled all over the world and been to resorts on stunning white-sand beaches, but somehow, nothing could top the sweet simplicity of Starlight Beach. It offered something that no amount of money could buy.

But then, she'd learned long ago that money couldn't buy happiness, could it?

A college-aged girl took her order and handed her an iced latte a few moments later. One sip went a long way in steadying Whitney's nerves, but they tensed again when she pushed through the door into the sunshine just as Derek was walking up the sidewalk.

"This is a surprise!" He gave his usual warm smile, but Whitney's felt tense and forced.

The last thing she wanted was to pretend that everything was okay when it was so far from that. She'd kept a poker face for so many years, with so many people, even her closest friends. And right now, after the shock of seeing Shelby's memorial and Tripp's handwritten card, she felt the mask slipping.

"Were you planning to sit for a bit?" Derek asked, just as a group of giggly teenage girls vacated the nearest table.

It could have easily been Whitney, Cassie, and Amanda all those years ago.

Whitney pulled her gaze from the top to consider her response. She could say no and wander around town instead, and still risk running into Derek again. Or she could go back to the cottage and be confronted with Amanda and Cassie, who probably weren't too pleased by the way she'd left them.

She went with the easier of the options, even though there was nothing easy about this day at all.

"For a bit." Until she figured out what to do next. She couldn't go back to the cottage until she'd cleared her head and processed what she'd seen. The marker. The flowers from Tripp.

But most of all she had to process the emotions that she had tried so hard to suppress all these years, and which were now bubbling dangerously close to the surface.

Derek's face broke into a grin. Evidently, his day wasn't ladened with any troubles. "Great. Mind if I join you? I just need a minute to order my usual."

His usual. Whitney should have known that the only coffee shop in all of Starlight Beach would still be a local hotspot. It was proof that she wasn't thinking clearly. She was thinking with her heart, not her head, something she tried never to do anymore.

She dropped onto a chair at the empty table while Derek went inside. She sipped her drink, idly watching an older woman break off pieces of a blueberry scone and toss the crumbs to the eager seagulls who hovered near her feet. She probably did this all the time, even though Whitney doubted the shop owners appreciated it much, and most had signs saying as much. A rule breaker with a soft heart, the woman was.

It made Whitney think of Tripp. Tripp, who had left that card. Did he do it because he suspected it would be found and read? Or did he do it out of his own goodness? She couldn't be sure. She'd lived for so long doing what she was supposed to do, being the devoted daughter, that she no longer even knew what was right for herself—or wrong.

"Oh, good, you're still here," Derek said gallantly when he stepped outside.

She gave him a sheepish smile. "I told you I would be."

"And you're a woman of your word," Derek said. Even though he meant it as a compliment, Whitney felt a tightening in her chest. She was loyal. At all costs. But to whom? More and more, she couldn't shake the feeling that she wasn't loyal to herself. "To be honest, I was afraid you wouldn't want to speak to me anymore," Derek continued, giving her a funny look.

Whitney frowned and set down her cup. "Oh? Why?"

"Because of how we left things earlier this morning. I'm sorry if I made you uncomfortable," Derek said. "I shouldn't have pushed you about your job."

He was the first person other than Tripp who ever had. Even Amanda and Cassie had kept whatever opinions they held to themselves, thinking that she was content, even happy because that's what she wanted them to believe. But she'd told Derek the truth—and she'd opened herself up to something she hadn't wanted to hear but needed to all the same.

"Why did you?" she suddenly asked. "Push me about it?"

"Because I care," he said simply, without any embarrassment.

"Please don't," she said. It came out automatically, without forethought, and the shock she saw on his face filled her with momentary shame until she reminded herself of why she'd said it. Why it needed to be said.

He couldn't care. Not about her. And she certainly couldn't allow herself to care about him.

"I mean…why should you? I'm just passing through this town," she said, her tone a little lighter, even if she struggled to look at the hurt in his eyes. She took a long sip from her straw, barely tasting the coffee.

Derek's brows drew together. "I guess I thought that you and I were starting to form a bit of a connection."

Whitney struggled to meet his eye, glancing again at the woman feeding the seagulls, her mind once again going to Tripp, of the reason he gave for being back here, the work he was doing for the youth—for himself. That she hadn't even known any of this until she'd run into him. And if she hadn't? She might never have known. She might have pushed Tripp away, but he'd pushed her away first.

It was what they did, the Palmers. It was how they survived. And it was the one thing they all sadly had in common. Maybe, the only thing.

"I'm sorry if I sent you the wrong message," Whitney said. She forced the words out, her heart hurting a little more with each one. She stared at her coffee, grateful for the shield of her sunglasses so Derek wouldn't see the tears that were welling behind them.

"I don't think I misunderstood anything," he pressed.

Whitney stared at him, knowing that he was telling the truth and that she was only being partially honest. With him—and with herself. For a moment, she dared to think of how it would feel to agree with him, to allow herself to fall. But that was a fantasy, not unlike the resignation letter that sat on her computer and would always remain.

It was a dream. And a wish that could never come true.

"I'm sorry, Derek. This was only ever supposed to be a week of fun. Nothing more." She glanced at him, seeing the hurt linger in his soft brown eyes, and swallowed hard, pushing back the sadness and disappointment that threatened to build up and make her say or do something she shouldn't. And couldn't.

Derek nodded, his expression resigned. "I see. So...that's all it was then? Fun?"

She pulled in a shaky breath, forcing herself to do what she had to, reminding herself why she had to keep her distance from this town and everyone in it. Today was proof of that.

"That's all it could ever be," she said sadly, but firmly, trying to convince herself more than him.

She stood, knowing when it was time to leave. She'd become an expert over the years of reading the room, gauging people's reactions and micro-expressions, looking for the slightest hint of a problem that she could fix before it happened.

But she couldn't fix a broken heart.

If she could have, she would have fixed Amanda's, all those years ago. Or done something, anything, to shield her from that pain.

Whitney pushed her way through the crowded sidewalk, back to where she'd parked the bicycle, the coffee cold in her hands, and the sun warm on her face. It was turning into a beautiful afternoon, even if she couldn't imagine being able to enjoy it.

She made a promise to herself a long time ago that she would never hurt anyone again. But somehow, she had.

And she'd hurt herself in the process.

WHITNEY SAT IN ONE OF the beach chairs, from late afternoon until dusk, staring at her laptop, catching up on work, trying to forget about Derek almost as much as she was trying to avoid facing her friends, even though she knew that it was inevitable.

Maybe, she always had. Maybe that's why she'd pushed them away, slowly at first, and later, intentionally, with more force.

Behind her, she heard the door to the house open and close, and then Amanda's voice calling out to her, holding no ill will for Whitney abandoning her earlier today.

Whitney closed her eyes against the tightening of her chest. Amanda was forgiving that way. But some things, she knew, were unforgivable.

"Hi," she said as Amanda settled onto the seat beside her.

"You get your work done?" Amanda asked.

Whitney tried to detect an edge in her friend's voice, something that might show Amanda knew she'd been lying, but there wasn't one. And she knew Amanda well enough to spot it.

"Yep." Another lie. Another knot in her stomach. "I'm sorry I left."

Amanda brushed her concern away. "I needed to be on my own. I sent Cassie away too."

Whitney was surprised by that, even if she didn't feel exactly let off the hook for her actions. "I didn't see her come back to the house."

"That's because I didn't come back right away." Cassie's voice cut across the silence and Whitney turned to see her approaching them, looking more troubled than when Whitney had left them this morning.

"Where'd you go?" Whitney was almost afraid to ask, thinking of what Cassie had revealed about Tripp. A crush, right under her nose!

Looking back, she supposed she shouldn't be surprised. Tripp was always a flirt as a teenager, and most of the girls fell for his charms. But Cassie falling for him was much different. And the only thing worse would be if Tripp fell for her too.

Whitney's mouth felt dry while she waited for Cassie to tell her where she'd been, even though she had a hunch she had gone to see Tripp. Would he have told her why he left those flowers and the card? Would he explain himself?

But Cassie just shrugged and said, "I walked around town for a while and eventually parked myself at the coffee shop. Forced myself to finish that dress design."

Whitney didn't even realize how relieved she was until a breath escaped her. She'd been at the coffee shop. But it was a reminder of how easily their paths could have crossed. How there was nowhere to hide in this town.

"Oh!" she managed to finally say. "Well, that's good. How'd it come out?"

"Good." Cassie was nodding. "I think the client will be happy."

"You don't look happy though," Amanda remarked.

Whitney picked up on the same observation. Cassie didn't seem remotely satisfied or even relieved to have this project off her plate.

"I just have a lot on my mind. It's been a long day for all of us. Now, I just need a nice night with my girls." Cassie smiled at them both, but Whitney thought she detected a hint of pain behind her usually bright eyes.

It could be a nice night, one of the last they'd have on this trip. One where they reminisced and talked about all the nice parts of their past, the ones that had happened right here, on this very beach. It would be so easy to do just that. Whitney could hug her friends goodbye in two days, promise to call or text soon, make a vague promise of another reunion next summer, somewhere that held no memories good or bad, and then go back to Boston. Back to her empty apartment and corner office with the promise of an even bigger one when her father eventually retired. She'd make up a story about where she'd been this past week. There would never be any mention of her having seen Tripp.

Life would all go on exactly like it always had. Like it had been planned. And maybe, eventually, it would all be okay.

But the problem was, it never was okay, was it? It was safe, but it was empty. And it was all so wrong.

"There's something I need to tell you," Whitney said, her heart starting to pound so hard that her chest felt tight.

"You sound serious," Amanda said warily.

Whitney closed her eyes, knowing that this was her last chance. She could make up an excuse, keep things light, and preserve the relationship, the way she always had.

Only what kind of relationship was that? One built on a lie. One that always made her keep her distance, never getting too close. To Amanda. To Cassie.

To anyone.

chapter twenty-two

AMANDA

AMANDA WASN'T SURE where this conversation was going, only that it wasn't like Whitney to let her guard down, even around them. Oh, sure, she did as a kid, back when she would wrinkle her nose at the mere mention of another one of her parents' stuffy dinner parties, but that was a long time ago, and over the years, she'd accepted that way of life, and never complained about it either. The only thing she ever complained about anymore was Tripp, and she kept it to a minimum, her feelings left vague and her comments made in passing, even now, after seeing him in town.

"You sound serious," Amanda said, wondering if Tripp had done something and if that was the reason why Whitney had run off today. Had the card led to a confrontation afterward?

"It is serious," Whitney said, blowing out a shaky breath. "It's something I've wanted to tell you for a long time, but I didn't think I could, and I didn't think it was my place, and maybe it still isn't, but it's something you need to know."

It wasn't like Whitney to talk so fast. Normally her words were measured. Controlled.

"You mean, there's been something you haven't told us? Something you've…kept from us?" Cassie asked in disbelief.

Whitney nodded. "I wanted to tell you, so many times. You have no idea how much."

"Then why didn't you?" Cassie asked, hurt creeping into her tone. "I thought we told each other everything."

Amanda and Cassie exchanged a glance, both probably realizing that wasn't true, at least not anymore. Once, when they all still lived here, sure, but problems grew with age, and distance didn't always make it easy to share.

"There's nothing you can't tell us," Amanda urged, offering Whitney a smile of encouragement. "You know that."

And she did, too. She'd told them about Ryan, and instead of feeling ashamed or embarrassed, she'd felt supported. Loved.

Whitney swallowed hard, and Amanda realized that this was the first time she'd seen her friend struggle to find her composure. Whitney was always so cool, so sure of herself.

But also, in recent years, so guarded. She didn't share her deepest feelings anymore; sometimes it was like she didn't have any. Like she'd closed off that part of herself that was open to love—or hurt.

"I know that you have always blamed yourself for what happened to Shelby," Whitney started. "But you know you didn't do it, Amanda. It wasn't your fault. Not really. And I should have told you that. A long time ago. Because you needed to hear it. You deserved to hear it."

Amanda shook her head forcefully, a tear already slipping down her cheek that she furiously swiped at. She knew what

Whitney meant; it was the same thing that Cassie had said so many times. Even Ryan. And Mark. But the voice of one person had always been the loudest, insisting on Amanda's part in the tragedy, punishing her for it. Even now, well after Amanda's mother had taken her last breath, she could hear her voice as if she were sitting right beside her.

"But I *was* responsible. I was supposed to be watching her."

"And you were," Whitney pressed, leaning forward in her chair. "You were a kid. And she was a kid. And accidents happen. The same thing might have happened on your mother's watch."

"My mother said it was my fault. And I believe her." More than believed her. Amanda had taken the scorn, and she'd punished herself, every day of her life ever since. She ate because it numbed the pain a little bit, but then the guilt set in and made her feel worse. She was a bad person.

She'd lost her sister.

She'd made her father run off.

No amount of taking care of her mother had earned her forgiveness. Was it any wonder that she'd lost her husband too?

It was punishment. It was what she deserved.

But even as she thought those words, heard them loud and clear in her mother's voice, a small part of her, the one she saw reflected in the eyes of both of her friends, knew that it wasn't completely true.

She was a good mother. A good friend.

She'd been a good sister. Tried to be a good daughter.

And despite what had happened in her marriage, she'd been a good wife too. Not perfect, but then, no one was.

"Amanda, you've carried that guilt all your life." Whitney's expression was pained, not the usual blank canvas with a whisper of a smile. "Maybe if your mother had someone else to blame, someone else to unleash her anger upon, you might not still be beating yourself up about it now."

Amanda hesitated, wondering anymore if this were true. For a while, she thought that if the person behind the wheel of the car could have been found then her mother would redirect her anger, but now, she wasn't so sure. Her mother had blamed her for so long, and no amount of effort had ever changed that. No amount of visits or gifts, car rides to medical appointments, or home-cooked meals had been enough.

"I don't know that," Amanda said. "And I never will."

Cassie reached out and held her hand. "But you can choose to forgive yourself, Amanda."

Amanda nodded, even though she knew she wasn't there quite yet. That would take time. But being here, with her friends, made it somehow feel possible. Even in Starlight Beach.

"We can all forgive ourselves," she said. Then, reaching out to hold Whitney's hand, she thought of how her friend had run from them this morning, unable to face that part of their past. "We all can."

Whitney licked her bottom lip and then slowly pulled her hand away, staring at Amanda in a way that made her stomach twist with nerves.

"The thing is," Whitney said slowly. "I don't know how you can ever forgive me."

They were here to put the past in the past and that's exactly what Amanda was doing. "There's nothing to forgive."

Whitney stayed perfectly still in her chair, only letting her eyes slide to Amanda and holding them there. "Oh, but there is. You weren't the only one who was there that day…"

"No," Amanda insisted, eager to rid her friends of the feelings that had plagued her for so long. "I never blamed either one of you. Shelby wasn't your responsibility. She was mine. My sister. And I—"

"You didn't kill your sister, Amanda." Whitney paused, but only long enough to take a breath. "And I know who did. I know who was driving the car that hit her."

There was a beat of silence, and then Cassie cried, "*What?*"

Amanda felt like she'd just been hit, slapped, or doused with a bucket of ice water, she didn't even know. All she knew was that the world had suddenly gone still and quiet. The only sound she could hear was the hammering of her heart in her chest.

"You know?" Amanda could barely whisper.

"I've always known," Whitney said, her expression lined with pain before she closed her eyes.

"You've known all this time?" Cassie flashed a look at Amanda, who was starting to tremble now. It was too much. Too much to think about. There was someone to blame. Someone was at fault. Whitney had known all this time and said nothing. Nothing! And who was she if she knew and never told? Was she ever even their friend? Did she ever even care?

"You've known all this time, and you never told us?" Cassie cried out.

Whitney nodded, looking miserable. "I wanted to tell you, believe me, I did. But…I couldn't."

"Couldn't?" Cassie was shouting now, her eyes blazing when she stared at Amanda, still frozen in her chair, listening, absorbing, but not able to speak. Not able to make sense of any of it.

"But you knew that Amanda was beating herself up for it! Her mother blamed her, every single day! She's carried this around with her for nearly *twenty years*! And all this time you knew? You could have gone to the police! You could have made this right!"

But here Amanda disagreed. There was no making this right. Her sister was gone. The outcome was still the same.

"Why didn't you go to the police?" Amanda managed to finally say, her voice coming out in barely a whisper.

Whitney turned her attention from Cassie back to Amanda, looking her steadily in the eye. She took a deep breath before speaking. "I couldn't. I was scared, and I didn't know what to do. And I'm so, so sorry. You have to believe me, Amanda, because I never intended for it to hurt you more."

"If not the police, then why didn't you tell *us*?" Cassie looked stricken. "You knew all this time and you kept this from us?"

"I *had* to," Whitney pleaded.

"Since when do we keep secrets from each other?" Cassie demanded.

"Since always," Whitney said, her tone shockingly firm. "Since the day that Shelby died."

Since the day that changed everything, for all of them. Amanda shook her head, replaying that day, the days and weeks that followed, the years of friendship that she'd trusted and depended on, held on to like a life raft until she'd finally let go three years ago.

Until Whitney had forced her to. Because she wanted her to, didn't she?

Amanda couldn't believe that she hadn't seen it until now.

"What happened?" Amanda asked, finally ready to revisit the events of that day. The full event, not just the part she'd known about it. She stared at her friend, who seemed to be silently pleading with her, begging her not to reveal the secret she'd kept from them. But no, bigger than a secret, worse than a secret. The truth she'd kept from them. "I *need* to know."

Whitney nodded and then looked down at her lap. "I didn't know until that night when I came home. I heard my parents arguing, through my father's study door. I assumed it was about me, about what I'd done, what we'd all done…" She stopped to meet Amanda's stare, and Amanda closed her eyes briefly, still remembering where she'd been and what she'd been doing when Shelby had been struck by that car.

That car. Whitney knew who had been driving it. And Amanda needed to know.

"They were whispering as I approached," Whitney continued. "I couldn't make it all out. But I knew they were talking about leaving town and going back to Boston. They said that there would be too much talk, that we couldn't stay here anymore."

"That's why they sold the house," Cassie said, urging her along.

Whitney's shoulders deflated as she looked down at her hands. "Yes, but it wasn't me that they were talking about."

"Who were they talking about?" Cassie sounded as confused as Amanda felt.

Whitney pulled in a big breath. "Tripp. They were talking about Tripp."

Amanda's and Cassie's eyes met, both wide. Neither of them blinked as they digested this information. Seconds seemed to pass when all Amanda could hear was the pounding of her heart.

"Tripp?" Amanda whispered.

"Tripp was the one who hit your sister." Whitney spoke the words so clearly, and stated the phrase so factually, that there was nothing else to do but believe her.

"Tripp was the driver?" Cassie, however, sounded doubtful, as if she couldn't place him at the scene of the crime, or maybe, Amanda thought, didn't want to.

"The dog ran out into the street," Whitney said. "Tripp swerved to avoid hitting it, and…"

Whitney didn't need to finish her sentence for Amanda to know what happened next. But Tripp! Tripp Palmer!

Tripp who had laid flowers at Shelby's memorial. Fresh ones. Likely not the first.

"He must have been…" Amanda tried to think of how much older Tripp was than them and failed.

"He'd just turned eighteen," Whitney said gravely.

Amanda felt like the wind had just been knocked out of her. It was the summer before he started at Harvard. The beginning of a carefully chosen, perfect life.

"You kept this from us," Cassie ground out, her tone turning angry. "For all these years."

"I was a kid," Whitney said. "My parents—"

"Your parents had the money to cover it up, right? To pay someone to take the car off their hands? To sell their fancy house and never come back to the scene of the crime? All to keep the Palmer reputation intact. That's what mattered above all else. Above anyone else?"

"I was sworn to secrecy," Whitney pleaded.

"I get that you were a kid, I do," Cassie huffed. "But you're an adult now and you have been for some time. You could have told us this years ago. You could have at least told Amanda! Why didn't you?" Cassie's face was red with anger.

"I wanted to!" Whitney cried. "So many times I wanted to! But—"

"But what? Family over friends? I thought *we* were your family, Whitney. I thought we were your sisters. More than just friends." Cassie was furious, shaking her head, her eyes narrowed. "I thought…" Her voice broke before she could finish.

"What?" Whitney pleaded. "What?"

"I thought we could trust you. I thought that we were connected. All of us. For the good and the bad." Cassie stared at her like a stranger. "I thought I knew you."

"No one knows me," Whitney finally said, her chin lifting as her features hardened once again. "Not even you. I made sure of that."

Now a single tear slipped down Cassie's face as she stared at Amanda. "Amanda?" Her voice was gentle and soft, so unlike the tone she'd used with Whitney.

Amanda seemed unsteady on her feet as she pushed out of her chair. "I'm going for a walk. By myself," she added, her voice firm enough to make Cassie stay where she was.

"Amanda," Whitney pleaded. "Please. Say something. Yell at me. Scream at me. Tell me you hate me, anything. Just…not silence. Please."

Amanda was already halfway up the porch stairs when she stopped, and without turning around she simply said, "I don't hate you, Whitney. I…understand. As best I can, as we say. But maybe that isn't enough."

Maybe it never had been.

AMANDA DIDN'T KNOW WHERE SHE was going, all she knew was that she had to get out of that house. She grabbed her bag from the counter where she'd left it, but she didn't bother with the car. She didn't trust herself to drive. Instead, she began walking toward town, her vision blinded by the emotions that blurred clear thought.

Tripp. It had been Tripp. And Whitney had known, all this time.

She'd sat there, in the days afterward, crying with Amanda, and again on that day just a few short weeks later when she'd had to leave town, only then it had been Amanda comforting her! And all that while, she knew that her parents weren't leaving town because of Whitney's part in Shelby's accident.

They were leaving because of Tripp.

Amanda was shaking as she started to run, faster than she even knew she could, when normally she struggled to catch her breath if she had to chase after a ball when she was playing with Trevor. She felt like she could run forever, into town, away from this town. But to where? No place felt safe anymore.

No one, either.

"Amanda!"

She could hear Cassie's voice behind her, but she didn't want to talk to her now, not when it was Cassie who brought Whitney here. Not when she'd made this awful revelation possible.

She kept running, picking up speed, until eventually Cassie stopped calling her name, and other noises from town replaced it.

She slipped into the nearest restaurant, only vaguely realizing that it was the same one she'd hidden in earlier that week, and settled in at the bar. She ordered a glass of white wine and then stared at it once the bartender set it in front of her. She didn't even want it. Didn't trust herself to hold the glass with her shaking hands. But she didn't know where else to go either.

She pushed away the drink, getting ready to leave and wander until she figured out her next steps when she saw Mark walk in through the open door. He stopped, grinned at her, and then frowned when he no doubt caught her expression.

"Hey," he said, after a few quick paces in her direction. "Everything okay?"

"Yes," Amanda said on autopilot, and then stopped and shook her head. She might not be able to go back to the cottage and talk to her friends right now, but Mark was a friend. And if she'd learned anything today it was that keeping things from your true friends only made things worse, not better. "Actually, no. No, things are very far from okay."

"Your ex?" Mark guessed.

Amanda shook her head again. Right now even her divorce felt like a small problem. "No. My...friends this time. I took your advice and opened up. And so did they."

"Wanna tell me about it?" Mark asked.

"Attorney-client privilege?" Amanda managed to joke, somehow.

"More like friend to friend," Mark said with a kind smile. He ordered a beer and settled onto the stool beside her. "Although, it sounds like my advice only made things worse."

Amanda considered how easy it would be to agree with him, but that would be placing blame where it wasn't deserved, and she'd spent enough time doing that.

"No," she insisted. "You were right. I had been keeping things from my friends. Turns out that we all were. But...I learned something, and I don't even know how to process it. Everything I've ever thought and believed....it all changed. It's like...I don't even know who I am anymore. If anything was ever real."

Amanda felt the tears prickle her eyes for the first time since Whitney's confession and she swallowed the lump in her throat, nodding as she gathered herself for the story.

She didn't name names. And she realized that by doing that, she had somehow already made a choice, one she'd decided as soon as Whitney had told her the awful story, when she'd said the name. Tripp. She wasn't going to report him. She wasn't going to snitch on him or drop his name and ruin his reputation.

Tripp wasn't an eighteen-year-old boy anymore. He was a grown man. A man who had left flowers at her sister's accident site.

A man whose life had not been easy. And now, she knew why.

Sometimes, living with yourself was punishment enough.

"So you finally know who did it," Mark concluded. He let out a low whistle. "How does that feel?"

Amanda felt her shoulders sink with the weight of the world. "Honestly, it feels horrible. I thought that it would take the pain away, but it doesn't change what happened. It doesn't bring back my sister. People were still hurt. Lives were damaged. And...after all this time, I still blame myself."

"But now you have the name of the person who actually was at fault. You can look back on that day and see it differently."

Amanda tried to do just that. To see Tripp, swerving to avoid her beloved childhood dog, panicking when Shelby came darting out of nowhere on her pink bicycle.

But all she saw was herself, at home, laughing as she flipped through fashion magazines with her friends. Without a care in the world.

"You're telling me to rewrite history?" She shook her head. "I don't think I can do that. I can't go back and change things. And my parents...my mother...I'm not sure this information would have mattered because the outcome would have still been the same."

"You've told yourself a single story about your past all this time," Mark said, giving her a gentle smile. "Now you get to decide your story for the future."

She nodded slowly. The future. She hadn't thought of it in so long. But now, once again, it was wide open, as big as the star-filled sky she'd once stared at as a child, daring to imagine something better. Something brighter.

Maybe, she still could.

chapter twenty-three
WHITNEY

L IGHT SHONE THROUGH the linen curtains of
Whitney's bedroom, confirming that it was a new day
and that the world hadn't stopped when her confession
was finally voiced. But somehow, it felt wrong that it hadn't. That
this secret she'd held on to for so long was finally released, out
into the universe, and nothing had changed at all.

Or had it?

From downstairs, she heard the chatter of Amanda and Cassie,
smelled the coffee percolating, and the bread being toasted. It was
the last day of their trip. Normally, they'd celebrate, make the
breakfast extra decadent like blueberry pancakes or thick wedges
of sugary French toast, and ward off feelings of loss and sadness
with plans for their next reunion.

This time tomorrow they'd all be packing, usually hugging
goodbye.

Only today, Whitney wasn't sure there would be a tomorrow.
Oh, the sun would still rise, a new day would spring, and life

would go on…but would her friendships?

And without Amanda and Cassie, what did she have?

Nothing. And that was what had kept her silent for so long. Not Tripp. Not even her parents.

She'd kept this secret because of her friends. Her sisters. And the fear of losing them.

Her body felt heavy with dread as she pushed the blanket off her and swung her legs over the side of the bed. She grabbed a cardigan and pulled it over her tee shirt, pausing in the hallway at the top of the stairs before she dared to walk down them. She'd gone up to her bedroom after Amanda had run off and Cassie chased after her. Not long afterward, she'd heard the front door open again, but it was only Cassie, who had retreated to her room as well. Even though Whitney's sleep had come fitfully, she'd never heard Amanda come back.

Whitney heard the conversation in the kitchen stop as she approached, but when she rounded the corner and entered, she saw Amanda standing at the island, cutting fruit, and Cassie behind her, pouring her coffee.

A hint of a smile—not of joy or happiness, but something deeper, something like love—lifted Amanda's mouth.

And it was only then, after years of holding on to this secret, fighting against her conscience, telling herself over and over again that it was what she had to do, what was best for everyone involved, that she started to cry.

She felt four arms wrap around her, holding her close, tears of sorrow mixed with those of relief. The worst was over. And now, maybe, they had a chance to move forward.

"I'm supposed to be comforting you," she insisted once they'd stepped back. "That's why I came here. To support *you.*"

"We're friends. We support each other. We always have. And we always will," Amanda said quietly, reaching out to give her arm a gentle squeeze.

Whitney stared at her friend. She knew that Amanda was a giving person—that she even worried at times that she was too giving, that she loved too much, and didn't love herself enough. But she'd somehow stopped to consider that Amanda loved her like that too. Even when she didn't deserve it.

"But how can you forgive me?" Whitney pressed, wiping her hand against her cheek. "I kept that secret—"

"You were a kid," Amanda insisted.

Whitney shook her head. "But I haven't been that girl for a long time."

"None of us have," Amanda said. "And isn't it about time we stopped living like we still are? One day changed so much for all of us, but it didn't change who we are. Or what we mean to each other."

"You mean you don't regret our friendship?" Whitney asked.

"Never," Amanda said. "I just regret the years we lost growing apart when we could have been there for each other. Both of us."

Whitney nodded quietly. So Amanda had figured it out then, that she'd tried, in vain, to push Amanda away. To make her hate her. To punish her. To see that she wasn't a good person after all.

But instead, she'd hurt the person she cared about most in this world. For a second time. And instead of feeling relieved that their relationship was finally over, that Amanda could stop thinking of her as the trusted, secret-sharing friend she'd idealized, Whitney had been filled with a longing to make things right. To make it all right. To turn back the clock and fix everything.

Except she didn't know how. Not for the past three years. Not for the past eighteen.

And certainly not now.

She knew that there was another scenario she had considered. That the truth sometimes hurt. A lot.

"You're not mad that I told you?"

Amanda hesitated, and for one awful second Whitney considered that she'd misjudged the situation, that she should never have shared the truth. That she should have protected her friends.

And her family.

But then Amanda shook her head. "I needed to know. And you needed to share. But…I think that there's someone else you need to talk to today," she said quietly.

Whitney nodded. She knew from the moment she said his name last night that she'd have to tell Tripp today that she'd told his secret.

"You must hate him," Whitney whispered, as the magnitude of what her brother had done came back, hitting her with full force. "He took a life and went on to live his."

Amanda tipped her head, pain filling her eyes, but there was something else there. An emotion that Whitney had seen before: concern. But more than that. Compassion.

Everyone in this room knew Tripp, from when he was a scrappy little kid who helped them schlep heavy buckets of water to their sandcastles, trying to fill the moat before the sand absorbed the liquid again, to the cheeky teenage boy who had caught Cassie's eye and made a lasting impression to this day. They'd heard about all his shortcomings: how he'd dropped out of college, took dead-end jobs that never lasted long, lost his marriage to his drinking problems, and somehow ended up here.

A man, who like herself, had held on to a dark secret for too many years, until it changed him.

Once, for the worst. But now, for the better.

"I feel sad for Tripp," Amanda said. "He didn't want this—none of it."

Whitney felt a single tear slip down her cheek. "You're a good person, Amanda."

Amanda started to protest, shaking her head, but this time, Whitney wasn't standing for it. Today, everything would change. For the better.

"No," she said firmly. "No more putting yourself down. No more blaming yourself. If anyone is to blame, it's me, for knowing the truth, keeping it from you, and allowing you to take the fault. To let you believe the words that your mother said."

"No," Amanda said after a long pause. "My mother chose to put her pain onto me. It was easier for her to blame me. I was a child. And as a mother myself I now know that was wrong. I know why she did it, but I no longer have to believe that it was true. I loved my sister. I would have done anything to protect her. It was an accident. A horrible, awful accident, and too many people got hurt in the process."

Whitney stared at her friend, knowing that she wasn't just talking about herself anymore. She was talking about all of them. Cassie, her, even Tripp.

One tragic event changed so many relationships, eventually nearly ending them.

But if Amanda had found it in her heart to give her a second chance, then maybe Whitney could find a way to do that too.

LIKE THEY ALL KNEW, TOO well at times, Starlight Beach was a very small town, one where the locals stuck together, one where newcomers were noticed, and recurring faces were welcomed. Whitney tried the camp first, but it wasn't open yet for the day, and neither were most of the places in town that she checked, places that had a history, that they'd once gone to together, back when they were still a family.

It wasn't until she began walking back toward the house that Whitney thought of the one place that had always brought them together, and brought them back here, year after year. Tripp walked this beach every day from what she could tell. Was it possible that he was walking by their old house? Would he even want to see it again after everything that had happened?

She couldn't be sure, but something inside her knew that it was possible. And that it was time for her to face the past once and for all.

She broke into a jog. Years of trying to outrun the demons in her head every morning made for a quick and steady pace, and she didn't stop until she'd passed Derek's house, the cottage, and the dozens of other homes that grew in size until there it was, high up on the dunes, sprawling against a wave of seagrass.

Home. She sucked in the cool morning sea breeze and stared up at the white house, into the large windows that filled most of the back of it, right up to the top left corner, where she used to sit on the built-in seat, leaning back against a stack of pillows, watching the waves crash against the sand.

She didn't know what she'd expected to feel. Longing. Sadness. Anger. She'd shut out those feelings for so long, but now, standing here, staring up at the sprawling house, remembering how it felt to run back up to it after a long day of play, leaving her footprints in the soft sand along with endless happy memories, she could only smile.

"It's beautiful, isn't it?" a voice said from behind her.

She turned, not surprised to see Tripp standing there, watching her carefully.

She sucked in a breath, swallowed hard, and nodded. She didn't trust herself to speak just yet. She didn't even know what to say.

"I walk by here a lot," Tripp said. "At first, I was just curious, but I also realized it was strangely comforting. To remember how things used to be. To focus on the good times, not just the bad."

"We did have some good times here," Whitney said softly. Better than any of the times they ever had in Boston. Better than any day they'd had since leaving this house behind for good.

"Do you remember how we used to play on rainy days?" Tripp's mouth curved into a smile.

Whitney laughed. "Hide and seek. You used to hide in the wardrobe behind the old trench coats and stick your feet in Dad's old rain boots so I couldn't find you."

"And you used to lie down on all the chairs tucked under the dining room table, hidden by the tablecloth," Tripp said with a chuckle.

Whitney stared at him as he approached, fighting the tears in her eyes. "You still played with me even when you were probably too old to."

"It's like I told you the other day, Whit. You're all I have. You're all I ever had. Being here, seeing this house again, well, for a while I can almost dare to think I can go back to the way it used to be."

Whitney felt her smile slip. Oh, how she wished they could do just that. For so many reasons.

"I didn't come here for the house. I was looking for you, actually," she said.

Tripp raised his eyebrows but then let out a heavy sigh.

"Cassie told you then," he finally said.

Whitney tipped her head. "Told me? Told me what?"

Tripp glanced at her, and she could see he was trying to gauge if she was telling the truth.

But she was. From here on out. Especially with the people she loved.

"Cassie's a great girl," Tripp said. "But she's also a great friend to you. So I made sure she wouldn't start thinking that I had any feelings for her."

Cassie hadn't mentioned this, but then, in light of everything that had happened yesterday, Whitney supposed that there wasn't an opportunity to share.

"Do you?" she asked her brother now, needing to know, wanting to protect her friend. "Have feelings for her?"

Tripp hesitated long enough for her to know the answer. "It doesn't matter. What matters is that she's your friend, Whitney. And you know that I'd never do anything to get in the way of that."

Whitney swallowed the lump in her throat. All this time, she thought she'd been the one who sacrificed so much, to pick up the pieces of Tripp's mess, to carry his secret and then later, the weight of the family legacy, all on her own.

But Tripp had sacrificed too.

"I told Amanda the truth," she said, unable to keep it inside any longer.

Tripp stared at her, long and hard, and she waited for the anger to come, or at least, an argument, but instead, Tripp's face broke out

into a smile, and all that coldness, all that distance that they'd kept
between them all these years broke down, and she saw a glimmer
of the boy he used to be. The one she'd loved, not resented.

The one who used to waggle his eyebrows when he snuck a plate
of food from one of their parents' many parties, and told her to
join him in the den, where they'd share it, watching a movie of
her choosing, even if it was a girly one. The one who taught her
to ride a bike because their parents were always too busy with
social events or work. The one who used to offer to bring her to
her friends' houses when he got his driver's license and let her ride
shotgun and pick the radio station. The one who used to laugh
like nobody else could ever laugh, whose smile made her smile,
and whose anger eventually became her own.

"Is she going to press charges?" he asked, sounding more interested rather than worried.

Whitney shook her head. "I don't think so." They hadn't discussed it, she hadn't dared to ask, but she knew Amanda, her
hopes and fears, and most of all, her heart. Amanda wasn't venge-
ful. Amanda was only full of love. Unlike Whitney, she hadn't
hardened herself to it.

Tripp dropped onto a dune, his gaze on the ocean.

"I've wanted to turn myself in so many times," he surprised
her by saying.

"Then why didn't you?" Whitney asked as she slowly took a seat
beside him. It couldn't possibly be because of the family name,
not when Tripp had made it so clear what he thought about that.

"Because of you," Tripp said, lifting an eyebrow.

"Me?" Whitney stared at him. "But—"

"Amanda and Cassie were your closest friends. Not just as kids, but now. You lost me. But you still had them. And I couldn't take them away from you, too."

Whitney stared at her brother, trying to make sense of it all. All this time, she'd told herself that Tripp was selfish, that she'd paid the ultimate price for protecting him, and all along, he'd been protecting her.

"I should get to the camp," Tripp apologized.

"I should have said it before, but you're doing a great thing with those kids." Whitney swallowed hard as she looked him in the eye. "I'm proud of you."

It was the first time she'd ever said the words, and maybe the first time she'd ever meant them.

And she didn't realize how much she needed to hear the same words said back to her until Tripp did just that.

"I'm proud of you," he said, setting a hand on her shoulder. "You did the right thing, Whitney. That took courage."

She wiped away a tear that had started to fall, but another one quickly followed, and this time, she didn't try to hold them back. She was tired of keeping her feelings bottled up inside.

"So you're not mad at me?" she said, relieved when Tripp shook his head.

"I told you I came back to this town for a second chance. To be a better person. If that means paying for what I've done, then so be it."

"What do you think Mom and Dad will say when they find out?" She wasn't worried anymore, not like she used to be, not about the consequences of the truth coming out. It had, and the world hadn't come to an end. If anything, her life felt like it was finally beginning.

But she knew that her parents had paid a price too, one that they probably hadn't calculated. They'd lost their only son, and maybe, if they decided it, they'd lose her too. She couldn't go back to that office, to the future they'd chosen for her, the one that served them so well but didn't serve her at all. Maybe she could have it both ways. Or maybe, she couldn't. All she knew was that she'd lived on their terms for over thirty years and now she had to start making decisions for herself.

"Maybe they never have to know," Tripp said. "Maybe it's better that way."

"For us?" There was no doubt that her father would be furious to hear that she'd come back to Starlight Beach, but revealing the secret that he'd gone to such lengths to cover up would probably be unforgivable.

And one look at Tripp told her so.

"For them," he said quietly. "Let them live with the decisions they made all those years ago. And let us live with the ones we've made today."

Whitney nodded. It was the kind thing to do. For everyone.

She looked back at the house. "It wasn't perfect. But it was pretty damn close."

And she wouldn't change it for the world. "We've lost a lot of time, Tripp," she said quietly, fighting back tears as she dared to stare properly, for the first time in years, at the face of the person she'd once loved most in this world.

"Doesn't mean it's too late, does it?" he asked, hope lifting his voice.

Whitney thought of the last time she'd properly talked to her brother, when she'd been free to love him without restraint, free to laugh without a care in the world, and be her true self with

Amanda and Cassie. When she didn't walk in fear, always doing what she was told so things weren't made worse, distancing herself from the people and places that mattered most because she didn't see any other way.

Of the loneliness that had taken over her daily existence. Of the secret that had held her back, kept her going, but never let her live.

She turned and looked at the water, and she inhaled the sweet, salty air, letting it fill her lungs, where the tight ball had once been, daring to remember the girl she'd once been, who had stood in the sand on this very beach and stared at the night sky and made wishes and believed that they might come true.

"No," she said with a smile. "I don't think it's too late at all. For either of us."

chapter twenty-four
AMANDA

AMANDA HAD PUT off visiting her childhood home for long enough, but today, she stood outside the two-story structure of the house she'd grown up in, not because she had to, but because it was time.

Mark, who had joined her, kept a respectful distance, standing back on the street, leaning against his car.

"I can wait outside if you'd like," he told her when she finally turned back to him.

She hesitated, and then nodded just once, before making her way up the three short steps to the front door, unlocking it with the key Mark had given her, because she'd never kept one once she'd moved out fifteen years ago.

When she'd left, she'd never wanted to return, and she'd kept that promise to herself, until now. Even when her mother had first gotten sick, it was Ryan who had made the trip to Starlight Beach to help her pack up her belongings and bring her back to their home in Connecticut.

The house was locked in time, no different than it had been the day that Amanda left home, but somehow, it all felt different.

Framed photos of happier moments still lined the staircase and the hallway leading to the kitchen. Ones from holidays and sun-filled days at the beach, ones with Amanda's father's arms wrapped around both of his daughters, or Amanda's mother holding Shelby on her lap at Christmas, Amanda leaning against the chair, beaming at the camera.

The living room, where the family used to gather most nights to watch television, and later, where Amanda's mother would sit alone in her armchair, staring out the window with a scowl, was still furnished, complete with the floral printed throw pillows from Amanda's childhood. The matching curtains had faded from the sun, evidence of time gone by, but everything else was the same.

It was like at any moment, Shelby would round the corner, her stuffed animal tucked under her arm, asking if Amanda wanted to play in the yard, or her father would carry the newspaper to his favorite armchair, a coffee mug steaming on the table beside him.

Amanda walked slowly into the kitchen, half expecting to see her mother there at the stove. It was almost impossible to believe that there was once a time when she would turn and smile when she saw Amanda enter the room, happy to offer the girls an after-school snack, or a warm cup of cocoa on a cold winter's day.

Somehow, all those memories had been replaced with the bad ones, the ones that had stayed and lingered. But being here now, looking at the round table where they'd all sat for breakfasts and dinners, she could almost hear the laughter rising up in the room.

Amanda closed her eyes for a moment and then turned, making her way back into the hallway and up the stairs that creaked from age. Her parents' room was at the front of the house, and then her own, and lastly at the end of the hallway, Shelby's.

She hadn't been allowed back into Shelby's room after the accident, and the door had remained closed, even when her mother sat inside it, alone. Now, Amanda paused with her hand on the brass knob, steadying her breath. She turned the knob slowly and pushed the door open into the sunny, lavender room that had belonged to her younger sister. The bed was perfectly made, the pillows plumped, and all of Shelby's favorite dolls were lined in a row.

She walked over now to the bed and sat on it, knowing that it would be the last time she did. That soon, any evidence that a sweet little girl had slept here would be gone. The furniture would be removed. The house would be sold. New memories would be made. Only happy ones, she hoped.

Amanda opened the bedside drawer, finding all the sorts of strange little things that children collected: tiny seashells, candy wrappers, a mood ring.

She closed the drawer and looked around, trying to memorize it, even though all she'd ever wanted to do was forget it. To push aside the memory of the little girl that she missed so much. The one that she'd failed to protect.

She'd thought it was easier that way, but she'd been so very wrong. About so many things, as it turned out.

Standing, Amanda reached back down and took one of the dolls. It had been Shelby's favorite, the one with the brown curls and the eyes that blinked. It had the fanciest dress, or so they'd both thought when they were kids. Now the doll seemed small, simple even. It was missing a shoe.

She hugged it to her chest and carried it to the door, taking one last look around the pretty room before closing it behind her.

She paused outside her own bedroom, wondering if her mother had cleared it out years ago.

It was now or never, she knew. With a turn of the knob, the door flung open, revealing the same brass bed that she'd slept in for the first eighteen years of her life. Unlike Shelby's room, Amanda's belonged to a teenage girl. The walls were lined with posters of rock groups and celebrities that had been popular fifteen years ago. A stack of yearbooks sat on the white dresser. There were no toys or dolls; they'd been forgotten about years earlier.

The closet was empty; she'd taken all of her clothes when she'd left. But Amanda lifted her arm and wiggled her fingers along the top shelf until they found the corner of something wooden. With relief, she pulled the frame carefully off its ledge, staring at the photo of her and Shelby that she'd hidden away so she couldn't be reminded of the playground on the beach, where they would spend hours swinging. She stared at it now, at the image of that sweet little girl, letting the hot tears slide down her cheeks and blur her vision.

She closed her eyes, listening for the voice she'd blocked out for so long. *Swing higher, Amanda!*

It would take some time to forgive herself. But she knew that her sister would want her to. She'd want Amanda to smile like she did in this photo, and she'd want her to focus on the good times. And remember. Remember it all.

Shelby would want her to soar.

Brushing the tears from her cheeks, Amanda turned to leave, but something stopped her. She squinted, then moved across the room to her dresser, which she knew had been cleared out just like her closet. But there, tucked beside the lamp, was the framed photo that she now reached for and pressed against her heart until she felt the ache in her chest finally lift. She'd forgotten it when she left home. She'd once thought that it was gone forever.

But here it was. In her hands.

A photo of three girls smiling, beaming at the camera, the very last photo of the Starlight Sisters in all their glory.

MARK WAS STILL WAITING FOR her outside when Amanda emerged with the few treasures she'd chosen to keep: the doll, the photo of her with Cassie and Whitney, and a box of family albums and framed photos of happier times.

The way she wanted to remember her family. All of them.

Mark's smile was one of understanding when he took the heavy box from her hands and set it in the back seat of her car, directly beside the box of her mother's belongings that she'd been unable to even look at before but now saw differently. Now, the memories were complete. And they weren't all so bad. Some were pretty wonderful.

"How are you feeling?" he asked when he'd closed the door.

"Honestly?" Amanda huffed out a breath, surprised with herself. "Better than I expected. I always feared going back into that house, but once I did, I saw it for what it once was. I was happy there for a while. We all were."

"You don't have to sell it," Mark said. "You could wait, think about it."

But Amanda shook her head. "That's not my home anymore. My home is with my son." She realized that she hadn't mentioned Ryan, her husband. Her soon-to-be ex-husband. Maybe Mark was right. Maybe, somehow, she was going to be all right.

Mark's smile left his eyes and he nodded. "I understand."

He did, she knew, but maybe not in the way that she'd meant. She opened her mouth to explain, but then stopped herself, knowing that now wasn't the time to rush anything, not when so much had happened in such a short amount of time. There was still a lot of uncertainty, and she'd need some time to settle everything here and back at the house she'd shared with Ryan.

She had a new future to consider. One that she was starting to imagine—so different from the one she'd once hoped for.

She turned back at the house, thinking of how she'd felt the last time she'd walked out the front door, a lost eighteen-year-old girl, and she wished she could go back and hug her younger self. To tell her that it would be all right. That all her wishes would come true—in time, and in their own way. That she'd find love. And acceptance. That she'd have a family.

Even if it wasn't the way she'd imagined it.

She'd known love. She'd found it and lost it more than once, but who was to say that it wouldn't happen again, if she dared to try? If she still wanted it.

And she did. Oh, how she did.

"This isn't goodbye," she said as she looked up at Mark. "I don't know what it is, but I just know that it's not goodbye."

"I was hoping you'd say that," he said, grinning until his eyes crinkled at the corners in a way that made her heart turn over. He opened his arms and pulled her in for a long, tight hug, and she closed her eyes at the warm pressure of his arms around her waist, pushing back that flicker of worry about her muffin top when he pulled her tighter, and she relaxed into his chest, taking comfort in a newfound friend, and in the reminder that good people were out there if you were willing to let them in.

"I'll see you tomorrow," she promised before getting back into her car. Mark took his vehicle, heading back to his office, while she took the long route, away from the street of Shelby's accident, the past growing more distant behind her.

Derek was outside collecting his mail when she got back to the cottage, and she flagged him down before he could slip inside his house.

"You were just the person I wanted to see," she said, hurrying up toward his front door.

"You've had a chance to look at the paperwork I left on the doormat?"

She had reviewed it, but that wasn't why she was here. "I am ready to sell. And I'd like to invest the money in another property."

"Here in town?" Derek looked surprised but no one was as surprised as she was. She was finally free of Starlight Beach and yet she wasn't ready to let it go just yet. Maybe, she just wanted to recapture it. To hold on to it the way it was, and the way it should have been and still could be.

"I'd like to buy something smaller, closer to the beach. Something with a view, at least. The beach was my happy place growing up. Maybe...maybe it will be my son's happy place too," she said. "When I look back on my childhood, the best times were spent right here, on the sand, with my two best friends at my side."

And with Shelby.

"So, do you think you can find me something that fits my budget?" she asked.

"I know the perfect place," Derek said confidently.

"Good." Amanda felt a surge of hope for the first time in so long that she was positively giddy, and joyous, and all she wanted to do was share the news with her friends. "I'm still heading out tomorrow. I have to get back for my son. But I don't live far, and I can come back next weekend to tour a few places."

"No tour necessary." Derek grinned. "You've already taken it."

Amanda frowned until she saw the twinkle in Derek's eyes. She glanced from the rental cottage to Derek. Surely, he couldn't mean this house? It was perfect. And it probably cost a fortune.

"Oh, but I couldn't afford this—"

"I happen to know the owner is willing to cut a deal," Derek replied. He held up a hand when she opened her mouth to protest. "My grandmother was the kindest woman I ever knew and my summers here with her were the most special weeks of my year. One of the last things she ever said to me before she passed away was that this cottage was meant to bring a second chance. It had given her one after my grandfather passed away. And it gave me one, every summer of my youth and again when it brought me here full-time. Now it's your turn. My grandmother would have wanted it this way."

Amanda's eyes filled with tears. "I don't know what to say. I didn't even know your grandmother."

"She knew you, though," Derek said with a sad smile. "She knew your story, Amanda. She was a reporter with the local newspaper, and she covered the events of that day. She worked for years to try to figure out who was the driver of the car."

He knew the story all this time, and he'd never mentioned it. Not even to Whitney. Amanda opened her mouth to ask why, but then she stopped because she already knew.

Some things were best left in the past. But some were not.

Amanda had a vague memory of an elderly woman with warm dark eyes, who always smiled at her when they passed each other in town. And as she thought of that, another image came to mind.

One of a little boy, maybe a couple of years older than herself, who had once chased Shelby's runaway kite down the beach, and happily returned it before running off again.

He'd made her sister smile that day. And she'd never forgotten it.

"I guess she never did uncover the truth," Amanda said quietly.

"Oh, I think she had her suspicions." Derek's gaze locked on Amanda's for a long moment. "Never could prove anything, though."

Amanda chewed her lip and carefully chose her words. "That must have been frustrating."

Derek nodded. "Gran always had a belief that when people were ready for the truth, it would come out."

"Your grandmother was a wise woman," Amanda said. "And a very kind one. Like her grandson."

A small smile of understanding passed between them and then Amanda huffed out a breath, taking a step back toward the rental cottage.

Toward her new home.

"If I don't see you before you leave, be sure to tell your friends goodbye for me," Derek said as she started to walk away.

Amanda turned and looked at him in surprise. "You're not going to tell Whitney yourself?"

Derek's expression seemed torn. "I'm not sure that I'm what Whitney's looking for."

Amanda knew that not so long ago, she might have agreed with him. She'd have thought that Whitney just cared about her corner office, working her way up the ladder of her father's company, traveling the world, and dining at trendy restaurants in expensive clothes.

But that wasn't what Whitney had wished for. Or what her heart wanted.

"I wouldn't give up on Whitney just yet," Amanda told him. "I haven't."

He smiled at her as if she'd just told him exactly what he needed to hear. And she smiled too because she needed to say it. Not just about her friend, but about herself.

She turned and looked at the cottage—her cottage. Her second chance.

She wasn't giving up on the future she'd always wanted. Not yet.

chapter twenty-five
CASSIE

C ASSIE STOOD AT the counter, pouring frozen margaritas into three glasses. This was it, the last night of their trip. They'd actually done it, returned to Starlight Beach, and now one of them was going to stay.

"A toast," she said, raising her drink. Her two friends each did the same.

"What are we toasting to?" Amanda asked.

"To your new home." Cassie looked around the space which was admittedly smaller than Amanda's house she shared with Ryan, but still large enough for her to eventually grow the family she'd always wanted. "Is it okay to admit that I'm a little surprised you're moving back here?"

"I surprised myself," Amanda replied. "Or maybe, this town did. All the good parts are still here. And the bad aren't taking up rent in my head any longer."

"Have you told Mark yet?" Whitney waggled her eyebrows suggestively. She was already looser than she'd been in years, and happier, too. A weight had been lifted from her.

From all of them.

Amanda shook her head. "I'll tell him tomorrow. But it will take a while before I'm ready to jump back into a relationship. I think that I need a little time to myself. To get to know myself better. To figure out my next steps. A career."

"Any thoughts?" Whitney asked. "I would tell you that I'd hire you but this time Monday I'll be unemployed along with you."

Cassie and Amanda both stared at their friend and Cassie didn't even care that her frozen drink was starting to melt in her hand.

"You're leaving the family business?" Cassie asked. "But—"

"No more buts," Whitney said firmly. "No more excuses. I just did what I thought I had to do, not what I wanted."

"But you said that's what you wanted. What you loved!" Cassie stared at her in disbelief.

"It's what I had to say to convince myself, I suppose. I never wanted to work for my father. And I certainly never wanted to make it my entire life."

"What do you want?" Amanda asked.

"It's been a long time since I've dared to ask myself that question," Whitney said, as a small smile started to form. "But I have some ideas."

Cassie could only wonder if those ideas involved Derek, but she decided to wait and see rather than push her friend into doing something she didn't want to or being someone she wasn't.

She'd done enough of that to herself.

"Then I propose a new toast," Amanda said, raising her glass. "To second chances."

Second chances. Cassie could drink to that, and she did, before blurting, "I sent the final dress design to my client today. She hasn't complained—yet."

"See? I knew you could do it!" Whitney grinned.

But Cassie didn't share her friend's enthusiasm. "I could. But I didn't want to. And I'm not going to do it again."

Amanda frowned as she set down her drink. "What do you mean?"

"I mean, that somewhere along the way I lost my love for what I do. And being back here, I started to find it again. I think I'd be happier making my own dresses, not just sketching and sewing to fit someone else's vision." Cassie gave a little smile. "You know, it's funny, but all this time I hid so much of my new life from my mother. I knew she wouldn't approve, and somehow, even though I never approved of so many of her choices, that bothered me. I think it's because I knew she saw through me. Right to the heart of me. And as much as I didn't believe it growing up, she did a good job raising me in her own way."

"She loved you," Amanda said quietly. "She still does. She just wants what's best for you. I'm a mother. I know."

"I wish I could say that about my parents." Whitney shook her head. "I have a feeling that I'll be cast off, like Tripp."

Amanda set a hand on Whitney's. "Are you okay with that?"

"I have to be," Whitney said slowly. "The other choice is to keep living a life I don't enjoy."

Cassie knew the feeling. And she knew that the decision had been made. For Whitney. And for herself.

"I have to call Grant before I go back to New York," Cassie said. "I owe it to him to tell him who I really am. That the woman he's known is just a version of myself, the person I thought I wanted to be. I never gave him a chance to get to know the real me. I guess I was afraid he wouldn't like who I was."

Amanda's expression was one of understanding. "We're all haunted by things people told us about ourselves when we were younger. But now we get to choose what we believe. We know who we are. And if we forget, we have each other to remind us."

"I'll toast to that," Whitney said, raising her glance again.

"And I have another announcement," Cassie said, feeling a bubble of excitement form in her stomach. She glanced at Amanda.

"You're not the only one who's going to be sticking around this town. I found a little shop that would be perfect for my brand, and I'm going to talk to Derek about the lease."

"Really?" Amanda's eyes widened along with her smile. "You and me. Together. Like old times!"

They both fell silent when they knew that it wouldn't be completely like old times. Not without Whitney. Not with what they'd lived through here.

"More like...new times," Cassie said slowly. "Better times."

"There's another person you need to talk to," Whitney said to Cassie. When Cassie didn't respond, she said, "Tripp."

Cassie felt her heart soar and then drop. She shook her head. "No. No, Tripp made it clear that he doesn't have any feelings for me."

"He said that to protect you. And me. Because he couldn't hide who he was from you, and he didn't want to, either." Whitney tipped her head. "He let his guard down around you."

"We both did. I can be myself around Tripp," Cassie explained. "And...I haven't been able to do that in a long time. But—"

"Not more buts," Whitney grinned until her eyes crinkled. "From now on, we stop holding ourselves back from the lives we really want to live."

"And we start living the ones we deserve," Amanda said, as they raised their glasses again.

THE NEXT MORNING, CASSIE LOADED her suitcase into the trunk of her rental car, hugged her friends goodbye, knowing that she wouldn't have to wait so long before seeing them again, and climbed into her car. But she didn't drive in the direction of Manhattan.

She drove in the direction of home.

Derek was waiting for her outside the shop that she'd spotted when she was in town with Whitney and looked at again after her terrible conversation with Tripp.

This time, the door was open, but Derek stood back on the sidewalk as she started to walk inside.

"Aren't you going to show me around? Try to convince me to take it or something?" she joked.

"Something tells me that you won't need much convincing," he said with a knowing smile.

He was right. The big bay window would be the perfect backdrop for her seasonal designs, and she had spent last night lying in bed, thinking about different themes she could use for the decorations. The space was brightly lit, and it would only take a couple of coats of creamy white paint to make it feel fresh again.

To make it feel like her own.

Like the person she was meant to be. Or always was.

"Suit yourself," she said, sliding past him to step inside, but she halted when she saw that she wasn't alone.

There, near the back of the room where she had envisioned a seating area and a three-way mirror, was Tripp.

"Tripp? What are you doing here?"

"Whitney told me where I could find you," he said to her, sinking his hands sheepishly into the pockets of his jeans.

Cassie realized that it wasn't the first time she'd seen the cocky grin fade and the mask slip. It was there, flashing through from time to time, but the Tripp she'd gotten to know this past week wasn't Tripp Palmer with the fancy, fast car and the big ego.

He was Whitney's brother, who had helped them build sandcastles, even when he was probably too old to want to participate. The boy who had run to fetch bandages the time she'd tripped on the sidewalk in town, even though it made him late for meeting his friends.

The one who liked her, just as she was.

And the one she liked, for the same reasons.

But then she thought of the other side of him she'd seen the other day. The coldness in his otherwise warm eyes, the set of his jaw, and the words he'd used to push her away.

"I didn't think you'd want to spend time with me anymore."

"All I wanted was to spend more time with you," Tripp said, his voice low, and his gaze never straying from hers. "But I couldn't tell you the truth, not until Whitney was ready. And I wasn't the person you thought that I was."

"That's where you're wrong," Cassie said, giving him a slow smile as she reached out to take his hand. "You're exactly who I think you are. Who you've always been. You're the kind of person that I want to be."

"Me?" He looked at her in confusion, but she just squeezed his hand tighter.

"Most people run away from the bad parts of their life." Cassie was one of them. But not anymore. "They try to change themselves into someone they don't even recognize just to convince themselves that something they weren't proud of never existed. But you didn't do that. You came back here. You've dedicated your life to being better, doing better, helping people."

"It will never change what I did," he said, narrowing his eyes.

"No, but it wasn't just you, Tripp. We were all a part of that day. We can all find a way to wonder how things might have been different." She wondered if Amanda's mother ever thought about how things might have been if she'd stayed home that day, instead of running to the store. If she punished herself or if it was just easier to punish someone else, even if it was her own daughter. To push away the person who could have comforted her the most.

It's what Whitney had done to all of them.

It's what she had done, too. To Willow.

"I've been thinking a lot about my mother lately," Cassie admitted. "She told me the other day that the happiest days of her life were spent here, in Starlight Beach, and I realized that somewhere along the way, I let the bad memories overshadow the good ones. There was so much good here, Tripp. There still is."

"What about New York?"

Cassie's conversation with Grant had confirmed what she already knew and just hadn't been ready to face until now. "There's nothing for me in New York. I was chasing a dream, but I was running in the wrong direction." She smiled as he reached down and took her other hand. "This is where I want to be. Where I belong."

"Then we have another thing in common," he said, his mouth quirking into one of those signature grins that always made her heart flutter and still did, even after all this time.

Things changed, but not everything, and she was glad for that.

"Do you think Whitney will ever forgive me?" he asked, his voice barely above a whisper.

"Whitney? But she already has," Cassie assured him, knowing it was true, and happy that it was.

"I meant...for kissing her best friend." His smile widened.

And there went Cassie's heart, swooping and soaring and dancing. And falling. Head first. "There's something my mother taught me at a very young age. It's better to beg forgiveness than ask for permission."

She lifted her chin until her lips met his, and then she closed her eyes as his arms slid around her waist, pulling her tight, right in the middle of her new shop in the heart of Starlight Beach, where all her wishes were finally coming true.

chapter twenty-six
WHITNEY

O NLY AMANDA AND Whitney were left in the house—something that just a week ago had felt downright terrifying. Now, however, Whitney was happy to have her friend to herself for a few minutes.

"You must be excited to see Trevor," Whitney said as Amanda came back from loading up her car. "Or I should say that he's probably excited to see you."

Amanda hesitated but then shook her head as if correcting a dark thought before it was allowed to take hold. "I think he will be. I just hope he doesn't take the news too hard when we sit him down and tell him about all the changes."

"Sometimes change is for the best," Whitney said gently. "And you've given him a lot to look forward to as well. Not every kid gets to grow up right here on the beach."

Amanda gave her a pointed look. "Says the girl who grew up with her own private beach."

"I'd rather have a shared beach," Whitney replied.

Amanda nodded. And then took a lingering look around the cottage. "It's strange to think that I don't have to say goodbye to this place now. Only to you."

"Not necessarily…" Whitney pulled in a breath, bracing herself for what she was about to say. "I've had some time to think about what's next for me, and I've decided that I can't quite walk away from the family business."

"Oh." Amanda did her best to look understanding but it was clear from the look in her eyes that she was disappointed. "So long as you're happy, Whitney."

Whitney knew that she meant it. Even if Whitney did decide to stay in a job that kept her from her friends, her brother, and even love, Amanda would still find it in her heart to support her.

That's all they'd ever wanted for each other. Happiness.

But they'd wanted something else, too. The best. And working for her father had only ever kept the best parts of Whitney hidden.

"I haven't been happy," Whitney told her. "Not in a very long time. And working for my father was only a small part of it. But seeing Tripp and what he's been doing here made me think of a new plan. A new future, I suppose."

She'd already run the idea by Tripp, and he was as excited as she was. They had so many thoughts that it was hard to narrow it down to a few words.

"We're going to expand what Tripp has built here, create a bigger cause, a foundation, one that gives back to the community, and to those who need a second chance."

Amanda eagerly nodded along. "And with your marketing background and connections, I'm sure you'll have no trouble getting funding."

"It will be a welcome challenge and you know I've never shied away from hard work. This time I'll be doing something that feels right."

"And right here in Starlight Beach! We'll all be together, every day. Summer will never have to end. It will be just like we always wished for, do you remember?"

This time, Whitney didn't deny that part of herself. She did remember. Every wish. Even the ones that were yet to come true.

Now, perhaps, they had a chance of doing just that.

Whitney hesitated, hoping her next words came out right, too.

"We'd like to name the foundation after Shelby. With your permission," Whitney added quickly. "We want her name to always be attached to something good. To know that she might be able to live on and that other people's lives can be made better, thanks to her."

Amanda's smile dropped as her eyes welled with tears, and for a moment, Whitney had the horrible feeling that she'd upset her friend—again. But Amanda's expression lifted as a single tear slipped down her cheek. "I...I don't know what to say. I can't think of a better way to honor Shelby."

"I can." Whitney set a hand on her friend's shoulder. "We want you to come on board."

"Me?" Amanda asked. "But I have no real work experience other than some clerical duties at Ryan's office."

"You run a household. You take care of everyone around you, sometimes at the expense of yourself," Whitney couldn't help but add, which sparked a small, guilty smile from Amanda. "What better training could there be?"

"But...it's a family company. You just said so," Amanda said.

"And isn't that what we are?" Whitney replied, pulling her friend—her sister—in for a long, much-needed embrace. And this time, she wasn't letting go.

AFTER CONSIDERING LEAVING SO MANY times this week, the irony wasn't lost on Whitney that she was the last to walk out of the house. She supposed that she could leave her key on the kitchen counter, as Cassie had done, but instead, she chose to walk it over to Derek personally.

She knew the first place to look for him would be the back porch, but today, like yesterday, it remained empty. Hoping that he was home, she went around to the street side, her heart speeding up when she spotted his car. Before she could lose her nerve, she hurried up to his door and knocked.

She knew better than to think he'd been expecting her or even hoping to see her. She'd pushed him away, the way she'd tried to with Amanda, the way she'd done with Tripp, and so many other people who came into her life and never stood a chance of getting to know her.

She'd closed so many doors and now, she was literally standing on his front step, hoping that he'd open his.

It wasn't a comfortable feeling, putting herself out there, taking a risk when she'd built such a safe world for herself all these years.

But it was an empty world. And it was a life she didn't want to go back to—and wouldn't, no matter what happened right now. She was staying, here in the town that had brought her true joy, friendship, and maybe even love.

Derek opened the door. His expression was unreadable.

"I…" She was fumbling with her words, something she only did in her personal life, it would seem. And she didn't want to mess this up any more than she already had. "I came to bring you your key."

"So you're leaving then?" He said it matter-of-factly. Confirmation, she supposed.

She nodded. She was leaving. But only long enough to find a replacement for her position in the company and pack up her rather empty apartment. It wouldn't be easy to tell her father she was resigning, but it couldn't be harder than living with the burden she'd carried for the past eighteen years.

She opened her mouth to tell Derek her plan when he gave a clipped nod. "Well, travel safe, then."

She closed her mouth again. So that was it, then. She'd pushed so many people away over the years, often with the hope that they wouldn't come running back, or maybe, secretly with the hope that, like Cassie and Amanda and even Tripp, they would.

But there were consequences to every action and every spoken word, and sometimes loss, too.

"Well, thank you," she said, stepping back.

She'd gone and done what she'd promised not to do. She'd hurt someone. And now she was paying the price by the ache in her chest.

She started to turn but Derek stopped her, putting a hand on her arm.

"You don't think I'm going to let you walk away that easily, now, do you?" he asked.

She turned to see the familiar warmth in his eyes, the smile that filled his entire face, and her entire heart.

"Derek," she whispered in disbelief.

He shrugged. "I was about to give up on you, but I spoke to your friend who convinced me not to."

Whitney shook her head, fighting off a wistful smile. "Cassie's like that. She sees the good in everything and everyone. It's something I've always admired about her. She's an eternal optimist."

"She sounds like an amazing friend," Derek commented. "Only she's not the one I'm referring to."

Whitney frowned at him, trying to make sense of what he was saying. "You mean—"

"Amanda," he said, nodding. "She certainly believes in you."

Whitney felt a lump rise in her throat, and she didn't even know how to respond.

"When was this?" she asked.

"Yesterday," he said.

Yesterday. Meaning even right after Whitney had told her friends the truth, Amanda still found it in her heart to believe in her. To want the best for her.

"Thank you," she managed to finally say. "For selling her the house." At a steep discount, they both knew. "She deserves to think about the future more than anyone I know."

Derek leaned against the doorjamb, his gaze locked with hers. "And what about you? What are your plans for the future? Do you think you'll get away from Boston again anytime soon?"

Whitney smiled her first real smile of the day. Of this trip. Maybe of the year. Her heart felt light, filled with newfound hope and infinite possibilities.

"I'm not going back to Boston. At least not to stay." She'd pack up her apartment first, not that it would take long. She didn't have many personal items, and the place had come furnished and would remain that way when she left it. She'd be all ready when she invited her father to lunch and told him her plans—or at least some of them.

Just thinking about it made her feel anxious, but thinking about not doing it made her feel worse.

"What about the family business?"

She couldn't fight the smile that started in her chest and bloomed on her face. "I'm going to stick with the family business, just in a different sort of way. I'm going to help Tripp grow what he's started here."

Derek's eyebrows shot up. "So you're going to need a place in town?"

"A place, and maybe a new friend, if you're around…"

"Oh, I'm around." His grin crinkled the corners of his eyes. "What made you change your mind?"

"I don't think I changed my mind," she said. "I think that for a long time, I didn't want to face the truth. And that included being honest with myself."

"You're going to follow your heart?" Derek asked.

"Better than that," Whitney took a step toward him and let him take her hand. "I'm going to open it."

EPILOGUE

THE SUN WAS low in the sky, casting a warm glow on Amanda's face as she walked out onto the back porch of her cottage, knowing that Trevor would be fine on his own for a few minutes, and that she didn't have to worry about him—too much.

Cassie and Whitney were already waiting for her on the beach chairs, but then, Whitney didn't have much of a walk these days, and most mornings Amanda and Whitney would wave to each other from their back porches over their morning coffee. It had been eight months since they'd all returned to Starlight Beach, and even though everything was different than it was this time last year, Amanda also knew that, somehow, it was better.

Trevor had settled into his new school and spent his afternoons combing the beach for shells or playing volleyball with neighboring kids. On the weekends when he visited his father and new baby brother, Amanda caught up with Cassie at the little apartment she had rented over her beautiful store, or, more recently, enjoyed a quiet dinner with Mark, who had slowly become much more than just a friend.

Other times, she was content to sit at home, listening to the sound of the waves crashing against the shore, reading a book, or just watching the gulls swoop and soar, wanting, for the first time in her life, for nothing.

Still, it was getting late, and a tradition was a tradition. And a promise was a promise. Her friends were waiting, and she wouldn't let them down.

Amanda walked down the porch steps, letting her feet sink into the warm sand as the women walked the short distance to the water, their eyes on the sky. It was the time of day when the beachcombers had left and the peals of children's laughter from a day of play were replaced with the rhythmic sound of rolling waves. Before the colors of the sunset completely faded and the first star appeared.

It was wishing hour.

Amanda wrapped her sweater tighter around her and stared patiently, wondering which of them would be the first to spot a star—until she saw it, high up, to the right, twinkling in all its glory, as if it were waving at her.

"Star light, star bright," she said, and they all smiled before closing their eyes, like they always did, since that very first time they'd played together, when life was still stretched out before them, unknown and full of possibilities.

Back then she'd wish for silly things, like a new bike, or a fancy dress, and later, for something deeper, bigger, something that had felt nearly out of reach.

Today was the first time she didn't make a wish for something different, or seemingly better, or for more of anything. But it was a wish all the same, and a wish from the heart.

"What did you wish for?" Cassie asked, like she always did, because they'd shared everything as children, and they still did.

"I wished that every day could be like this one," Amanda said, feeling her heart swell with fulfillment.

Because she knew, maybe for the first time, that this wish had already come true.

ABOUT THE AUTHOR

Olivia Miles is a *USA Today* bestselling author of heartwarming women's fiction and small-town contemporary romance. She has frequently been ranked as an Amazon Top 100 author and Kindle All Star, and her books have appeared on several bestseller lists, including Amazon, Barnes & Noble, BookScan, and *USA Today*. After growing up in New England and later living in Montreal, Olivia traded salt water for fresh water, and now lives on the shore of Lake Michigan with her family and an adorable pair of dogs.

Visit www.OliviaMilesBooks.com for more.

ABOUT THE AUTHOR